BOOMERANG

~

NEVER DIE

BOOMERANG

NEVER DIE

TWO NOVELS BY
Barry Hannah

With an introduction by Rick Bass

BANNER BOOKS
University Press of Mississippi/Jackson

Boomerang was first published in 1989 by Houghton
Mifflin/Seymour Lawrence
Copyright © Barry Hannah
Never Die was first published in 1991 by Houghton
Mifflin/Seymour Lawrence
Copyright © Barry Hannah
Introduction Copyright © 1993 by Rick Bass
Manufactured in the United States of America

Boomerang and *Never Die* are works of fiction. Names, characters,
places, and incidents either are the product of the author's
imagination or are used fictitiously.

97 96 95 94   4 3 2 1

The paper in this book meets the guidelines for permanence and
durability of the Committee on Production Guidelines for Book
Longevity of the Council on Library Resources.

Library of Congress Cataloging-in-Publication Data

Hannah, Barry.
  [Boomerang]
  Boomerang ; &, Never die : two novels / by Barry Hannah;
  with an introduction by Rick Bass.
      p. cm. — (Banner books)
  ISBN 0-87805-702-1
  1. Authors, American—Mississippi—Fiction. 2. Frontier and
  pioneer life—West (U.S.)—Fiction. I. Hannah, Barry.
  Never die. 1994. II. Title III. Title: Boomerang ; and,
  Never die. IV. Title: Boomerang. V. Title: Never die. VI.
  Series: Banner books (Jackson, Miss.)
  PS3558.A476A6 1994
  813'.54—dc20
                                                    94-7877
                                                      CIP
British Library Cataloging-in-Publication data available

INTRODUCTION

I want you to imagine, for a moment, a world without Barry Hannah: how dangerous it would be. A world in which the self-important, the brusque, the shallow, the greedy, and the cowardly were not only free to roam unchecked, but a world in which these types were perhaps encouraged to prosper and multiply.

Hannah, of course, is the great dog-handler in modern literature. He soothes and pets the ailing and the defenseless, snarls at the crude and the savage, and jerks the choke-collar on the misbehaving legions of the power-mad. If only every bad guy in the country were wearing a shock collar, with Barry Hannah in charge of administering the voltage.

Some days when I have a bad encounter with some useless cretin, someone to whom the word *respect* or *courtesy* is utterly alien, it is enough for me to think how Barry Hannah would loathe that individual—how he would get it all right, that poor sap's life, in a single line—and it makes me feel better, just thinking of it. He's like a big brother in that regard, always ready to kick the moral shit out of bullies.

Nobody could ever have had it luckier or better than I did, drifting into Jackson, Mississippi, when I did, in

1979. I hadn't studied writing in college, but the great local bookstore—Lemuria—saw to it that I made up for lost time by telling me what to buy and what to read. They referred to all the authors by their first names: Eudora. Reynolds. Willie. Jim. Tom. Susan. Walker. Shelby. Barry.

So I read *The Moviegoer* and *The Second Coming* and learned about bravery in the face of malaise; read O'Connor and learned about bravery in the face of death; read Faulkner and learned about being your own boss and liking the ways of the woods perhaps more than the ways of the people. I read Miss Welty and learned about the care of storytelling—the notion of a certain reverence for the act. And I read Barry Hannah and learned that you can say anything, can think anything—that nothing needs to be proven or debated; it only has to have logic to it. In this manner, I got the best of both worlds. I read the awe-strikingly beautiful descriptive passages from Miss Welty about a bird dog's panting pink tongue being the color of fading roses, and about the sound the locusts make in the evening in the summer—a sound like grain being poured in a metal bucket—and then I read Barry.

Geronimo Rex, to be precise. A scene in which the narrator is hoping to couple with his beloved, parading around her room naked. "My Lord," cried the narrator's intended target, "it looks like you've been wounded! Something they rammed through you from behind!"

That was good for me. I knew you had to be deft and delicate, to write well. I did not yet know that sometimes you also had to be able to be rough and coarse.

Never, to my knowledge, has an American writer taken

such pleasure in the act of writing sentences. He typically starts with a first sentence that freezes you and then accelerates, as if that sentence has just snatched your purse, or something more significant. ("The other day we cornered a man, a lout named Reggy John. It was in a barn near the Kansas and Missouri border. The weather was freezing and moist. John was unarmed and covered with cow manure.")

But this game goes nowhere—pulling favorite Hannah lines from his works—for they're all amazing. We all have our favorites. In discussing Hannah's sentences—and ultimately, his stories, his books—you must use words like *jolt* and *electricity* and *dizzying*. *Zigzag, jazzy,* and the like. Regular mortal words for which Hannah himself would have no patience.

You have a wonderful thing here, two of Barry Hannah's books in one volume. He might like it were I to say that you could hold one in each hand, a left and a right, like two breasts, or perhaps like the dancing testicles of his gunslinger in *Never Die.* For a fact, Hannah's work is hooked pretty firmly to both the earthy and spiritual pleasures that bodies can provide. But he doesn't stop there, of course; that would be the simple ravings of a fiend, a sex maniac.

What I think he may be, instead, is a love maniac. Certainly *Boomerang* is the sweetest of his books, one of the sweetest books ever written. It is a poet's litany of his blessings, his friends—his celebrations for the living and lamentations for the too-soon passed. The old man Yelverston embodies all the characteristics our species is capable of on our best days: sterling loyalty, a masculine muscularity and feminine sensitivity, an almost Christlike amount of for-giveness. *Boomerang*'s not going to replace the Bible, but like that book, it holds a lot of love and war in it. One shudders to think of Christianity today had the prophets studied with (and perhaps read) Barry Hannah.

I think the scholarly procedure for these kinds of things—writing an introduction to another writer's work—calls typically for the introducer to en-capsulate the works forthcoming. I wouldn't dare. Nor could I possibly. *It's about this tiny but sincere child, growing up in Mississippi.* No. *It's about this woman who gets her hand shotgunned* . . . . No. *It's about* . . . .

Forget it. Read the damn thing. It's his most atypical work. It's his lightest work—by which I mean it is the work that contains (for me) the most light, the most goodness.

Much has been made of the bad Barry, the hostage to alcohol, rage, and despair. I know it's politically incorrect and often just a plain bad idea to pardon all but the most severe antics of the hard drinker with the dismissive wave—"Oh, that's just so-and-so"—but back when the bottle was kicking his (and everyone else's around him) ass, I and many others would hold out belief in him, knowing, as one of his readers, that he'd been burdened with a hugeness of talent and a hugeness of heart and perception that would crush any of the rest of us like a gumdrop. I understood with trembling lucidity the loaded courage of his narrator in *Hey Jack*, who describes Jack's character in the following passage: "He was barely carrying his weight. I thought he was going to fall. But he didn't. 'They gave me and you a certain hell, Homer,' he said to me. 'They made us know everything.'"

So I admire the sheer day-to-day burden there must be for a writer of Hannah's electric talent, having to

viii

carry around—all the time—all that sizzle and blaze, that fury. And I think that as a reader I understood early on—even in only the most abstract way—the courage of Hannah himself when, in the end of his short novel, *Ray*, his narrator charges headlong into the maelstrom that lies just ahead. Clearly, there are no whiners in Hannah's corps. "*Sabers, gentlemen, sabers!*"

But this is all fawning friendship. Some of the bad-Barry stories are frankly very good. The student in Tuscaloosa who kept giving him grief, kept smart-talking him in class. Barry deciding to take the student for a drive after class, down to the end of a lonely dirt road, and pulling a *gun* on the student and telling him to cut the crap. So goes the story. Barry shooting holes in the rotten floorboard of his old car to drain the rainwater that was collecting there. Barry menacing his classes with saxophone riffs that perhaps made them wish for the gun. Barry howling and shooting flaming arrows over the roofs of houses: holding that city and everything—*everything*—at siege. Sorting it out. Trying to get out from under that stranglehold.

Another passed-down tale: a student getting her story back from Barry, with the honest criticism on it: *This just isn't interesting.*

As I understand it, the student, a whiner, complained, *What can I do to make it be interesting?*

The cruelest advice I ever heard, but also the best—advice that I do not think I could have withstood had it been given to me directly, but which I have remembered. Barry, I am told, looked long and hard at the student, decided she was earnest about becoming a better writer, and told her the truth, told her Jack's and Homer's truth: "Try making yourself a more interesting person."

The student—as would have any of us—reportedly dissolved into tears.

This is all the bad Barry, the Barry-of-the-Past. These rumors and acid tales are told here not so much for sensationalism's sake (for, frankly, these are the tame ones, the very tame), but rather, to place the sweet Barry-of-the-Present in context. His job has never been that of mollycoddling society or of mollycoddling anything, except perhaps for stray dogs.

For those interested in the author rather than or in addition to his work, it is my understanding from all reports that the Barry-of-the-Present has gotten the pin in the bitter, desperate wrestling match with the bilious toxins of too-much knowledge, too-much *juice*. These days the most rage I hear about Barry Hannah venting loose into the world (outside of his continuing life habit of turning English sentences on their head) is his Tasmanian Devil's relationship with the tennis courts, turning the Oxford air blue with the inventiveness of his profanity and supplications. Even the frat boys blush, early on a Sunday morning, to hear Mr. Hannah's roars against the injustice of the foul line.

I believe that from here on out all the rage is going to be in the sentences. No more pistol-brandishing.

Certainly in Hannah's work there are pistols, swords, flowers, penises, vaginas, breasts, mouths, and other instruments of passion. In *Never Die*, the ripcord seems to have been pulled loose on all passion; the small Texas town of Nitburg (circa 1910) is a town of incest and murder, a society in which all of the noble traits so espoused in *Boomerang* have fallen away, victims of sloth and a lack of endurance of spirit. And what is revealed in Nitburg—the rotting floorboard beneath a shiftless, insincere veneer—is significant and ugly. There are a couple of decapitations, the likes of which may not soon leave your memory. And then after the heads are cut off, it gets worse: the sliding-away of any hopes for civility. Art takes it on the chin, too—perhaps one of the truest indicators of a loss of humanity. The crooning balladeer in *Never Die*, Fernando Muré, the story's only good guy, has his kneecaps crushed by a dwarf. (The dwarf is a recurring character in Hannah's fiction that I've come to see as a metaphor for the most small-minded of critics.) The dwarf in *Never Die* is once again an enemy of art, an enemy of tenderness. He's in love with a monkey—a metaphor, perhaps, for unevolved (or degenerating) humanity.

But this kind of mumbo-jumbo, deconstruction and explication, is too dry to bring honor to Hannah's work. His work is fuller than full, ringing with a magic that cannot and should not be analyzed: the magic of language and the grace of the best. One hears the word "genius" associated with very few story writers, but it is a word that has probably been used more often in Barry Hannah's company than in that of any other writer.

These words are getting in the way of what awaits: the characters of Yelverston and Nitburg, powered by the essence of Hannah. One of the pleasures of writing this introduction was the excuse to re-read these works. Let anyone who does not wish to read about love, friendship, loyalty, heroism, or the desperate joy of being alive, step aside now. Here comes the master.

Rick Bass

BOOMERANG

For David Marion Holman
1951-1988
And for my wife Susan

TINY

We were such tiny people in the Quisenberrys' pecan orchard.

We were so tiny but we were sincere. The Quisenberrys' house looked like a showboat on the Mississippi River, and when we were tiny we fought and we had secret intrigues. We built a fort out of railroad ties. The kids would roam out and find pecans and horse apples and a stick of dynamite.

There were Reds and Nazis out there.

We knew about dynamite. We once announced a rule that you couldn't come back to the fort unless you had something wonderful to tell. Our fort was very private.

We threw walnuts at each other. The Stovalls had a walnut grove. One night I was running around even more than usual. Mrs. Mell and her daughter Moochie tried to make me slow down. Moochie pulled down her pants and said, I'll show you mine if you'll show me yours. What a wonderful night that was, near the Stovalls' fishpond. It was a concrete pond with goldfish and big lily pads in it. But nothing would slow me down. Moochie's mother was a beautiful woman who worked in the drugstore. Mrs. Mell was the most beautiful woman I could imagine, outside of my aunts, Bertha and Bernice.

In my back yard Tommy Poates was in an Admiral television box moving slowly ahead, attacking the rest of us with an automatic rubber gun. Rod Flagler had brought in the idea of the automatic rubber gun from Culver City, California. The television box was as large as a refrigerator. Every time we ran up close, we got stung. We all dressed in short pants and nothing else. Fairly soon we learned not to get stung. Edward Ratliff set the box on fire with lighter fluid. It was quite amazing to see Tommy get out of the flaming box. Darn it, I'd never thought of that.

Preacher's kids lived in the barracks below us. Later I heard they were so poor they had to eat cold cereal for lunch. We fought them too. And hated them. All those preacher's kids were good athletes. They were never in the band, they were horrible skinny people with bad complexions. That's not true. That's a hideous statement. They were good and swift. And they were mean. We fought them with mudballs and threw cane spears at them. They were down there beyond the tall cane patch and they had nothing to eat and we were glad.

But one afternoon in Clinton I was standing out in the back yard of Edward Ratliff's house, helping him mow the tremendous acre of his yard. I was standing there in my shorts and bare chest. I thought I'd been stung by a hornet, but looked at my stomach and saw I'd been hit by a shot from an air rifle. The preacher's kids were giggling through the bushes. My god, they were all across the fence, laughing. I had no weapons on me. I was stupefied. All I could find near me was the boomerang I ordered out of the back of a comic book, $1.98. It took a couple weeks to save the dough. I went and got the boomerang and knelt over and pulled it out of the grass. There was nothing to do with it. There were bushes between us and the stormwire fence. There were plum trees and standing corn between me and the fellow who shot me. A lot of honeysuckle too. I looked over there and heard two of them giggling. The red welt on my belly was growing and still smarted terribly. When I threw the boomerang it went very high over them and then made a lovely twist, coming back. It just made it back to the Ratliffs' lawn. Maybe the guys never saw it, but it was a nice toss. I was learning to control it. It would almost come back to you, as promised in the ad. It would sail and then make a little return. Back into the St. Augustine grass. The preacher's kids would never have a lawn of St. Augustine grass.

3

They would never have anything except themselves and their air rifles, I thought. God, how I hated them.

But they were good. When we bought our own air rifles, they were ready. We had Daisys and we were out there behind the trees in the great pecan orchard. We had on plastic glasses too. What I mean is that two out of our six had on plastic glasses. The preacher's kids were behind the cane patch, all ganged up, shooting their air rifles at us. Even I knew this was dumb. They had three air rifles and we had six. We were moving up and getting behind the big trees so nothing could hit us. But everybody was chicken about being hit by beebees. I did not become the Pfc or the Sergeant at this point. I had my plastic glasses and my leather coat. Then I went into the meadow on my knees and started firing my Daisy over and over. Far in the back was Ratliff with his pellet gun that would penetrate a squirrel, but I wanted this to be a fair fight and I waved him back.

I received fire. All of them were shooting at me. But I was not being harmed. I caught a beebee in my right eyepiece. Moved ahead. Then the others came up. We had six guns to their three. So we started moving on them very slowly. They were out of beebees. Then we began moving very fast. They were in the back of the cane but then they fled.

———

I saw the boy who had shot me and started running after him. He had no shirt on and very thin blond legs. He was racing away toward his miserable barracks apartment and I aimed and shot him in the back. He went in the bottom apartment, howling with pain. I wanted to shoot him again. I shot him in the legs. I could hear him running on the stairs. And then he slammed the door. I gave it up when I heard his mother shriek.

Out there in September with the sun getting colder, in the gravel parking lot, looking at the stained yellow asbestos shingles where he lived, I took off my goggles. Thank god, I said to myself, I'm not him.

Later on I met David Bass, one of the preacher's kids, in Square Books here in Oxford. He smiled and said, Remember me? Certainly I did. He was older but he was still smiling, looking a little ragged around the eyes. He was coaching a ball team in Mississippi somewhere. I forget the town.

He was the fastest football player on the junior high team. You just handed him the ball and he would run away from everybody. He would go by the grasping end and then flee through the helpless linebackers down the field. We beat some teams 77–0 when I was the tiny quarterback, throwing over the taller boys to David Bass or Henry O'Neill. We took everybody. My head was always too little for my big plastic white helmet.

But we were the Clinton Arrows, not to be messed with.

An old man came off the sidelines to congratulate me one afternoon.

I was all sweaty in my white and red uniform. He hobbled up beside me and wanted to take my hand. I was nothing. I was five foot one. He told me I was the best passer he'd ever seen. The truth was I was so tiny I lateraled or handed off or threw it. I didn't like big people tackling me. I knew I had no future in athletics. I was going into music and my own poems. Quisenberry was second-string quarterback. But he was eating a lot of protein food and taking the weight course from Joe Weider. I gave the ball to him for the history of the Clinton Arrow football team. Eventually he broke all the records.

□ □

Then there was a new guy came in our class named Horace Newcomb. He could recite "The Wreck of the Hesperus" cold, standing up in the class. My whole future life opened up when I heard him do that. What a thing to be able to do in junior high, I thought. What a showoff. Newcomb was tall and had hornrim glasses. In the band he played tuba. I was on cornet. Wyatt Newman was on viola, not with the band but over in Jackson with the symphony. I'd never heard of the instrument. In the band he played tuba also. The big guys in the band played tuba. Art Lee played cornet. William Quisenberry played clarinet. John Quisenberry played cornet, though he was becoming more the star quarterback. Then there was Joe Brown, a clear genius from Union, Miss. He was pale—thin, too. His arms were like the limbs of a mimosa. His forehead was high and he already knew about botany.

OXFORD

There is a tall black man walking slowly through the alleys of this town, wearing glasses. He goes slowly. You would never think he was looking for anything especially. But he has the big plastic bag. He's looking for beer cans. Next to him is a slim young German shepherd on a rope, a dog with blue eyes, trotting alongside. They must be fine friends. The man walks with difficulty. He has a cane. He has gray hair. He must be sixty. The dog is young and steps delicately around the pavement and the grass. The man has dignity. He does not want your pity. His beloved dog prances back and forth around him, helping him scent the beer cans. This is a college town and the beer cans lie everywhere. I believe he might get a penny apiece for them at the recycling plant.

❑ ❑

An overprivileged young man from Kentucky killed his girlfriend. He strangled her and left her in the room, passed out, then awoke to find something wrong. Awoke to the horror of himself. His attitude was the same as that of many rich spoiled kids at the university: Don't get in my way. They throw the beer cans everywhere so the tall black dignified man can make a living.

The jury gave the young man life. His Kentucky parents were horrified. They hired a bodyguard for him at Parchman so that the criminals wouldn't sodomize him like he did the girl, who told my nephew once she'd smoked dope every day since she was thirteen. No drugs were mentioned in the trial, although everybody knew drugs were involved. My son was in class with the killer. He brought his helmet into class, from his motorcycle, said my son.

My son they call the best guitarist in north Mississippi.

He neither smokes nor drinks. What a great improvement over me. He just stands up there and plays. As if nothing ever happened but his guitar, as if there were no history beyond himself. He doesn't know how to fight. Like our little Lhasa apso dog, Joseph, he just wasn't trained that way. In fact he has prevented me from violence several times.

❑ ❑

When I came to this town I was homesick after twenty years away from my home state. My hometown is three hours from here but this place was close enough. I had been on my last frightening flight to space, and I returned my rank to the pool. At the last I even poured my last little half vial of coke down the toilet.

I was here as a bachelor, and then my son joined me to go to the college.

The sun comes up like a purple diamond. The wet smoke in the air falls away, and there is the country. When you are meeting your next wife the house smells like charred embers and it's a two-story cottage with dry grass and the croquet tour you'd set out for your other two kids, Ted and Lee. There are a number of things here under the big blue long-clouded sky. Mainly there is music. My kids are all crazy about music. They come in with their tapes and their albums.

Right behind us they were grinding out a field to plant. I was paying $300 a month for privacy and then all the Muchles come here ripping up my back yard. I felt like a tenant farmer. Certain people don't care what they do to you as long as they are making a buck. What landlords.

I saw my future wife and declared my love at the Hoka. I was not doing too well. In depression I had spray-painted my kitchen and my car silver. I was wearing swimming trunks and a herringbone sports jacket. She was sitting with friends in a corner booth. I was trying to get some food down, so I ordered a salad, but I was eating it with my hands, she says. She was sitting there with her regal blond hair and her big gray eyes. I never even noticed her friends. We met them later but I had no idea who they were. The Hoka is an old warehouse made into a bohemian café with a movie house in the other half. Ron Shapiro, from St. Louis, owns and runs it. He works with a partner named Jim Dees. Dees begged my future wife to come over and sit with me, after I'd begged him to do it. I told her I had a plane and a boat, total lies. I asked her to marry me. All I asked was that she be rich and have a covered garage. She was not only poor but she was less than zero. When I got back on my feet I was in her kitchen and saw her pouring ketchup from one of those large cafeteria-sized jars. I almost broke down and cried for her poverty. She had two teenaged children and they didn't know what was happening with me in the house, having been on their couch for three days.

❑ ❑

The man leans on his cane to pick up a can.

He could be a professor. He looks like a man floating on serene thoughts after his immense history of thinking and deciding. He moves along slowly, no hurry. It's just money, it's just pennies, it's just to get by. My own old man moves along with a cane now, at eighty-four. He has a cancer — a big tumor off the bone near the spleen. But it's in control, after his neutron treatments in Houston, and the old man still walks along slowly, looking at the mysteries on the side of the road.

Where does the old black man live? What does he eat? What does the dog do at the home? Does it stay inside with him or sleep outside near the steps? Does the old black man ever read the newspapers?

I don't want to know, really.

I asked about him one afternoon, from Ollie Caruthers. I was sorry I asked. Ollie told me the old man carries a loaded .25 in his back pocket all the time. Maybe that's why he always looks so serene and philosophical. Lately he got brushed by a car, walking along some road looking for beer cans. He got laid up. I wanted to take him some food and offer my respects. But since I heard about the .25 I don't anymore. He's just as scared as the rest of us. I'm terribly sorry to hear it.

❑ ❑

A dude with no hopes, no prospects, alcoholic, twenty-four, eighth-grade dropout, white, got a divorce. He found a job taking care of the dogs at the animal shelter. I bought him a car and he started loving the dogs. He had ten of his own back at his mother's house, where he was staying now, though many nights he slept in the little Subaru. Then he quit the dog shelter because of personal differences with everybody. He simply left the place without telling anybody. He left dying puppies out in their own manure. He couldn't stand the women of the Humane Society. I have to hold it in because I'm president of the Humane Society now. All the women are sighing martyrs. They don't know how sighing they are, bossy and sometimes insane. But I am full of error myself.

❑ ❑

Wondering about the lady—eighty-four—who hardly ever leaves her kitchen. There is nothing in the town that interests her anymore. The old brick streets and the "old town," as they call it—Clinton, Mississippi—have been surrounded by subdivisions and the increasing Baptist church, with its ugly red bricks. There is an evangelism that reaches to Southeast Asia and heals the diseases of the natives and gives them hope itself, beyond their fatalism. The money is given from the purses of the old women and their reluctant husbands. Churches with their stacked bricks claiming all the view where there used to be great oaks and calm green meadows. The town has almost been changed into an asphalt maze running between two-story rectangles. She has no more interest in the town except for the mail she receives at the post office. She taught me modern poetry. Her husband, long dead now, taught me History of Civilization — an ambitious course, but he taught it to me. He'd been a war correspondent in World War One. He taught me about Spain and North Africa. He taught me about Paris and Germany. He taught me about China. He had a stiff posture and he wore nice long-collared shirts we heard were made in London.

That was when Mississippi College was good.

That was when J. Edgar Simmons was there.

That was when Louis Dollarship gave me praise.

That was when Annabell Jenkins was the prima donna of the eighteenth century.

That was when Tom Boswell taught a great class in Roman Ritual and Religion and we went over to his apartment and had pizza and beer afterward.

❏ ❏

When we went out fishing, big cottonmouth moccasins were everywhere in the ponds and the lakes. Russell Williams and I were fishing in a boat on Lake Garaway. There was a snake lying on a little limb just this side of a big log. Russell threw over the log, where he let the "wounded minnow" — a topwater plug with spinners — lie so as to attract an enormous bass. He jerked the line softly a couple of times. Then the snake coiled up around the plug. Russell jerked it and he had him. He reeled it in. Snakes are harmless creatures, they say — yeah.

Now that I'm an adult they don't mess with me so much. You take a .410 shotgun and blow their heads off. They sure messed with you when you were a kid. Jim Harrison saw one wounded in the tail and it bit itself over and over. Shoot, shoot, shoot, is what I say.

UNCLES

A few weeks ago old Uncle Babe comes in with his cane. He can't sit in the sun because, he says, he's had forty skin cancers removed in the last couple of years. My old man asked him how his old friends were doing.

"They're all half dead," said Uncle Babe.

He was going back to his bedroom and my mother asked him what he had to say.

"Damn," he said.

"Well, that's not nice," said my mother, a deep Baptist lady. Uncle Babe has vicious arthritis.

I put up his shirts and pants in the closet and set his grip-bag on the cedar chest. He was sleeping in that high bed I slept in all through my teenage years. Outside the window were the oak trees, all bare now in the late warming month of March. There was the clayey ground on which no grass would ever grow. I'd mowed and raked this yard hundreds of times. I knew every inch of it like the back of my hand, from the St. Augustine grass in the front to the patches of ivy in the very back. I was a mad boy, angry about everything except my trumpet, which I played out of the open windows of my bedroom. I'd play in the air and try to make something happen in vacant air. Rafael Mendez was my idol. I tried to play the whole Arban book. My notes pierced out in the air with a sweet revenge on reality. The neighbors were kind not to complain. I was quite a howling, stumbling attack of sound. I dreamed long trumpet sounds and made my tone as sweet as possible.

In the last days of being swift and tiny, I recall raking the leaves and running the mower, increasing my muscles and taking a sweat break while the teenaged girls circled my house with their new driver's licenses. I wasn't that wonderful, but there were only about five blocks to go around in Clinton. The town was still running wild with Baptists and their happy morbid meetings. We had heard a rumor of five Catholics in town. Maybe twelve Episcopals too. Members of these churches made graven images and served them. Also they drank.

But I knew the lakes and the muddy creeks and some music and I had forgotten caring about religion one way or another.

There was a place where I could go with my own war. I would line up plastic soldiers against the door and shut it and then shoot my Daisy beebee gun against the door. The ricochets, coming right toward my face, were the enemy firing back. One of the beebees chipped my tooth and there was blood in my mouth. At that point I knew the enemy would fire back and I wanted no part of war anymore.

□ □

When we were in our tuxedos and were playing in the Jackson Symphony Orchestra, riding over there in Wyatt Newman's old Jaguar sedan, we rode past the smart hedges around Murrah High School auditorium. We'd picked up a very tall gentle percussionist named Hugh. That was back in the main part of Jackson, on North State Street. We passed a ragged man selling papers. The newspapers in Jackson were right-wing racist documents. Even I knew it. Just as I know today that Mississippi College is owned by frowning fat Christians. The school has gone away. In my tuxedo, I lit up a Picayune and stared out at the man selling papers.

"Look at that poot peddling papers," I said.

There was a huge silence in the car.

When we let Hugh out at the back of the auditorium, Joe Brown said to me, "Do you realize that what you said about the 'poot peddling papers' is everything that Hugh is against? That kind of insensitivity is what keeps him so nervous."

I guess I was wrong and Brown was right. Hugh was so tall and had an Adam's apple like Ichabod

Crane. He was shaking all the time, too. But he played perfect kettledrums, never understated, never overstated. Brown was his understudy, I guess, sometimes doing a roll on a snare drum when the orchestra did an adventurous symphony. I was third chair and did about ten notes an hour. I was in my tuxedo but I was bored to a condition of glassiness.

I was such a factotum in the orchestra that they got me to go out and get some little lady's harp from her house and haul it in. Her name was Lina Kellum, I believe. Three of us would go to her house and haul out this enormous harp. Her husband was the flute player, first chair, and he was so much better than the rest of us that he was always angry. Somebody told me he was Jewish. He was the first Jewish guy I ever met. His wife Lina weighed about ninety and she had an enormous flowing gown on her. She was so grateful about our lifting the great harp into the station wagon and getting it to the auditorium that we ignored the trouble.

She was a fine harp player, although I thought the instrument was ridiculous.

Twenty years later I saw a woman in Venice, California, strumming a giant harp like Lina's near the ocean. She had on a gown too and she was sprawled out there straddling her instrument, with her record albums for sale. Behind me, on roller skates, was a mulatto in a turban playing Jimi Hendrix tunes with a pighead amp wrapped on him and an old Fender Stratocaster, playing it as he skated, turning back and forth on his wheels, self-charged, squatting and rising as he rolled along. A white rock-and-roll band was going just a hundred yards away. The guys were so ugly and white they looked like they'd been doing nothing but shooting heroin and living in a cave for two years. All of us wanted music.

I was there trying to write a good screenplay with music in it for Robert Altman. With all my striving, I had only grown to five feet nine inches' height. A giant black in a lavender latex outfit, white Stetson hat on his head, with a white cane to guide him on his skates, rolled up beside me. He had great muscles in his arms and his legs that you only get in a penitentiary.

"You're him, ain't you?" he demanded.

"Who?"

"Him, baby. You're him, ain't you?"

I wasn't drinking then and had a tan and he had mistaken me for the television star John Ritter. Then he looked at me through his sunglasses a while longer. When he saw I wasn't John Ritter the disgust began accumulating in his eyes.

"You ain't nobody," he said.

"Don't get angry," I begged him. He was getting enraged.

I've always avoided fights by ignoring the looming person in my face. I looked down the boardwalk at the mulatto man playing Jimi Hendrix as he squatted and rose and then twisted on his skates. It was the Olympics of the weird out here in California, and I was just a small boy from Mississippi, so broke I had no ride except the green Triumph motorcycle lent me by John Quisenberry, Annapolis graduate, heroic Phantom pilot in Vietnam. Under the great Dick Prenshaw we made beautiful music in the Clinton High band. Now Quiz was a newly married lawyer in L.A. Our common memory was "Eroica" and winning "superior" in the state band contest.

When I was working with the kind and brilliant Robert Altman in his wooden mansion by the sea, I was in a tower of Plexiglas with sea gulls flying around me and the Pacific rolling under the house like a white man's dream of peace. I had a typewriter and there was a Spanish maid who would bring me coffee. But it was too nice and I had to turn on the radio. Altman came up and asked me how could I work with the radio on that loud.

I needed the music, the tinny loud music, to remind me of all the trouble in the world. I missed my kids so much, I wanted to hear how other people hurt too. I could not accept paradise. I had to drag in the bad music and the cigarettes. I had to foul up the air and my ears. With no whiskey, what else was there to talk about? What about all my pitiful little songs and my tiny eloquence, back on trumpet in the Jackson Symphony Orchestra and in the Mississippi Lions All-State Band?

What if I was wrong and I was nothing, exactly nothing?

❏ ❏

Neil, a tall skinny guy, and Krebs, a short little man with a big nose, squared off in the alley next to the Dutch Bar, 1959. Art Krebs left the bar telling us he's had it with Neil and wants to have it out. They came back in after about fifteen minutes — nobody messed up, no bruises. "What happened?" I asked Neil while Krebs was getting another beer.

"Krebs paid me five dollars not to hit him," said Neil.

Krebs retired as a major in the army about six years ago. Tommy Poates, the guy we burned up in the television box, is probably a full colonel in the air force by now. Quisenberry is a commander in the Navy Reserve Air Force. Only two out of our class have died, and they are both women. Ann Gill in an air crash with the Olympic wrestling team. Jenny O'Neill, Henry's wife, with heart disease in Houston, lying on the operating table.

❏ ❏

"What if this *is* heaven?" I asked Horace Newcomb one night while we were riding around drinking beer. "What if all those who don't drink beer will never know heaven, and this is it?"

"That's a good idea," said Newcomb. "That's a very good idea."

What a feeling those first beers gave us, cruising in my parents' Bonneville, my brother's Plymouth Fury convertible, my brother's '57 Thunderbird. My family always had the best cars. The old man was so poor in the Depression he always wanted a good car.

One afternoon Gomar Wallace and I were fishing right next to the boat ramp at Elwood Ratliff's pond. We'd just come out to hang around the good country and have some fun if we could. We brought a couple of poles and some crickets. The big bream started hitting out at the end of the ramp. We kept hauling them in. They were really big bluegills and shellcrackers. We'd hit a bed of them. We had about forty when we went home. That was in the days when we'd clean them and my mother would cook them right up. Gomar's father died early. Then his brother was killed by a farmer on the wrong side of a four-lane highway—49—coming back from the Gulf Coast. Their family has had such bad luck, I cry.

NAMES IN PASSION

Krebs. I am not sentimental about departures. But I thought it would be interesting to report that Krebs shot his own leg before any of the rest of us were armed. That was when Quisenberry was throwing footballs through a swinging tire down in his pecan grove. He was lifting weights on the Joe Weider course. He lent me a puller to strengthen my arms.

The great villain in this piece was Hoyt Weems, who made everybody disgusted with themselves. He was the football coach. They've named a football field after him now in Clinton. Weems hated tiny guys like me. He was a tank sergeant, maybe, in World War Two. He was supposed to teach me science. Weems owes me about $50,000 for personal abuse. He received salary and taught me nothing except self-disgust. He was a raw, tough, ugly soldier, who wanted to talk about people burning up alive in tanks. Neither of my uncles in World War Two were like him. They were level creatures.

Krebs was with us at the Strong River. Wyatt had brought along his Argentine Mauser. Carl Lee had the bazooka. His father had just died and he was going wild for armaments. I had my double-barrel .410 and a .22 Mossberg with a scope, lent to me by John Kitchings. O'Neill had maybe a .22. Krebs had grenades. He was the only real veteran with us, since he'd shot himself in the leg.

The Strong River was a beauty with big rocks and white rushing water, pooling back up in deep holes where the streams ran in, like where we camped on a bluff with our beds dug out elaborately in the bank and tarpaulins over them. I think Newman had discovered the Strong on one of his travels. It was down in Simpson County, about forty miles south of Clinton. But it felt like the tropics. Horace Newcomb was there with us a couple of times. He carried no weapons. He was tall and gangly and very smart. His dad was a postman, a veteran of World War Two who had quit Camels and begun going to the Baptist church very seriously. I can't recall whether Joe Brown was out there on the camp or not. His stepfather was the head of the Mississippi National Guard. We had a wonderful stew going by the pool on the little white beach. You got the water boiling and dumped in meat, potatoes, carrots, onions, and at the last, sardines. George Patterson was there. His father owned the Army/Navy surplus store. You walked in there and smelled Cosmoline and treated tarpaulins.

Newman was out in the river with a piece of Ivory

25

soap floating near his palm. He was naked. New-man was a big fellow with a hairy bod and he was maybe the only one of us who was not ashamed of himself naked. The river was firm and green around him. I lined up the scope on the Mossberg and shot away the bar of Ivory just as he was reaching for it. It was a miracle shot. He raised his fist at me, pretending to be outraged, but the big smile broke out on his face. What a shame that none of the rest of them saw it. Later I took a quart of oleo into the tent to have my satisfaction with dream women. We had a trotline running under the bridge, baited with pork livers. The stars came out and were brilliant and heavy in the air. The stew was big and manly. We were sober and deeply sincere, although you had to tell lies to have any class around here. Newman was writing endless poems to some woman in Nashville. I had my dream lover in Natchez. My god, she was long-legged and brunette and nothing but little songs came out of her mouth. In church the preacher would be talking about Jehovah and heaven and the judged, etc., and I was out there in the balcony pew in my suit writing poems to my dream woman in my head.

❏ ❏

Just a few years ago, when I was a bachelor and very lonely, I went out to a private lake, snuck in, and had a line out in the water with a minnow on it, way down. I'd heard there was a thirty-pound catfish here. My life was over with Vera, a cellist at the university. I always knew we had nothing going, and she did too. I went to all her cello playing with the Memphis Symphony. She traveled around with me when I gave readings. I loved the cello, I loved her Porsche. Then I went out to west Texas and found out her people. They were just wealthy. My parents didn't know everything but at least they were courteous. I tried to teach Vera to fish and know the lakes but once she saw a moccasin swallow the bream we'd caught, she went out of her mind. Vera and her sister, a failed painter, had been spoiled so much they could only see a white room with other people paying for them to go to Switzerland and get another privileged view of the world. Vera was denied tenure at the university mainly because, as she said, she was "no good with people." I stood up for her, but I never knew the main issue was she was "no good with people."

I was sitting there fishing and nothing was biting, and it was very hot, extremely hot in July, when this young lad of about seven walked up to me and said: "There's a big snake on my pole." At that time I had a .25 automatic in my tackle kit. I had a silver automatic in my kit and I walked down the dam with the gun. The little boy was right. There was a snake coiled around his cane pole. Its head was in the water. What a hell of a snake it was. Back at Wyatt Newman's pond, when Newman was think-

27

ing Eastern and about to go into the Navy Band, he said: "You can't kill anything. They just regenerate!" I thought about this. It rose its head and I blew its head off. A lucky first shot.

The child said to me: "Are you with the army?"

"No."

"Are you with the police?"

"No."

"Who are you, mister?"

"I'm with the army of myself," I told him. "It's just you and me, son."

We sat there all the rest of the afternoon and eventually he got a good five-pound catfish.

I've missed my daughter Lee a long time now. Also my son Teddy. Lee used to ride on the back of my Harley, reading a book. She trusted her dad so much after we went out to Sardis Lake she was sitting there reading her book when I looked back. She knew I was a safe pilot on my big Harley. And I was. Nothing could happen to us on my Harley. The thing about the Harley is you know every tire rim, every movement on the wheel, every gauge: You're perfect.

I've missed my daughter Lee and son Ted a long time now. Lee was waiting late one afternoon on a dam at Elwood Ratliff's lake when all the rest had left. She was still holding her little pole with the cricket on the hook, nothing had been happening for the rest of us, but she believed in her father, me, and the mosquitoes were biting her all over, but she was hanging in. It was almost too dark to see. Something took her cork down. It pulled her little body and she pulled back. She waded into the water and pulled the long cane pole back. Then she had it and she knew she had it. She backed up on the bank. Same thing when Ted brought antlers from the woods, proud as if he'd won the Nobel Prize.

Lee, my daughter, landed it. It was a redgill. A shellcracker. The biggest bream I'd ever seen. When it was flopping there on the dam, she looked down and saw it between her feet. She did not want to eat it or even have it. She just wanted to look at it a while and let it go. Which we did.

❑ ❑

Old Mama Hannah, who had no money and no home, was living with our Uncle Wayne and Aunt Jeannie Alliston down at Bay St. Louis. I had famous times as a youth in Bay St. Louis. There were shrimp and crabs and flounders in the seawater. Mama Hannah had no house, no money, and she lived from home to home. That was in the days when the children took care of their parents. My old man had to drop out of Ole Miss to take care of his parents. He was a smart man but he had to go back and take care of his parents. He was rooming with Senator Eastland (in the future) and they already had their stationery written up together as future lawyers, but my old man had his dreams shattered and had to go back home to take care of his parents.

On the the sea wall they're just catching a few crabs. I'm there. I've always been there. The high wind is coming in, and there are white spouts in the bay. My grandmother hangs into a big flounder on her cane pole. She's got it and the flounder's got her. She starts calling *whoop whoop whoop! Whoop!* Then Mama Hannah has got the flounder on the sea wall, big lover of a meal, and my granny brought it in.

Mama Hannah talked about it for three years. She'd brought a big meal into the house. Late at night, when everybody else was asleep, they told me that Mama Hannah was dancing to a country band on the television. Her hair was beautifully white and long and she had spirited eyes. She wrapped the hair around her head in a close way with combs in it. When she was put in the grave I saw my old man with his beautiful white hair sitting by the graveside. It was over in Forest, Mississippi. All the rest of the relatives were there, but I only remember my father and his elegant white hair and his courtly bearing. That's where I came from, Scott County, in the middle of the state. Pines, oaks, ashes, going crazy with squirrels.

My uncle ran Roosevelt State Park. My word, how I loved to visit with Aunt Bertha and Uncle Slim

and all their boys. I swam in the lake with Ted
Hannah and caught bream and watched the speed-
boats going by. The Lodge was an exquisite place,
with its dance floor and the juke box. The trees
leaning in close to the lanes at twilight. The World
War Two tank sitting there for us all to climb
around and get in. The real business. The WPA or
the CCC or somebody did the parks all over the
states in the Depression. We had cabins and stone
lodges, giving people work. My Aunt Bertha would
cook us fried squirrels and slaw and potatoes. At
night we had a Jeep to run around in. Off the diving
platform Mrs. Something got parked and caught a
six-pound bass, but my cousin Ted told me never
to tell anybody else; this was a secret thing. There
was a name I heard, maybe I was kin to it: Tadlock.
We had cousins all over the county. At that time
"Searchin' " was on the juke box and I saw a lot of
older people dancing. It was done by the Coasters.
Pretty soon after that, Elvis broke out. But what a
lovely place Roosevelt State Park was to visit. All
the Hannahs. Tommy and Ray and Robert Oliver
and Ted.

❑ ❑

Quisenberry called for me to be a pallbearer at
his father's funeral. What an honor that was. His
father was World War One. I never knew the
man that much. He was silent when we played
around him. Later, John told me that he had a

temper. They were afraid of crossing him or he would erupt. Mrs. Quisenberry, Bea, was the wit of the neighborhood. She invented Cowboy Salad. It was macaroni and cheese and we all would have hated it except Mrs. Bea called it Cowboy Salad. Down at the Quisenberrys' house we had also a butter-and-sugar sandwich. Aunt Rosa and Uncle Curry were still there then, moving slow and wise.

The Ratliffs took us down to Florida. We caught so many redfish and red snapper that we paid for the whole trip. Mr. Ratliff never said much, but he had a magic around him about fish. He is in his nineties now and a veteran of World War One. One day we were out at old Mr. Elwood's lake. There were a lot of fish caught but a lot of moccasins were there too. Uncle Elwood got out his rifle and got one of them running in the water. He knocked off its head. Forever after that I've knocked off their heads. The herons were landing and the little happy small airplanes were going above us in the blue air and light cumulus. Hey baby!

◻ ◻

My first wife worked hard for me and rushed me into marriage. She was an army brat who thought my parents were rich. She was a painter and a lover and a wife, but foremost she made sure we were married. She hated all my friends. She had the great talent for taking the heart out of any situation that gave me joy. She had no friends. Everything scared her.

But now she is better.

She has a new husband and she is proud at her school. When you can't live life, school is a great skill. Take that into a zone and into another zone. A lot of people sit back in life and have their overview. Compared to my underview, where I scout, under the bleachers, for what life has dropped.

When I was fifteen, I already thought about a great uncle whose name would be something like Yelverston. When I went down to the coast I would see the great uncles, with their important boats in the water. A dad cannot win against the great uncles. Can never win. Yelverston launches the craft and goes out laughing with his friends. It's a brown cedarwood boat with a white cabin, cruising the waves and the people laughing. Yelverston was in my dreams when I was there and he was so far away. When I finally met him at Syd and Harry's and his son had been killed, and he was sixty-two and I was forty-six, I thought, All right, uncle, tell me everything and I will be your nephew, learning in the new distance. We don't have that many years to go. Things are shortening up. One of us has got to be wise.

Then I was struck by one of those meditative states, with no action, that affects men and women.

I could not participate in reality anymore. Could not.

There is a day for everybody who ever practiced cruelty. The boomerang, if you throw it well, as I did yesterday, almost comes back into your palm.

Every good deed and every good word sails out into the hedges and over the grass and comes to sit in your front yard. Only the creeps forget a good deed. We are all so loaded up with what our good mothers did in the past that we walk through life like darlings.

LOST PILOTS

Uncle Bootsy was lost over the Amazon, piloting his big plane. He was just twenty-three when he died. My Uncle Cicero Eugene told me about him. Bootsy never smoked and was a strapping good-looker. He played football at Mississippi Southern and then married a beauty named Hazeline. He wrestled a bear to the ground when he was a teen-ager and the handler wouldn't let him try for the five dollars again. He was after Rommel and the Nazis in North Africa, and before he left he laughed and told my old man that the Germans didn't have a chance, what with all our planes and fly-boys and materiel. In fact he laughed about al-most everything, said Uncle Cicero Eugene and my dad. But then his plane went down in the jungles. I have told this story before, many times, but my mother's crying is what stays with me. When I was just a tiny guy my mother would break into tears about her baby brother Bootsy. He has been listed as missing since 1942. We always expected him to show up, laughing. Maybe smelling like smoke from his B-25, but definitely there. He had always been so lucky and handsome and good. When he was a little boy a window blew in during a storm. Big shards of glass covered him. He was still sleeping and did not suffer a single cut. The Delta winds were still whipping around over the cotton. The sisters and Gran King and Daddy King, the plantation manager, were standing there looking at a miracle. The storm left with the silence of a vacuum and a green sky overhead. It went back into Arkansas across the river and poured itself into Texas.

Daddy King was known for his fairness to blacks. What a fine old grandfather he was. He died in the same room where I was sleeping. He'd had a stroke and he'd been blind for several years. But he loved baseball and strawberry ice cream. He laughed a great deal and he had pretty white hair too, combed back. He had liver spots on his face, and he was the handsomest old man I ever saw, although that is said about many grandpops. He would reach out his noble speckled hand to me and want to feel the glove when I was going down to play baseball.

But he had that laugh, most of all. I suppose Bootsy had it too, because Cicero Eugene had it and Annis Lloyd had it (she was my aunt in Baton Rouge), and the laugh through the years is the only thing that saved me, even when I was in Bryce, state home for the nuts. Because of drinking and shooting. I had a nasty laugh then and I was a roaming drunk with weapons in my hand. I thought I was enormously sensitive and a hero but I was also scaring hell out of everybody I loved. That was in Alabama. It was not fun to be in the nuthouse for five days, with the tall loony black guy coming by stealing your clothes while you were trying to get some rest. He wore my shoes on his enormous feet, and they were hanging on his toes. Like Kesey says, those black orderlies will boss you around too. They've been waiting all their lives to get whitey in this position. It's a dirty horror. One little white guy told me he lived on cigarettes and Cokes for two months. He'd been in alcoholic dry-out wards sixteen times. I got a lawyer and got out. Still owe the lawyer three hundred. All my family wanted me to go to Atlanta to a dry-out clinic for impaired professionals. They were there, my brother Bobby. I gave him the finger when I walked out. I'd passed all the tests and I was *compos mentis*. All I needed was some bacon and eggs and a good night in bed with a woman. Forever after that I've asked Bobby to forgive me. He has. He and Grace have forgiven and forgiven me.

❑ ❑

1988.
    Went to the fellows' house behind me, went over to have a breather and some of Ollie's ribs. Ollie is

a black guy about thirty-five who claims he was in Vietnam, handling the M-60 machine gun. Maybe it's true. But he is doing a swell job at the animal shelter, he and Maryl. Ollie cooks great ribs. I could smell them at one A.M. I walked over there to see Terry and Ollie and catch some ribs. About two A.M. the electricity went out of the neighborhood and we were back to the nineteenth century, with just a little fire going in the yard. Willie Morris came over. Hadn't seen him in five months. It was pitch black except for the fire. He'd been working on a novel on the Bogue Chitto River, near McComb in the south of the state.

We walked back to see my wife, who was sleeping. With the help of Willie's lighter we found her. When she came out to the fire she looked smacking with her blond hair all ruffled out and her eyes dazed. She was in her baby-blue gown with white figures around the throat. She had our flashlight and went back to the house to get our dogs Joseph and Missy. We wanted to give them some rib bones. The little black female puppy we call Missy was given us by Mr. Levi at the Jitney Jungle. It sat on the table and ate a rib bone so ravenously that Willie Morris broke into tears.

"Look at her. Look at her. Look how she wants to *live!*" he said over and over. She was crawling into his arms. She had not been weened when Mr. Levi found her. Her mother was probably killed. She had white feet and a look from her eyes like all the good dogs do: What's next, friend? "Look how she wants to live!" said Willie.

Willie, who had just given a hundred and forty to the animal shelter, wanted to give a hundred more. Willie Morris has an enormous heart made of pure gold, like the beautiful old sluts in the western tales. He told me I must write a story called "The Animal Shelter," about the immense cruelty to dogs by human beings. Since I was listening, I recalled some blacks putting a lit cigarette to a puppy's tummy. I recalled white county people shooting the forelegs off a dog when they were through hunting with it, leaving it out to hobble near the highway where some person might, just might, pick it up and call the Humane Society. Who in America can ever quit the Humane Society?

❑ ❑

The aforementioned dude Wayne who was working with the animal shelter for a while. I bought him a car for $500 and he was supposed to pay it back with his work. Has an eighth-grade education, alcoholism, a divorce, and lives with his mother at age twenty-four. He quit and told me he'd pay back the car. For two months I never heard. So I woke up Ollie and the wife and I called him so I could go down there to pick up the car because he told me if I wanted it I had to come get it. I couldn't understand his directions so I asked if somebody else in the house could talk to me. He hung up. We went out on Old Taylor Road and I stopped by a black woman's house to check on the directions. Then I called him again and since we were near his place he was a little more pleasant. Where they lived was down a long gravel road in a sixty-foot trailer. The car was a little Subaru about '75 vintage. I knocked on the trailer door. His mother told me Wayne was out back. The mobile home sat on grated earth. I'd only met Wayne once before and he sounded so angry over the phone now my wife had brought along the .45. I went in back of the trailer and there was Wayne. He's gained about fifteen pounds. He's about five three, one of the few people I could actually physically beat up. I told him he was looking good. Down in the back about fifty yards was a garden. He and this man with tattoos all over his arms, maybe his stepfather, were sharpening some tool. The car needed a jump start so Wayne came out and jumped it and after a few times it was ready to go and Ollie drove off with it. Wayne had taken the tag off the car and I had to pay him for that and the jumper cables. Wayne was a cheat, a scoundrel, a liar, but he was proud of it. I was watching the man with the tattoos more than Wayne. They finally got the title for the car out of the trailer after thirty minutes. I was watching for sudden movements from the tattooed man, but he was the sanest one there. Some obese child of ten or so wallowed up and watched us, spitting a lot. We must have been something to hate there in our little silver Chrysler LeBaron convertible, which I couldn't afford. I really wanted out of there but Wayne finally came out with the title. I wished him luck. He told me I was the one that was going to need luck. He said something about the nigger who took the car. That wasn't a nigger, I told him. That was a sergeant from Vietnam. Oh *excuse me!* he said.

I hadn't seen real scoundrelism close up for a long time.

It was tough to be a repo man. But all the while, I knew that Wayne's pride was at stake and the tattooed man, Lester, was keeping him calm. I remembered the garden down from the trailer. It was neatly arranged and just starting with some shoots. I believe Lester was trying to give me a hand.

That was Sunday morning.

□ □

Another Sunday, 1988.

All this day I've worried about what to do with this third marriage. It is a cold day in April and my wife has never offered to lick me or serve me food. She is on the picket line of feminism. My god, I've hired Ollie to put the azaleas out. It looks like a bad spring to me. Many Confederates and Yankees have fought over this land. I've told about flying jets in Vietnam so long and so faithfully, I think I deserve a woman on her knees. Besides, she has wonderful blond hair. I will snap my fingers almost anywhere, and there she is, on her knees. But she's on the picket line now. I never took her to Shiloh. I never took her to Graceland. Yes, yes. There's so much I've not done for her yet.

She's off the picket line now. My great sullen manliness is controlling her and she has no self-esteem anymore, which is exactly the way I want it. I am a terrible man.

Her beauty almost slaughters me.

In fact, I move through life without a conscience. Years ago, Wyatt Newman, who played viola and lived out in the country, took care enough to make some peach wine out at his place. He was writing poetry to his woman in Nashville, playing the viola, and being harrier and more mature than the rest of us. He had the old Jaguar sedan in which we went over to the Jackson Symphony. One thing that Newman taught me early was that endless note-books of rhyming quartets don't necessarily mean anything. While Newman was making his wine on the sly, Horace Newcomb came out to the place. We had rigged up a blank .22 and Newman's hand full of ketchup. It happened in the kitchen. Newman started yelling at me really hysterically about some matter. I had the rifle already in my hand and said I'd heard this too long and wasn't going to take any more. Newman was really large and when he charged at me I lifted the rifle and shot him in the stomach. He grabbed his waist with the ketchup and staggered down. Newcomb was ter-ribly alarmed. He couldn't believe it. Newman twisted all over the linoleum floor and blood was flying everywhere. Poor Horace had his mouth open and his hornrims went out on his nose. Newman would never quit dying. Finally we all laughed and it was over. What a relief to the brilliant and sensitive Horace. We went out and smelled the nectar of Newman's peach wine in the well house. It wouldn't really be ready for another two weeks, he told us. My word, how Newman loved the fine things. None of us had ever had a fine wine. None of us, in fact, had had *a* wine. When it was ready, right before the senior prom, I went out with Wyatt and hid the bottle under some leaves in the dam of Lake Garaway. It was near the road so all he had to do was drive the Jaguar right by it, step out, and lift it up. When I was at home I could get no rest. I couldn't stand it. So I drove out to the lake and pissed in Wyatt's wine. I knew he would want to go by the bottle for a trial before the prom, so I and Art Lee — who in his sorrow used to try to run over dogs on country roads — and maybe Krebs went out to make the test with Newman.

Newman took a big slug. He choked and spat out what he could, knowing immediately what had happened. He chased me all the way down the dam and I was laughing so helplessly in the moonlight I couldn't run anymore. He pounded me and pounded me until he was tired. But I loved it.

When I was in the first grade I got run over by a car and maybe that fouled my head, even though all I got out of the accident was a dislocated thumb. There was a hill next to our house that ran to the main highway. It was a brick street and you could look at the cars making their cautious turns into our narrow brick street. We would sit on an encyclopedia with a roller skate under it and race down the hill. We had great carts with big ball-bearing wheels on them, as in the Soapbox Derby. Cars were a great nuisance coming toward us. I liked to get a big auto tire and roll it down the hill toward the cars, hoping to cause a wreck. By the time the driver got out to complain, there would be no kids at all around. There would be quiet. But we hid where we could see. We hid under the houses, where only cats went, and looked through the grates.

I am looking at the television and seeing Navratilova and Lendl, from Czechoslovakia. Without their millions and the hired teams of dogs and friends, they could be dead for weeks and we wouldn't know it.

Look at the heroes lately.

Look at the heroes who are human and then you know what was there.

I have no conscience, I guess. After the hideous Sundays I've had in our godless clime with all these males on the pulpit screaming and taking, I must rescue our women. There's only one way to do it, ladies: make a big pot roast with onions, carrots, and potatoes in it and then get naked except for your high-heeled shoes, if you've got any legs and fanny left. He'll eat the roast and then sleep, dreaming about some bitch five counties away. You've done everything to please him but it's not enough. Good thing I finally get up and take care of the little woman, heh, heh.

My wife ripped off the tubes when she had pneumonia and came and got me, because she knew I was lonely and distressed. She came up to Syd and Harry's and said, Here I am. She was off the IV, and we made love and petted our dog Joseph, the Lhasa apso, a Tibetan temple dog, bred in Arkansas. He's just solid love and fur. He does not know how to fight. He gives the alarm when strangers are near the house. Apparently that's all the breed was ever good for. Susan is a beautiful, short, nicely breasted woman with hot gray eyes and pretty feet. She went back to the hospital at eleven P.M. She was covered with flowers and presents, but she still had pneumonia. The last time we got into a real fight she socked my fifty-dollar flight glasses into my eyes and busted them. I knocked her down and began kicking her, but then we called the law: our friend Ron Shapiro. Would you please come stop this? So Shapiro comes up and just listens and then it's all over.

What a drag. Now I've got to get all sensitive and write again.

The three of us—Susan, David Smith, and I— went down to see the bingo game. David had a tape of Chuck Berry on. The ride was merry, with all the green fields and the little homes stuck on top of the small fields where the little hills were. The Chuck Berry tape was going on, and I loved it.

I saw Chuck at the National Guard Armory in Jackson, Miss., 1959. He was singing such a nasty song and I was dancing with a girl. The lyrics were so filthy neither one of us would acknowledge them. Two days later he was arrested in Meridian for asking a white girl for a date. I continued on with my white sports coat and drove the Thunderbird lent to me by my brother. My date and I were so shy of each other we barely touched. Even a kiss was out of the question. God knows why she came with me. She was a poor girl named Sandra who lived on Clinton Boulevard. She had good looks and so did her big sister. They lived across the road from the nice cemetery with a lake in the middle of it. I snuck in a lot of ponds and fished but I never snuck in that one because of respect for the dead.

On Clinton Boulevard was another lake. I remember, always, the afternoon I took my first wife out to fish with me. She was angry and pale. She stood there and watched me fish for thirty minutes, then she said she'd had enough. She cursed nature and generally wore a frown. I was embarrassed by her, but we had a baby. I thought we could get together as husband and wife if she went fishing with me, but she didn't like the outdoors. Her favorite sport was being indoors and being depressed on the couch. Now in 1988 I hope she's better.

At some air base in some desert, with no trees and the hot wind whipping by the houses, where there was barely a bush, somebody's mother got out a butcher's knife and wouldn't talk to the kids. She was silent for a week. She was nuts when her husband was gone. Worse, she became an intense Christian.

It is terrible to see a woman become religious. Jesus on the telephone, etc. Jesus sleeps with her. Jesus is asking her to *join* him. There is no record of Jesus making love with anybody. But he is the eternal lover and he died on the cross. Even worse was his friend Peter who got crucified upside down. Those were severe times, and the Iranians have proved in the last days how nasty it was. They send children against tanks. Moslems, baby, are ready for heaven. They die to be next to Mohammed. Mohammed on the phone, children. He's calling collect from somewhere in the sky. Only forty thousand can be there but he still calls collect.

The other day I tried to run through a hot Southern day, even in a Jeep with Rick Kelley. We were fishing, in a way. I had my old Confederate cap on, like Stonewall Jackson wore. He never imbibed or swore like I did, and I know why he slowed down in the Valley campaign, when the Confederates were almost triumphant and could have taken

47

McClellan and Washington, D.C. He was sunsick.
He was just *sun*sick. I threw up and sat down in the
hot sun when Rick Kelley and I were fishing, even
just fishing in the shade. But I had had enough of
asking idiots where the pond was, and when the
pond was there I could barely see it for the old sick
sun all around me.

MODERN

When I saw the Hollywood streets I was with my son, who was looking for a Les Paul guitar. We were traveling on the Triumph motorcycle. Finally found the guitar in a shop in San Pedro, where I was living. We were standing in a pawnshop and the fellow that owned it said no, no, he could not give us at the price we offered. This was a famous guitar. Po had just finished high school and I wanted him to have the Les Paul. So we quit the deal and mounted the motorcycle. But the guy came out in the street, almost crying, and said he would take the money I offered him for the guitar. We went away with it, Po holding the guitar on the back of the motorcycle. I have bought ten different guitars for my son, maybe, but this is the one I remember.

We drove back to Mississippi through the deserts and at the end of July, probably 120 degrees out there. When we got to Dallas and on to Shreveport,

---

49

I could smell the trees and it was the South, my beloved South. Home again. Back to Clinton, Miss. We were in my red van. For a while the gas wasn't working and we had to stop in Tucson, Arizona. A nice young guy there fixed it for about twenty dollars.

I love expert mechanics. These men with grease on their hands. When Ron Shapiro and I were going to Montana, there was a problem with the van. It was outside of Amarillo in Groom, Texas, where there was nothing to look at but the scrub plants and deserts and fences. This skinny guy rolled in after a kid had taken the front end of the van apart. The man in the car knew the problem. It was in the dashboard. He put the van back together and charged only twenty-five bucks. Let's hear it for the few good mechanics left in the world. Hurrah! Hurrah! Shapiro bought this huge plastic housefly to put in his restaurant.

We left Groom and went up to Aspen, Colorado. On the New Mexico border I had to take a leak and saw two rainbows in front of me on the prairie. There were the lonely rainbows and we got to witness them. Then we went five miles an hour over Independence Pass. And I mean five miles an hour, at night. I could hear the right front bearing going out on my wheel. It was almost done for, but God was watching out for us. He was tired but he was watching and it was, actually, fun.

When we got to Aspen and met the movie stars

and Hunter Thompson, I was pretty stupid. I'd been sober a long time and I thought that was the problem, so I, like a simple boy who had never had much of it, sought the cocaine. A bowl at least, from Mex Eller, who admired my work. Met Jack Nicholson and Michael Douglas, both delightful and civil people, but was too cranked to comprehend them. Forgive me.

❑ ❑

Yelverston was a man before he was a man. He was early at everything. He was a good ballplayer but he was never too good. He was married to Ruth and then he looked over the territory. He went up in a plane with Ruth and they looked over the territory near Galveston, Texas. It was an old Cessna with no windows and you could hear the engine roaring, shaking the plane. Yelverston was just thirty, but he knew what he wanted. There was some vodka when they got back. She was pregnant and she wouldn't drink any of it.

May 13, Friday, 1988.
Just a minute. David Holman has died on the golf course. This date will always register in my mind. I heard it at Syd and Harry's from Bob Haws. David had the thick glasses and the mustache and the cheerful word. He'd had a heart attack before and he had lost a lot of weight on his trip to the Carolinas last summer. His wife JoElla and his baby

———

51

son Jeff, two, lit up this little town and university. David was a fine teacher of Southern Literature. His father was the famous scholar from Chapel Hill, David's home. David wanted to cut his own path. So he did. He taught his classes beautifully and he knew good literature and music like the back of his hand. He was only thirty-seven when he died.

Today my son graduates from Ole Miss. His girl also graduates. We'll see the commencement and then my wife Susan and I will go to the funeral home to bid David's lovely body adieu. He used to sneak cigarettes from me, and we always talked about playing golf together. I was always going to get my old man's clubs and go out with him, even as the terrible golfer I was. He called five different people to play golf with him in the morning. But he went out by himself with his new clubs and died around eleven. They found him out there, alone, doing what he was bound to. Maybe he knew. Maybe he knew he was going to end up on the fairway, on the practice tee. Maybe he was playing for little Jeff his son, and for my son, Po, and for me, and for JoElla his wife—to go away with your sport shoes on, trying to get the ball to go into the sky and hit God's dumb foot.

The next day my son graduated from the university with a degree in journalism after an endless agonizing ceremony. I and my wife poured into the exits of the coliseum along with other irritated parents who wanted a smoke and a drink of water. For years we had been paying and hoping for this degree. We had been through the girlfriends and the boyfriends and the money and the worry. My daughter came with her mother. Lee was quite lovely in her high heels, her own high school graduation coming up in Tuscaloosa. She is now the "young lady," as all fond parents call their seventeen-year-old daughters. There is much to weep about in pal David Holman's death. There was the memorial at Waller Funeral Home, where his precious body lay in the casket, bound for Chapel Hill, North Carolina, the next day. That he will never see his son graduate. That we shall never hear his encouraging words again. Smiling, is what one of his students recalls. He always came to class smiling. My wife saw him at graduation last year, in the coliseum. "What are you doing here?" she asked him. "Just came to see my kids graduate," he said. He meant his students. The only thing he hated was mediocrity. That was the only thing I ever saw him angry about. Like good friend Ron Shapiro; you never heard a discouraging word from him.

❑ ❑

Think back, think back, and then come back to where it's always been, at the WPA lodge, the community center above the Hoka theater and restaurant on the hill near the water tower. When was the last time you played bingo? Bingo happens for the Humane Society. Sgt. Ashford, of the Water Valley V.F.W., in charge. The bingo board is up and the sound system is here courtesy of Stuart Cole, my neighbor, the refreshments provided by Ron Shapiro. Last time I played I was fourteen at a Catholic thing in Bay St. Louis, Mississippi, on the coast where the Catholics roam and put some spirit into the town. All the old boys from the V.F.W. have their brown World War Two hats on. Shapiro walks over and says to me: "Man, this is America, ain't it?" We cleared $130 for the dogs and cats. Everybody seemed to have a good time. The mayor, John Leslie, came, played a bit, and went back home. Leslie has been a fine mayor. He loves the animal cause too, he and his wife Elizabeth. "Everything is possible," says John. "Just wait a while, and everything is possible." He gave us a big building for the new shelter. Now all we need is money and good cages and good runs and air conditioning. Dr. Bob Guy and Dr. Harland contribute their time and energy at low fees. The town is giving, wants to help. We will get the great shelter.

□ □

I have been drunk some and Willie Morris has been drunk some, but Willie gave $140 for the animals. Willie's heart has never been in doubt. He makes this little town swell with his dreams. Willie wishes the best for white black yellow and the animals, and his great soul lies over two o'clock A.M. as in that painting by Chagall with the face lying on the town. He does not have time to fix his teeth, he does not have a worrying wife like me, he does not have the carefully made house with its appointments and the toothbrushes and the vitamin tablets and the nooky. But he continues, like a truck of love, spilling love on the highway. Down to McComb in the beauty round the Bogue Chitto. Writing his novel. Getting the lines straight from the moon and the weeds near the river. The both of us have come back to this pretty and humane town to practice secular humanism as hard as we can. That is when we're just staring out of windows trying to see even the rough face of God in the clouds or in the vapor over the oil spots in the parking lot of the Jitney Jungle.

Yelverston was a man of sixty-two years. His son had gotten married after he'd finished Yale. The girl was perfect. They'd lived together for three years and then got married near the grape arbor of an old friend of Yelverston's in Ocean Springs. Yelverston was divorced but his wife was also there, with her new younger husband, and Yelverston liked the man, and felt aglow with a new appreciation of his old wife, who looked elegant and friendly in her yellow gown, with the trim ankles he'd always adored. Everybody was paid for and happy. It was sublime how his ex-wife smiled and said just the nice soft things to inquirers, never trying to bully the conversation. He went off into a rose garden and wept for his good fortune. He had three million and a half and he was very satisfied that he had no more envy, sorrow, or littleness in him. He was tan and had only a little stomach and he had no wife at all. The sun was coming over the low limbs of the live oak and through the Spanish moss and shot on ahead with an orange glow over the roses and azaleas. He looked backward to see his son and his bride, a slim girl with nice breasts in her wedding gown. Life could hardly be better. The girl even had a crush on *him* and he knew it. He looked back to the tables full of seafood and the black men in livery standing around them. You could live here for a month on the soft-shell crabs and the scallops themselves, he thought. You could live off the West Indies slaw falling out of the bowl. Plus the lobsters the little kids are slobbering over. Jimmy Buffett came up close to Yelverston and strolled around, in his red moccasins. "Didn't I buy you?" asked Buffett. "No," said Yelverston.

Yelverston met with an older friend of his son's who was a publisher for a North Carolina small press. They met at Primo's restaurant, in Jackson. Young Ben took Yelverston along with him to meet Mona Neary, the genius of American literature. It was at a house near some college. The young publisher Ben knocked on the door and then knocked again. There was no answer but they heard a rustling out back and walked back quietly to see the actual lady, Mona Neary, a legend of world literature, leaning over some tomato plants with some scissors. They moved along the fence silently and Ben was about to call out to her when she fell into the tomato plants and farted violently over and over. Not only was she a legend but she was a blameless legend of world literature and her sensitivity toward all humankind was deep and wise. She could write about an old darkie on a bicycle as if somebody gave a shit. Yelverston was embarrassed and so was Ben and they hustled back to the front door as if they had never been there. They waited around a while and then Yelverston got tired and fired up a Pall Mall. The old woman opened the front door and said: "Well. Welcome." She poured them great tea glasses full of bourbon and then went out to the kitchen a long time. Ben wanted her to do one of her old stories on Japanese paper, very special edition. It was about BeeBee and Juju getting married. They got married in the Delta, where everybody was especially stupid but deep. Ben and Yelverston waited for Mona Neary, and finally she came back, claiming she had a headache. She had been blameless and sensitive so long, and Yelverston felt for her. Ben told Yelverston when they got in the rented Cadillac that Mona was tough as nails and hated heterosexual male writers. Yelverston really didn't care that much anymore.

He was hoping he would not have to be bent over and mutilated by the burden of history when he got old. How awful, he thought, to be so smart and so old.

□ □

Yelverston went to North Dakota for a conference and saw the B-52s at the SAC base. They took him down the tarmac and he looked in at the planes with crews on ready. They were earnest young men with short haircuts. They were younger than his son, most of them. With these great jet engines and these awful munitions. There were some older men with gray crewcuts who Yelverston presumed were pilots or hydrogen-bomb experts. There was a terribly short little man in a sweater and a colonel's badge on him. The man was only five feet tall. His hair was coal black and he was a colonel. He was explaining about security and what he couldn't show them. Yelverston was six feet three inches tall. There was this deep croaking voice beneath him. He could not even see the man's name tag. "At the ready moment, conditions . . ." What the hell was the little man saying? Then Yelverston went back with the executives to the Best Western motel, where there was a cheese and wine gathering near the indoor pool. Norman Mailer and Alex Haley were there, and they were right fellows, he was glad to meet them. Kelly Skampton was there. She wore cowboy boots but lived in Charlottesville and had big teeth. She dropped a French phrase and Yelverston moved away.

"I saw you at the base," a young woman said to him.

She was the wife of one of the air force pilots and she was well formed. It was a mixture of the literary conference and the circuit board people and the air force. The young woman was tall and the short colonel was really drunk but he came just to her nipples and started his deep voice. To Yelverston she looked like the hoyden, the cruel coy one of his youth around the desks of Meridian High School. He was striking up a Pall Mall when she backed away from the colonel and pushed her rear against his pants.

He went out with her to the miserable apartment where she lived. She was showing him photograph after photograph of B-52s in in the air. "What horrible boredom," Yelverston said.

They drove back to the motel where his clothes were all lying around the room like he was a slob.

"Don't be quick," she said.

He was slow but his heart wasn't there. There was a forty-eight-year-old woman, British, back at home in Connecticut who loved him and waited for him and could take him full up her bottom while she gasped more more more.

The next day the girl was gone and he was lying on the wild bed staring at the pair of high heels she'd left behind, when the phone rang and he found out his son was dead.

There was a pint of Jack Daniel's in his suitcase

———

and he found it and drank it down almost immediately. Then he went to the bathroom and threw up. His son had been murdered along the Tombigbee waterway by dope pirates who were running free. His son's wife had been wounded by a shotgun. She was in the Tupelo hospital. Most of her right hand was gone. Yelverston could not weep. He wanted to but he sat on the bed with his heart beating all the way up in his throat. For an hour he sat there, wanting to be dead. Then he picked up the phone and dialed it.

□ □

Yelverston talked to the sheriff after the funeral. The sheriff had attended the funeral himself and Yelverston was touched. Here in Ocean Springs, where his son and his bride had danced radiant and gorgeous, they buried Yelverston's lad. He had expressed a desire to his wife that he never wanted to leave the Mississippi coast. This was her home, and he wanted it to be his too. So that was fine with Yelverston, who had lived in Pascagoula in the forties and dealt with the shipyards. Yelverston's wife was angry with him the fifteen years they lived together. Now at the funeral she resumed her anger and simply glared at him. Maybe it was his fault. He was a strong-willed man and maybe he had not taught his son enough about survival, too busy getting his own way. They had shot a few guns together, but only at beer cans and alligators. And they never tried to hit the snout or the eyes, just let him know they were there.

Yelverston was looking around for her young new husband but he couldn't find him. She kept glaring at him as he walked away and took his car back to the motel. The car was a beige Mercury Cougar without even a radio. He was ashamed of his money and his success and he wanted to be obscure. The words of the kind sheriff were in his mind and he lay back and took a long nap. He was so tired and so weak and so guilty he could not stand it anymore and he was released into a peaceful nap of no more than two hours, when he awoke to a light rapping on his door. He was in his shorts and he lifted himself and got his robe. His stomach had gotten a little large and he sucked it in. His eyes were wide and he was racing with a blessed peace when he opened the door.

It was his ex-wife: father, mother, son, morning when you watched your son with his little neck leaning out of his highchair and first ate his cereal. All of it except the frown and the hate was gone from her face and she had got so lean with dark circles under her eyes she finally looked human suddenly to Yelverston. She was ancient. She was lovely. There was a mist falling in back of her in the miserable hallway of the motel.

"Come in," he said.

"Well, darling, what are we going to do about this?" she said. She'd gone over to the bed next to his and sat down. She was almost too skinny now, and if his eyes blinked and he had a rotten attitude about her, she could be seen as a slut who needed a drink and some money. Going back in history he could see himself only as a man with big legs who had never stopped running from one task toward another. He had worked in California and had a woman who introduced him to marijuana in 1950 but he could not stop running. He hated the marijuana because it made him giggle for no reason. He was running, baby, off. He had big muscular legs and he didn't even smoke until he was thirty. At twenty-eight he had his first drink, a martini, in Washington, D.C. It was terrible but he drank it straight down and ever since he drank it he was in another zone. He was in a zone where the little stuff didn't touch him anymore. He was very friendly and never angry. He arranged bowling pins in his fireplace. He would shoot a beebee gun at them instead of bowling, and the beebees would bounce back at him and he would dodge them. Every time he shot at the bowling ball and the pins in his fireplace, with the fire roaring behind, something would come back to him. He was smiling once when a beebee hit his front tooth.

"Well?" she called from the bed. She was so haggard and though blonded looked nothing as good as his forty-eight-year-old British woman in Connecticut, whom he could barely recall now.

Yelverston was just in his robe and his shorts, with his gray hair splattered apart.

"Tell me what the sheriff told you," she said.
She wanted vengeance just like he did.

I finally met Yelverston one night at Syd and Harry's when the music was raging but he looked so sad and distinguished we went downstairs to talk.

The next day my wife and I went over to Tuscaloosa to see my daughter graduate from County High School. I'd made the trip a thousand times on 45 to 82 and had called my old friend Pat Hermann up to have dinner with us at the Red Lobster. He and Jeannie were having trouble with their daughter Sophie, who had run away to Nashville. We met at the Red Lobster with my handsome son Teddy, and my sweet faithful wife Susan, with her hair swept back and the big rose on her bosom and her black shirt and her black hose. Old Pat came in with his gray hair like mine.

In the symphony you announce men like Pat Hermann with a soft chorus of trumpets. He comes in with his Mexico sandals and what a great thing to see my old Chaucerian buddy. We'd eaten all the seafood in the place and I was stunned by all the langostinos. With the butter and the salad. Tuscaloosa is about five avenues with racing cars and the light rain coming down. There was a five-car pileup on the avenue just after we left. My son Teddy was once in a wreck at a light when somebody hit him. He had long hair and the cops did all they could to blame it on him. But they took his blood alcohol and he had nothing. He had an earring but he had no dope. Old Pat and I and Susan were talking and then we had to go to the commencement, to look at daughter Lee graduate in the Alabama coliseum. There was a lot to talk about but I remember only one big parent, younger than I was, black, with oiled curls coming down, and he had a chain on him with a gold emblem of the state of Texas on his chest, with further gold chains going down to his stomach. He had some kind of fancy boots too, baby. He was from afar and he was here to see somebody graduate. All I had was a brown suit with a smart tie. But let me take this moment to embrace all of Alabama. Just like my ultrabad state, Mississippi. We're all so fucking terrible, no wonder it took four years of hideous war to get Lee up there and give up his sword.

THE TIME

March, 1988.

Giving a party lunch for Jim Harrison and his wife Linda. Our publisher Seymour Lawrence and his companion Joan Williams pull in front of our shack in a white stretch limo with a black chauffeur, all the way from Memphis airport. Sam's got diabetes. Got to watch the sweets and the drinks.

He started getting thirsty. I was dressed above my range. I'd got a $35 tie and kerchief, but Sam in the stretch limo had already beaten me. Everybody in the neighborhood, including the black guys down at the ice plant, were stretching their necks out. The cars were all down the street for Jim Harrison but they had never seen a Cadillac this long in their lives and I hadn't either. Sam said how he never wanted a stretch limo.

I heard wonderful stories from Harrison. His little daughter was lovely and absorbed the town. His wife Linda was regal, dismissing my drunken

65

overtures. Harrison wrote a note back saying we might all someday fish in a wooden rowboat and drink Diet Pepsi. He means take it quiet and be off the stuff. What a dream. I want it. What a lovely dream.

My wife Susan sent her son David to live with his father in Easley, South Carolina, where he would have all the advantages. It cut her heart. But it was a dream of David on the green and white team kicking the ball and having his beautiful girlfriends. As his father provided. David goes ahead as the golden son.

I remember when Bobby and Ralph were drafted into Korea. My mother was crying in the dining room as the tall boys stood in front of her. They were going down to Biloxi to fight again. It wasn't over. She'd lost her baby brother Bootsy in the last war and here were her sons going again. I was a tiny guy, as usual, holding back my horrible needs for the moment. I recall that Ralph, when we were building the house and I was getting in the way, got a great nail in his foot and went leaping and howling away to another room. I never knew much about Ralph except he was a good quiet guy, my foster brother. He became the millionaire in Texas and paid for my second honeymoon. We had the catamaran and saw the porpoises in Florida, and my mother went out with us and saw the porpoises.

My dad was there near the ocean. But there was something terribly wrong about my second marriage. I could never get it right. We had a big house and thousands to look at but I could not bear the big legacy of physicians and wives who never taught their kids any guts or sense. My second wife was a beautiful book-burner from Nebraska. She had enough of me and threw me out.

❑ ❑

Before us there were tribes of people wandering around deciding what to eat or fuck or own. Billions of people went across this planet, asking each other "Did you get any last night?" Then came religion and all the long-winded phony bastards like Plato. The guy that wrote Leviticus should be shot for boredom. Then came gunpowder and steel. The Europeans occurred with tea and gunpowder. Some of the afternoons were tedious and so they began killing thousands of each other to own shit. Then came Pearl Harbor. Then came America and Uncle Joe, who only killed seven million of his own people for, get this, an idea. Commie against Free. The preachers are still going at it. Jimmy Swaggart said on the television that he would sweep out a lonely mission with a broom for the rest of his life if that's what God called him to do. He liked to "make love" to a New Orleans prostitute while her little daughter watched. I dare the man to quit Baton Rouge and sweep out a lonely mission for the rest of his life. I dare him. If he will do that I'll fly down to where he is and play him some of those hellish tapes of his cousin Jerry Lee Lewis and help him sweep.

◻ ◻

All my nephews and nieces are a blessing to me endlessly. They have cheered me through the hopeless and stunned times. I owe thanks to my sister, Dot, and I owe much to my great giving ex-brother-in-law John Kitchings, who has been nothing but a prince to me. All of us together have been divorced twelve times and we are looking for the thirteenth wife. We are stumbling forward toward the great big bass pond of the mind, with gentleman Pappy sitting in the lawn chair looking for the seven-pound bass. Being both rude and deaf, so incredibly rude that the rest of us are just awed at looking at a type that could only have come from the Great Depression. Pappy is like the Confederate army. So awesome in his rudeness. Pappy is a 120 and still smokes. Cancer has attacked him but just given up. Pappy wants his children and grandchildren and great-grandchildren all around him, bringing him their hugs and their good news and their snapshots of even furthermore babies. He wants all the little children to swarm into his bosom and put their little hands in his hand with its speckled fingers. He eats a banana and has had his bacon and eggs for 120 years every morning. He picked up golf in his fifties and he had pretty tan legs, nailing the ball straight ahead and short, then putting pretty well. I saw him pitch one into the hole from about forty yards out one afternoon, on a green with a horrible left incline. He was so happy and his friends were so happy, I felt proud of the old dude and will remember the afternoon forever. In fact, I love my father into the deepest fathoms.

During Korea my brother played for the Choctaws of Mississippi College, number 86 on the football team. I saw him recover an aerial fumble and run fifty yards for a touchdown, into the zone with the crowd roaring in little Robinson Stadium. My brother was six feet two and I frankly don't recall that much about him since he was eleven years older except that he accidentally hit me in the chin with a swingblade when I was a toddler down in, what? — Pascagoula. The blood spurted and Mother howled and I've still got the scar on my chin. There were palm trees around and the wind hit them and made the branches clack together while the moon out on the sea did its best to light up Nazi U-boats and Japanese submarines.

Yelverston was a young man from Mobile then, very entrenched with Roosevelt's Democrats already. Yelverston had a mild heart attack when he was twenty as a basketball player and was disqualified from the war. When he first saw the destroyers under construction in Ingall's shipyard, his mind fastened on them as miracles. They went up so fast. He stood on the deck and felt the ship and its guns coming alive under him. He could feel in his body that there was nothing wrong with him. He looked out at the gray muddy channel. Within minutes, it seemed to him, there would be sailors and their captain, all armed, going into the war. He had a moment on one of the destroyers when all the noise and all the welders, painters, riveters went into his bloodstream and everybody's health was connected with his heart — the sun scalding the edges of the yard, and the gulls lowering and shivering in the outward breeze of the tide going back to the moon.

They were still looking for invasions by German and Jap when I was a toddler. Everybody was ready. After Pearl, anything might happen. The teenagers were ready with their .22s and shotguns. Blackouts were maintained and everybody was looking for a traitor, so I understand.

But when I went back down to visit Bay St. Louis in the fifties with my relatives the Allistons there was nothing but the bliss of the heavy cool salty nights. Big blue crabs in your net and fighting croakers on and speckled trout on your fishing rod. The freezer was full of shrimp and flounders. Oysters, big and meaty and succulent. Tomatoes huge as two fists and four deep green watermelons sitting on the floor under the television. By that time we just had to scare ourselves, with a horror show from New Orleans called *Lights Out!* We trembled, baby.

I had seen some spooky movies at the Hilltop Theater in Clinton, but these were coming into your own home. We had Dracula and Frankenstein and the Wolfman and something called *Children of Blood*, a C-minus wreck maybe today, but it was the first time that people of my own age were shown as evil and ate their parents. My girl cousin, Catherine, had fits of anguish during the horror shows, and we would calm her down. She was horribly afraid of lightning and thunder. She was a lovely blond woman when we were just kids. We'd hit the sheets, Woody and I, afraid in delicious safety. It was a marvelous thing to be close to Woody, Sut, Catherine, Uncle Wayne, and Aunt Jeannie.

It got hot sometimes at night and sometimes Woody and I slept on the porch, which ran around two sides of the house. Nobody had any money, nobody had any big dreams, nobody had an inkling of disaster.

On August 17th, 1969, the hurricane Camille hit Pass Christian and the southwest Mississippi coast with a force of 250 mph, the strongest storm ever registered on the North American continent. My Uncle Wayne was with the State Health Service and suffered a heart attack while working to relieve the victims. Water came all over the towns and corpses from graveyards hung in the trees.

Phil Beidler and I visited Uncle Wayne and Aunt Jeannie in 1978 and he was still talking about the hurricane. Uncle Wayne had had his thorax removed because of cancer and he just whispered to us. He liked the house cool and his watermelons, but once before when I'd been there and wanted to catch some fish, to catch up on our old times, Uncle got us a boat and we went out, but we didn't catch anything. He spoke with a whisper all the time and he was bald-headed, wearing glasses. Nobody ever had a better uncle than Uncle Wayne. In that brown water with his little boat and him in his flannel shirt. Nobody ever even had a better uncle.

DELTA IS THIRTY MILES WEST

Ron Shapiro, with his white bent Oldsmobile convertible, has a home anywhere he goes. I have seen Ron fall asleep on a slab of concrete in New Mexico and Wyoming and Colorado. He keeps a log of good sayings with him. He's Jewish, from St. Louis. Was in the dry-cleaning or tux-rentals business up there, but his dad died early and I believe Ron is committed to having music and parties and now, like the rest of us, to making a living as long as the past doesn't take its toll. The past will cost you fifty dollars a day in worry if you let it, and Shapiro knows that only the day with your friends and neighbors really matters.

My wife and I were beating the hell out of each other one morning, as mentioned earlier, and the wife called Ron. I'd slapped her a few times and she'd brought out a baseball bat and we were both miserable. Earlier we had on love music and Susan had the house looking superb, even with our thirteen pets running in and out of the place. We have thousands of memories of our kids and the sanctity of our poor dwellings with our children close to us. Shapiro came right up and just understood. Did nothing but stand there with his long hippie hair and his bright black eyes and said, "I'm here, guys." I went down to the Hoka for a while and had a lunch of stir-fry and bacon. Then went ahead to my screwdrivers and my great tales of the war. I have a need to tell people about all the wars and Quisenberry's heroism. Very strange how I read antiwar poems when I was teaching at Clemson and pled with Quiz not to fight. Now Susan's got the Vietnam Memorial going at the university museums with the warriors coming in to speak of their experiences. Col. Flo Yoste is providing tapes of the air force doing its duty. Shapiro did his duty as a clerk-typist in Korea. He told me once that the girls over there were so available and easy that he could never really recondition himself to America. But when I talked with him at the Hoka, he smiled and said how lovely it would be to have a feisty woman like Susan who got out a baseball bat and knocked your fifty-dollar flight glasses into your eyes.

I seem to be talking about nothing but war and the threat of calamity.

The calamity is that we get only seventy-five years to know everything and that we knew more by our guts when we were young than we do

with all these books and years and children behind us.

I remember the great pride I had in being a pallbearer at Quisenberry's father's funeral. I had visited him at the nursing home. Quiz called me about
his father's death and I didn't have a working automobile. I had only my great Harley-Davidson and
I got on my flight suit, put my formal brown suit
in the bag, and drove down through a hell of a rain
to be a pallbearer. What an honor it was. I met
Jerry Lyons and Ed Ratliff and Billy Quisenberry
again, and we traded stories. The Lyons family
were always a sweet bunch of people. They lived
near the Dicklies, who were awful people. Peter
Dicklie and O. B. Leader were sociopathic scum,
especially when they got their cowardly little souls
together. They liked to beat up drunken people
and steal, along with Cal Richardson.

There was a girl named Marie Hoppe, the daughter of brass in the air force or something. She
wanted to get naked and use profanity. She had a
crush on me and told a friend of mine that if I
would just take her out once and respect her, she
would get naked and do everything on the next
date. She had no breasts, unlike Martha Barnett,
who was a flute player. And Liz Meeter, whose family is so violently right-wing religious in the Pres-
byterian church they don't give anybody a chance.
Liz was the biggest tease in high school and so stone

dumb you would see her going by the house in a station wagon with even more children, increasing the race as Abraham said.

Behind my house lived the Tighes, nephews of the most deceiving wretched governor that Mississippi ever had. My father roomed with Jim Eastland at Ole Miss. Eastland the seg millionaire, the power. I suppose when you give everybody a chance and a personal interview they all might have their charm, as Pappy said Eastland did. One of the others of Pappy's great friends was the president of Mississippi College, R. L. McLemore. Pappy and R. L. and their wives went to Russia together. They went through the straits of Finland, etc. My pappy tried to discuss real estate with gray-faced Russians who had no idea what he was talking about. R. L. and his wife were historians. He had a heart condition that finally took him and his wife was hit by a car not too long afterwards. He was a fine president and a scholar who appreciated world literature. We knew him as Doctor Mac.

What a sorry damned thing it is to see the preachers get in politics. They shame the church of Christ, which has always been a small body of believers who never even thought about having a Buick. Shapiro, the Jew, is much more the Christian than any of them. He brings love to the crowd and good food. Asks almost nothing for himself, until the bills are owed. He brings the architecture around himself, the architecture of good will and never a discouraging word, as in the song "Home on the Range." Shapiro is home on the range. Yeah, he is our native son, who can fall asleep even with cocaine in Aspen, Colorado, with Semmes Luckett and our friends out there.

They were filming at the Ole Miss motel when my wife and I went down and watched. I was stoned, I guess, from some anger over the missed plane ride, and insulted the director and the producer. But when I saw Treat Williams in a pink pirate's blouse doing some moves around the motel room with Ally Sheedy, I knew that this was really misinformed. A man wearing a pink pirate's blouse, after an Elvis concert in the fifties, would be stomped to death like a rabid dog. So this I told Treat. We went up and ate in the community center and by the way they have exquisite food on the movie lots. They are swell people. I've got a little money and some time now and so I think I'll just go write a stupid and misinformed story about all their hometowns. Costing nobody nothing. I *need* pickled pig's feet! I *need* to eat Updike's books and abuse Connecticut, Massachusetts, Vermont.

When I saw daughter Lee graduate from County High in Tuscaloosa, I and son Teddy and Pat Hermann tried to have a little party for her at the Best Western motel. I bought some chips and nuts and eighteen beers, but Teddy had only one and Lee was tired. She wanted me to see her Volkswagen Rabbit out in the parking lot. She was the smallest graduate in the class of 450. She was my last child and I always wanted a daughter. She is tiny and has missed her dad these many years. We will never recover the afternoon when we came back from Sardis Lake and she rode behind me on the Harley, leaning back and reading her novel. She used to sleep with me but then my mother and my wife told me that was not right, as she had breasts now and was a young lady.

I went through the lovely town of Olive, Miss., the other afternoon and thought of a certain reformed alcoholic doctor there. Get this. His daughter's report on him was that he was so smart he had to drink himself dumb to be a citizen of the community. What a loyal interpretation of the father!

We went through Columbus and I had to go into the Army/Navy surplus store. Columbus is where the air base is and I also wanted to go out and see some of the new air force jets take off. There was no deal there. They had security and I knew nobody on the base except Col. Edwards and that was late and thirdhand. But back to the Army/Navy surplus store. I bought a three-dollar shirt but I wanted the stuff they wouldn't sell. They had a snow-white German helmet from World War Two. They had a Spanish paratrooper's helmet, black leather with a gold heraldic device on the front. This was made so any spotlight would pick him out and the enemy could shoot him through the head when he landed. They also had a good boomerang on the counter and the price was only $2.98. After all these years, the price had gone up only a dollar. The better one was black and cost seven bucks. But I wasn't feeling very warlike then.

My wife and I had made some whoopie in the cruel old town of Tuscaloosa and we'd had a good breakfast with my kids and Pat Hermann at Wright's Bakery, where Lee gave me the news that she'd run out of gas last night and had to walk a mile, buy some milk, and empty it out so as to get gas from a hysterical Arabian at a late-night mart, and she got home at one. This is the U.S.A., night watchers. Arabs own the oil and they come over here wanting the other end of the pump. They also want white dumb wives, some of them. One of them came to Ole Miss and has killed both his American wives. They have pride and a certain attitude, you see. Several people have written long history books explaining how the Persians have a proud culture and it is all our fault. Shit.

Ayatollah rock and rolla. With a religious idea he sends thousands of children in front of tanks. The pope is a good number too. Goes down to Africa and tells them to multiply. This earth is not our real home. Die at nine months old with a swollen

———

79

belly and flies all over you and that will prove it. Sally What's-her-name for the Christian Children's Fund arrived bloated in 1980 in her Mercedes with chauffeur with the doctor who was running the alcohol clinic in San Pedro. He was a meaningful guy, a smart man about alcohol and he helped me. But then Sally showed up to dance with the ex-drunks and she looked like a blond pig. She was eating enough for seven children herself. For just fifty cents a day you can feed one twentieth of me. And the whining voice. The voice that even makes you dismiss starving Peruvian children. Michael Jackson and the rest come in, "We Are the Children" etc. Michael says God wrote the lyrics. Like God replaced his original face with that of Diana Ross. But god knows we need our rich phony celebrities. Some food got to some mouths and that is the bottom line, eh?

DOGS

The dogs at the animal shelter have been infected with distemper. Twenty-seven of them had to go down two weeks ago. Now twenty new dogs have to go down. All the trouble and all the food and the care that Ollie and Maryl have been giving avails nought. All the creatures with their front feet lifted to you, man's best friend multiplied by forty, wanting you for their lifetime pal. Please, please.

There's a cruel old alcoholic fart down at the Gin named Pete who said he would pass by a crushed human being in the road but could not help but stop for a dog in need. He was talking through the vodka of course. He wouldn't stop for anything if it got in the way of his next drink. He wants to tell the story of his education and his girlfriend and the contacts he has. He says that his "moniker" is "Fast Pete," earned by his expertship on the pool table. He also mentioned that "Nosferatu" was simply German for *vampire*. He was trying to impress me and all the hungover slobs in the Gin. Mickey has been down there for centuries but he just gives the encouraging hand and never even mentions his poems, which are quite good. A stone wino, he doesn't try to impress anybody. Come on come on come on come on come on don't you know me I've always been there just your brilliant pal let me give you some advice all I know about the interworld situation have another yes let me pay for it must come up to my house where I can show all the pictures and all the culture and the music in my very private precious house have I told you the number of gooks I killed? Man, have I had wives. Have I had money? Have I known some stars? Can you understand Faulkner, I have to make a big effort. Sorry I vomited.

Almost all the news is in and the class of '60, Clinton High, has been an exceptional class. Despite Coach Hoyt and Emma Wills and Superintendent Milkness, we did get educated. Despite Coach Hooks and the enormous insensitivity of Billy Nick Farte and the enormous worthless Coach Nichols, many of us have lived lives of substance. Lois Blackwell was the one. And Mrs. King in Latin. And last, *sine qua non*, superlative, Dick Prenshaw. He and Mrs. Blackwell told us about a whole different world.

He and Barnett, the student assistant from the college. Barnett wore a blue suit and was always talking about sucking his wife's pussy. We saw Barnett's senior recital when he played a really difficult piece by Rafael Mendez that ended on a high E above high C. He did the whole thing brilliantly but it was one of those that depended on the last ultrahigh E. Barnett had his jaws out and hips ready but the E wouldn't come. He just sort of became a balloon around his trumpet, and nothing happened. It was total silence and all of us afriended of Barnett looked away into the shameful aisles. I was giggling but I am a low bastard anyway. I looked over to Barnett's good-looking wife and could not believe he had said that about her. She seemed so innocent but on the other hand you looked at her ankles and her impatient feet. I had never imagined love like that and I wanted to lasso with my tie her ankles in their black stockings. I would pull off both her stockings and set them on fire. By that time I had possessed five lovely women on campus but I had never even looked. None of them though had the long black eyelashes of Barnett's wife. All of them just waited with their legs. With my trumpet and the little jazz band there was no trouble in finding women. They wore madras blouses and brown Weejuns with no socks and tan legs. But I had never been a lover. Barnett wore a goatee. He looked like a beatnik, but he described his beard as a "womb broom." I was my full height but I was so tiny compared to all the real men. I wasn't filling out all through even if I had my way with college girls. One thing you made sure to do was go to Youth for Christ, where the crippled minister to youth, Chester Swor, gave his antisex sermons. I was with girls larger than I was and they would get hot while he talked about "an errant hand, a willing thigh." I was a man in his tie sitting next to them and they didn't consider me real sex. I know that now. But we went by the ice cream place and had sherbet on Monument Street or whatever it was, in sight of the state capitol building, and they (two of them) drew my hand under their skirts. I would look straight ahead and then I would look at the pretty flushed face. I was in control. I owned them. They were in a helpless state when my fingers reached down under. There was only one who was good. She was going with a fullback from Ole Miss but we made love again and again. Her name was Arlene. When she was through with me she threw me away like a rag doll. Sudden and no mercy. I was a nobody, except now I could play the trumpet fairly well and had a European lover. She was hot one day and cold the next.

All through high school and college I had only the horn and my aloofness from the others. I was a horrible snob and the poems I wrote were difficult. They got even more difficult after J. Edgar Simmons taught me.

I saw J. Edgar dying in the V.A. hospital in Jackson, 1980. He put his poor slip-in shoes on backward and I thought he was ready to go down and have a cup of coffee with me. The attendant came up and said no. He wasn't ready to go anywhere. He barely recognized me and he thought I was from Texas. El Paso, where he'd taught last. His poems were about drinking too much wine and seeing Osiris at the roller derby and he had projected this work called *Hamlet Jones*. He wanted me to write interstitial chapters for all his books. I knew J. Edgar was crazy in 1963 but they gave him a bad deal at Mississippi College. The fact is the college needed a crazy poet. His book of poems *Driving to Biloxi* was nominated for the National Book Award. I saw him in a shopping mall in Jackson not long before his internment in the V.A. hospital. He was big-bellied and angry-looking in an orange shirt. I almost stopped and said hello but he looked very angry. He was an incessant smoker, as I became later.

You ever notice how easy it is not to meet an intense man from your past? How easy not to stop and take his hand, this weird genius who has the nonsequential connections to the universe? I was terrible. I should have divorced my wife right then and there and joined forces with him in the ugly mall. His wife and his mother had just died and he needed me and I didn't know it.

We didn't spend enough time with any of our friends who are dead when they were alive, we never are good enough and we never can be the old declaration God Is Love. Some shaky old bastard comes out of the depot wanting a smoke or a quarter and you turn him down. Horace Newcomb's father was a mild man who was caught in the Battle of the Bulge in December '44. He must always be remembered, especially on Memorial Day which was yesterday. He had a café in Sardis, Miss. Suddenly he felt religion and gave up his Camels and joined the Baptist church. He was a postman in a suburb off Clinton Boulevard and his son and daughter were smart as whips. But Mr. Newcomb never forced religion on anybody and he was just a congenial man in the house. Like my old man. It's the middle-aged women who take it so awfully seriously. Sometimes I think the whole movement for the churches is carried on by aging women who have found out when their children are gone that they have absolutely nothing inside except their beautiful dead son Jesus.

We moved too fast and had no time with the real people, we tiny and fast people.

When we were guys in the high school band at Clinton, we had a director named Dick Prenshaw. He was a laughing guy with great wisdom in him and we became musicians under his care. He was the one who cut off the wire because the principal gave his messages during our rehearsal. You cannot realize what an awful thing it is to have a dumbo principal breaking in.

Brown and Newman and Newcomb and me and Quisenberry and Hammond and Spiro and Kay

Sumrall and Ralph Parks and Sidney Odom and
Charles Harrison and Nancy Lumkin and Kaye and
the other Nancy and Jeff and Tim. With Prenshaw,
we all made straight "superiors" in the state band
contest. Jerry Lynn Bullock. Yes her, and Martha
Barnett, and I forget all the proud kids, wait: Art
Lee. We all were proud and march on because of
Doc Prenshaw. I played my guts out for him and
made the Lions All-State Band. Prenshaw had the
first Volkswagen in town. He was an adventurous
sort. I went riding with him around town and he
already knew how to do it. He would pass by the
normal citizens in Clinton, Miss., and say: "Yes.
Hello. Smiling at you. Kiss my ass."

He knew what. In Mississippi we had superb
bands, but at that time the Horn Lake band was
the worst in the state. Prenshaw would call a few
of the little captains of the Clinton band in just to
hear them. Prenshaw was a genius. He knew that
if he and you heard the worst you would know how
much better to be. We sat there and heard them in
our proud red-black-and-white outfits. Horn Lake
went against all sensitivities. They were out of tune
and loud and out of time. The Forest, Miss., band
came on, under Hal Polk. They were wonderful.
Then we came on and I think we did "Eroica" and
another two good ones. Rusty McIntire on baritone.
It takes manhood and good feeling to be a musician.
It takes constant stupidity to be a preacher or an
athlete.

Nobody much died. Called it quits. Nobody died.

Talk about smart-asses. We had the corner on smart-assism and I for one had become vile and profane in my thoughts, along with Brown, Newman, Lee, several others. We were messing around with a reel-to-reel tape and decided to have our own show. A tape recording of reality was a new thing to me. I had only three classes the spring of 1960 and spent most of my time in the band room. Coach Smith saw me leaving through the window one morning during "home room," as they called the stupid fifty minutes you spent looking at maybe half a poem by Keats or a *Field & Stream*.

I had a sort of band going and we had all the equipment in the band room. I had learned a few licks on the drums and saw the advantages of being a drummer. There was a girl who wanted to be on stage very much and I and two others went around supporting her in these talent pageants by creating a barroom scene while she sang "Frankie and Johnny." Being the drummer, I could look at her legs and the black dress emphasizing her breasts, and her Hungarian looks. We had been boyfriend and girlfriend when she was in junior high. Her mother was a stage mother and a half, a big-bosomed woman who pushed and pushed her to be somebody, to be famous. I whopped on the back-beat of "Frankie and Johnny" and the bass and the piano went around following her really wretched voice, but what high heels and breasts and black hair. Her mother had made her a public whore with a flat voice at age sixteen. At this time I pitied her and kept up the drums and got the other fellows there. Even when I was a college freshman I came back, because she was nowhere and I knew it, but she loved me and her past was horrible. She used to wear scarves on her throat.

Doug Hutton once mentioned in the basketball gym, where he was a great star, that when I went with her "head to head your foot's in it, and toe to toe your head's in it." That meant I was a short fellow and Doug was envious. High school guys can be awfully cruel, especially when they're around their coaches. Doug scored fifty points when Clinton High won in the state basketball contest and now he is married to Mary Sue Broome. He was a genius on the floor for Clinton and then Mississippi State. He was maybe five eleven, but quick and brilliant on the court. He could turn backways and slam it in 1961. We've met since near the Baptist church in Clinton, where he was teaching a Sunday school class. He and I in our suits, and he describing me as the only really famous person he knows. We were all awful in high school. There was a locally rich real estate salesman, a twenty-three-year-old senior in high school. His sister would lie on a mattress in the Mississippi College gym and take eight or twelve guys on. She was fat and wore glasses but she didn't want to miss out on anything.

Across the street from where I lived they had a gathering of hoods. Later I understood they were talking about whether to kill me or not. Luckily they all got drunk and just stole the hubcaps off my dad's Pontiac Bonneville, 1959. They did it twice and then I loaded up the automatic twelve and waited in the dark of our garage. I waited until two A.M. and was very sleepy, so I lit up a Picayune. There was a screeching outside and a guy got out of the car, knocking over the garbage can. He was at the back of the great long Pontiac when I got there. I knew who he was and I let off two quick ones near his legs and then the other two right past both ears. The car started up and left him. He went out in the middle of the street, staggering around, begging me not to shoot him. He fell down and started whimpering and throwing up. He had a hell of a lot of beer in him. I put the muzzle on the back of his head. Ever since that night he has been almost totally deaf and has left me alone. Luckily it was New Year's Eve and when my dad asked me about the loud sound I said it was some jerks celebrating too late and too near the house, with cherry bombs.

We made a vile tape in the band room. All the instruments were around us and we met at night. We'd seen the wrestling on teevee and we combined it with everything we knew about Barnett Jones, who "sucked pussy," and on to the big fat beatnik Negro I had seen sitting on the rim of the fountain in Washington Square near N.Y.U. when I was in the Mississippi Lions All-State Band, who told me,

"You want some of this?" I asked him what it was and he said, "Mary Jane, young baby." So I had my first weed. He told me after I'd coughed a little bit: "You know, baby, I know I lead a basically non-existent life and I want to go home." "But I'm from nowhere," I told him. "I'm from Clinton, Mississippi." "That's my home. Just four miles south. I'm from Raymond. I've had enough. Would you please take me home?" I walked off from him. Later that night I heard him read his poems in the Gaslight Café on MacDougal Street: "Stamp out the purple worm. Stamp out the purple worm! Oh Tarzan and bananas, let me go back in the shack where my mother was and there was no jazz and no sunglasses!"

They had a wrestling match going on but a guy would get thrown off and the baritone horn would sound and you would hear some slurping noises. Then you would hear the crowd roar as if there were thousands there. "Just a little cunt juice," the wrestler said. Bass drum. "I never eat much but entire cows and a field of lettuce and cunt juice." The other wrestler is a slimmer guy who knows the "science" of wrestling. He is assisted by an electrical shot in the balls when he makes a bad move. The fat guy flies at him but he ducks and rams the man's head into the pole, causing a huge expulsion of cunt juice and turnip greens. The crowd goes wild. Come in three trombones in a Bach chorus for no reason. Then the fat guy awakes and starts slamming the man of science. But his pants fall off and he has a one-inch cock and thousands see. Etc. Man of science kicks him in his huge horselike balls and shame happens. The fat guy's mother and father are there, from Joplin, Missouri. They both come into the ring and stomp the head of their son while the man of science has his way with the mother and then the referee has his way.

The principal found the tape and made an announcement over the intercom: "This recording is so vile and vicious, I do not have the courage to tell the parents of the children." That was poor Mr. Barnes. He finally got so old he drove a car through an entire pedestrian block. Never touched the liquor or the cigarettes.

Mrs. Barnes was a good teacher and loved my son Teddy at the church party where my dear mother took him. Reminds me how good Mrs. Bunyard was in the third grade when she let me write my stories and draw all over my tablet. Mrs. Bunyard saved me and my imagination, as did Mrs. Lee, Mrs. Harrison, Mrs. Burroughs, Mrs. Crane. Looking back, it was the women who put up for me when everybody else was saying get ready to be a Real Guy and make a living by being the same old things we are.

My foster brother Ralph was an ROTC from Ole Miss. He was at Lockburn Air Base, Columbus, Ohio. In 1954 we had photos of the Russians moving from house to house. Crypto messages, friends. They briefed SAC men on their targets. Gary Powers and the U-2. Enough said?

Everett Dial was going into the war but Dr. Dial knew a senator or somebody and pulled strings. Dr. Dial hated Roosevelt, the Democrats, Negroes, smoking, drinking, but he loved the little children. He was a doctor in Greek and Granny Dial had these wonderful meals, always: chicken, vegetables from the garden. Dr. Dial hated anything that would stimulate a man but he drank Dr. Pepper, which was loaded with caffeine. And still is. The Dials are fine honorable people, especially Murphy and Jane in Atlanta. John Dial, who has given and given to me and my family, is the famous uterine cancer specialist from Jackson, Miss. Many young men go to the universities and come back with their orthodox religion shot apart, Dr. Dial told me. While Granny made the milkshakes for my little children. With all this time gone by, nothing matters except Granny's milkshakes and the sweet smile in Doc's eye as he saw my little children in his house.

When brother Ralph came back to Clinton he met Joe Albritton, who had dragged Homer Ainsworth back from Pork Chop Hill in Korea. Joe loved speed and stock cars. Brother Ralph was going to go in with him and race stock cars. But Joe Albritton got in a wreck at the entrance to the Cotton Bowl on old Highway 80 and got killed. He came all the way back from Korea and got slaughtered five miles from his home.

Nothing is ever as you have explained it. Everybody is better off and worse than you could know in your furthest dreams.

Brother Ralph went off to be a millionaire buyer in Richardson, Texas, and his wife Meridith and his boys took care of Pappy in Houston when he was having cancer therapy at Anderson Hospital.

THINKING

I'm staying in, thinking about my people. Everybody is better than I am. I've bought everything
for peace. Susan and I have a new king-size bed.
My life is bountiful. It is like the Garden of Eden
with a woman who is so good-looking I took a Po-
laroid picture of her lying in a bed in Biloxi with
her breasts showing and showed it to my close
friends. Sharing her beauty, although I hate her
often. She challenges the thing: the *thing*. The thing
itself.

Old moon comes over the ocean, blessing the blacks
and the Indians and the white people. It touches
my wife Susan and me when she goes to the couch
in the red silk camisole. She's on the brown velvet
couch with her legs in my lap and I take off the
pants with her little feet and toes around the original engine, har. A waltz was in order but I had no
good clothes and we put on John Lennon's "Imag-

---

ine" and sat back. All the animals in the house came around us, knowing that something was happening. When we were in Columbus, Miss., at the Army/Navy store, the new boomerang, black and fiber glass, cost $5.98 and I bought it. It's still here in the room with its wrapper. It looks awfully lethal. It almost throbs but I won't take it out of its wrapper. Until the right time, which will be in deep Florida on the beach where Sam Lawrence has invited us and we will find our way there to the tropics in our Chrysler LeBaron convertible, looking all over Florida like Newman, Rankin, Lee, and I when we were fifteen in the Chevy Belair.

We overdid it immediately when we were fifteen but on the way back when we were all sunburned to hell and tired of hot bright Florida, we stopped at a motel and I was looking at the ocean which I was tired of at that point. But some teenagers were running around and I saw this taller older person with his back turned take this really fast spiral of a football on the back of his head. The football was thrown viciously hard and he never knew it was coming. He fell over but he was not quite knocked out and he got up howling about the person who could have done that to him. I was lighting a Winston with my feet up on the parapet. I started laughing so hard I almost vomited. Then the guy went off moaning that his ear was hurt. They were from Ohio, two cars full of them, and their voices were

so horrible in the evening I just had to laugh. I was
burnt to a crisp and needing the air conditioning
but Newman came upstairs and asked me: "Did you
see that guy get hit with that spiral?" He was col-
lapsing in laughter too.

At a high school party out in the country off Clinton
Boulevard there was this older brother of Claudine
who was going to entertain us. He put on an Indian
blanket and played the ukelele. Even worse, he was
a sincere Christer who wanted to sing "Kum Ba
Yah" — an African song reported from the mission
fields. There was a lot of watermelon around. He
was still in the Indian blanket with the ukelele when
he got in silhouette under a lawn light. Four of us
threw at his head but only I hit him. The spray off
his head was beautiful. Later in the night I had a
date with a woman who was three inches taller than
I was. I had a smart car, as usual, but she was a real
"woman." She lived near the Clinton Country Club
on the boulevard. She was three inches taller than
I was and already looked like a flight stewardess. I
tooled around the handsome midnight and drove
close to a fence on the north side of the club with
a ditch of willows nearby. I let the top down off the
Plymouth Fury and lit up a Picayune. By then I
had some fame as a trumpet man and poet. I was
wearing a white sports coat with a limp rose on the
lapel. She was holding this little orange corsage I'd
given her. The blue clear night poured in.

"How about my sucking your pussy?" I asked her. In getting this date, we had perhaps exchanged twenty words.

She hit me so hard right in the face that my blue sunglasses flew off. I saw some stars.

"How come you look twenty-five when the rest of us look like kids?" I said to her, relighting a Picayune. She looked away at the moon. She took her own pack of Oasis cigarettes out.

Then she started crying. Oh my god.

"Here. Have a light," I said. I was feeling sorry for her although she'd broken the hearts of many football players. She just wouldn't put out, even though she looked already like a mother of three.

"Who do you think I am?" she asked me.

"I have no idea. Why'd you go out with me?"

"I had nothing better to do."

It was a wonderful night for love and maybe I could have been charming, but I said: "Get out and walk."

"I can't believe this."

Maybe it was a mile to her house. I left her in the road and went back to Claudine's party. It now strikes me that everybody who lived along Clinton Boulevard was desperate and unsettled. People died early and grew up early and pretended early and men sexually abused their daughters early. I was left in a house with a beautiful mother one afternoon, mother of one of my classmates. She came on to me, asking me to save her. I threw away my cigarette and fled in the Plymouth Fury. She'd told me she had an ulcer, her son had an ulcer, her husband had an ulcer. All she did was lie in the back yard and get a tan, using iodine and saltwater solution.

Yelverston came through town looking different from the rest. There was a fury in him and he told me he'd lost a lot of weight lately. He had news from the sheriff in Tupelo now and from his friend the sheriff in Ocean Springs. He'd gone out to look at the Tennessee–Tombigbee waterway and it was nothing but a dull channel between sides of slate. He didn't know where to begin. But he had bought a speedboat loaded with food, water, and two cut-off automatic sixteen gauges. His wife was waiting out in the car. Or, he said, his ex-wife. I thought he was out of his gourd, though I'd read about his son's death in the newspaper weeks back. He was taking one Jack Daniels after another. I said, Well, what about a helicopter, and he told me: "Don't you know I've already thought about that?" But he put a hand on my shoulder and said, "Lad."

I was forty-six and was not a lad. I was a writer here at the school and he knew it. He wanted me to meet his wife down in the car. His ex-wife. She was out walking around the famous courthouse and reading the Faulkner quote on the plaque about how much the county courthouse meant. Yeah. It gives many lawyers employment. March on, legions of the violated and ripped-off. March on, lawyers and your money. Center of the squalid quid pro quo and random justice. His ex-wife, I forget her name, but she looked pretty good in her long black coat and black shoes underneath with a flash of silver buckle. Things in nature gather round, es-pying the architecture where the fences and the benches squat out with a dignity ungiven until this very moment, this last hope for justice in the wild driven land the cunt with a hot seed on fire etc. Women exchangeable like shells coming back and thrown off in the weeds from a howitzer lanyarded by three poor fuckers from Germany or the U.S.A. or does it matter—the exchangeable women like thrown-out vessels wherein used to place some cock, etc.—where the shit is the end of this sen-tence, Faulkner?

She was a handsome woman and I shook her hand and she was very happy to meet me.

"Good luck," I said.

Yelverston was some drunk but he kept calling me lad. He had a driven look. He got in the long yellow car and they went off. Then I saw the police come around and arrest Blanche, Ollie, Jamie, and Buck for bringing drinks outdoors. They just wanted to look and then they were nailed by the cops. The police get $136 for the city like this and they get to write something up on their miserable biographies.

——

I always smile at the cops around here and there are a few good ones. I even saw one in the bookstore once.

Yelverston's wife was *Ruth*, again. I've got to remember her name. She was a woman with class and you could see it in her walk. There is a certain life to a woman's step. I've seen that thing happen in women since I was fifteen. No matter what has happened or who has been with them, they have a certain lift in their step.

It is like watching a friend come in, like my son, who walks through the house with some step in his sneakers. He owns the earth and doesn't even know it.

The night perishes and the morning comes back with its dumb challenge like Bukowski with the red eyes, looking for a winner at Anita. When I was in San Pedro in 1980 I was clear of the stuff and did not dare try to contact Bukowski, even if he would meet me. I went down and heard a Mexican band in a bar, two trumpets and a bass guitar and seven other string instruments. My god did I want a tequila or at least a beer.

But my son came out and I was fine in the little apartment with a color teevee. We were getting around on Quisenberry's Triumph and we ate down at the 22nd Street dock in a white Mexican restaurant. Basil, the South African, went with us. He was riding his Kawasaki. Basil told me he was so sick with alcohol he couldn't even take down water and just threw up bile for a week when he tried to get off the stuff. But now we were eating everything on the bay.

What was the show we watched, me and my son? *Baretta*. Tony. *Tony*, Po and I would call out. Robert Blake had that cockatoo and his dad and we loved it. Quiz and his wife Kathy were very hospitable to us. We ate with them up in Westwood and in Venice, watching the sea and having our coffee. Elliot Lewitt was generous to us all. For a while we were roaming around Southern California, just having it. Money and the Pacific.

❑ ❑

Back in the fond smoky days of youth Yelverston was never a youth at all. He was dealing, he was selling in his neighborhood in Mobile. He and his girl pal made puppets and gave shows for which they charged a nickel. Most children had never heard about a bank account but Yelverston had and he owned one. He did not eat fish but he would go out fishing in the bay and then come back and sell speckled trout and mullet to his neighbors after smoking them on an oil-can grill in his back yard. Yelverston's father was like Elvis Presley's. He retired at thirty-five for vague reasons, the more solid one being that he didn't believe in work, not any longer. Yelverston went to bed smelling of smoked fish and yearning to help his father even more. He would think about his poor tired papa who had worked in the grocery store so long and had an arthritic back and sore feet. Though Yelverston saw him dance and go hunting for ducks when he wanted to. These things made Papa happy and all his diseases suddenly went away. Yelverston's uncle was a rich man who lived in Hattiesburg, Mississippi, and he would come in and chide Yelverston's father as he lay back in his rocking chair. He would leave two hundred-dollar bills behind him on the kitchen counter and everybody, especially Yelverston's mother, was embarrassed to pick them up. But they did. Yelverston was selling boats, big boats, when he was seventeen. He would buy a bad one and then fix it up and sell it for thrice what he'd paid.

❏ ❏

Yelverston was valedictorian of his class. His uncle bought him the suit he was standing in as he gave the address to his class for three minutes. He was a good-looking man of eighteen, with unruly brown hair that he could never comb correctly. He could not even find a natural part in his hair. His uncle and his mother, Ellen, were in the audience. The band had just played "Pomp and Circumstance" very well. There were a lot of good musicians in his high school and he had wished often that he could be among them.

Yelverston had made at least a dollar off of everybody in the class. The teachers and superintendent loved him. He had made almost straight *A*'s. In science classes, when the teacher was absent, he had taken up the book and taught the class better than the teacher had. He could read very well. He knew math awfully well. He had ten and a half thousand in the bank that he never told his rich uncle about. He was paying the last mortgage note on his parents' house. He could not recall what he said when he was valedictorian. It was something about poverty was your own fault and you should fix up your own house. Something about never asking for anything, never begging. Some message against cigarettes and how idle they were. The band cut in and he was swept away by his swarming friends. He had treated them all right when he was making money from them. The principal of the school owed him $500 for a boat. The daughter of the mayor owed him $2000. He got his diploma and marched out with the rest of the kids, only he was not a kid and he knew it. He went forward in his gown.

Yelverston moved and moved and made money. He never met a woman who slowed him down until he was in Arlington, Va. They needed him at the Roosevelt administration then and he had had a heart attack. He was only twenty but he had a heart attack. He was selling the port to the senator. It was such an amazing deal that would make him rich forever and while he was enjoying it he had a heart attack. Now he was even richer than his uncle, and his parents would have a respectable home. Poor papa with his disease, and his mother, Ellen, who had to live with his father, who was now, Yelverston realized, a lazy bastard with a foul temper. His father's first name was Larles. What kind of name was that? Yelverston realized his own first name suddenly when he was twenty. It was Barton. Barton Benton Yelverston.

A number of years went past and he was even richer and had a wife. For a while they couldn't conceive and then they asked a doctor's advice about it. His wife had to turn backwards to him so he could get the sperm all in her. Haunted moments when they had no music because neither of them had ever heard much music. They ground away in slow silence, thinking they were alone, in the dark. Then they had a son who once he was walking went and fed himself directly. He went ahead and did it. They watched him. He had his own little imperial strength.

The little man went ahead and did his business. Things would occur to him that nobody had ever mentioned and he would act on them. He moved along and he had his little schemes. He went through the day with his own agenda, as Yelverston said. He was always a strange boy and not especially beautiful, but he had a deliberate motion and he cared not for his toys and all the extra candy and silver spoons that Ellen brought him. He didn't want the big house especially and went fishing with little black boys when he was eight. He made himself a special fish bait, which was a roach covered with glue, hardened, and he trolled it through the bayou with great results, and he didn't have to change baits much. He just trolled it along with his long cane pole and he brought home seven or ten big bluegills and then cleaned them himself. He would take hours cleaning them. Ruth finally recognized that he was studying the anatomy of the fish. He was using a magnifying glass and working under a bright light in the utility room off the garage. He had found a *scalpel* from somewhere. He and one of the little colored boys, who was also interested in anatomy. Yelverston began eating fish when his little son caught them. He suddenly found them delicious. The little boy brought the flesh in supremely clean and Ruth would throw them into the hot oil with cornmeal on them, onions sizzling around them. With some lemon and ketchup, they were very tasty. Also when the little one was asleep Yelverston and Ruth would have nightlong enormous affections for each other, running into dawn, where they were thinking of the beauty of anatomy and the holiness of man and woman.

OXFORD

June '88.

Had coffee with JoElla Holman, the widow of David who died on the golf course. He's also left behind his little son Jeff. She told me she was going to go back to Chapel Hill, where David's buried and she has people, but she didn't feel like moving from their little house because of feeling for David and what they had here together. She was tidying up all the loose ends of the business. Little Jeff knew his father was not coming back and he was becoming anxious. David used to come into Square Books with Jeff on his stomach in one of those slings. What a proud father he was. His pride will continue into little Jeff. JoElla has a wonderful dignity to her. David loved her to the bone. He talked and talked about his amazing wife JoElla. He never had too much whiskey and just occasionally borrowed a cigarette from me, so as to feel like a regular guy. He loved good lit so much, he laughed when something was wonderful. He was sailing with the natural high of being himself and distinguished. His father was Hugh Holman, who wrote the handbook for the literary terms and was the great scholar at Chapel Hill. David was cutting his own track as a thinker and a young father. Every day, he would go to JoElla and ask her: "Do you feel loved?" He would give her a big hug. He did the same for me, as his friend. Do you feel loved, Barry? He always had a smile and the encouraging word. He adored Susan too. Do you feel loved today? With his thick glasses and his smile. He still comes into Square Books, a ghost with brilliance coming off of him now that he is merely dead. Since David has died I take nobody's life for granted. Everybody has a shine coming off them. Most are doing their best but not all of them. Some of them are still landed in the altitudes where they think that passing a dollar and keeping the status quo is a nice thing. Pres. Reagan has made a lot of shits like that feel comfortable. I'm not that political, but when so many criminals show up at once and want my dollar, I get angry.

The hideous man who stabbed the other 128 times in a trailer. There was a fight over a woman. Drugs were involved. He stabbed the other so much he fell apart. When he was out on bail he got behind some old guy at a stoplight. When the old guy was stalling in front of him, he dragged the old guy out and beat him up. Bobby Marks represented the killer. Marks is a good-looking lawyer making a living, has a fast smile, and like most lawyers who get their fee doesn't give a headache about whom he is setting loose on the streets. As long as it's the law. As the law requires. I would like to watch some of these lawyers react when the scum they have released collects around their back yard and starts looking at their baby daughters. I was down at Ireland's bar listening to my son on guitar. The murderer's father got up and danced like a low weird Greek back and forth in front of the band. Really, he was a joy. He was light on his feet and he was gliding back and forth like a balloon. He was dancing away from his son the murderer.

Buck and Dees were fishing in one of the creeks off Sardis Reservoir one afternoon. They were calmly fishing and then they looked up on the bluff and this fellow was yelling. He had on a full camouflage outfit and he was wanting them to see his minnows. He kept calling to them. No white man calls for another white man to come look at his minnows. Buck went up and looked at the minnows but he knew something was wrong. The man was on drugs of a serious nature or he was insane. The facts prove out that he was serious on drugs, but just marijuana. He had seen *Rambo* as he said later, and he and another loser went on College Hill Road within two weeks. He broke into a man's house and stole a high-powered rifle, perhaps a .278 — what the hell does it matter? — and came out on the road and shot into a car, killing a four-year-old child, right through the windshield. No doubt he had been deranged for a long while and when Buddy East and the police caught him and his buddy on some muddy motorcycle, he explained he was going back to town for more dope. He'd seen *Rambo* and he just wanted to shoot somebody.

I was reading Hunter Thompson's new book, *Generation of Swine*. There was some old Jeep in a pasture with plastic explosives in it. Hunter is a mature fifty, I think. Yet grown men were shooting at the Jeep to see it explode. Things get slow. Rick Kelley and I went out and shot four snakes in Jerry Hoar's pond the other midday because things were slow. We were letting off the twenty gauge at all squirming things. But nobody ever thought about blasting into a car with a family in it. This killing was so random and heinous it made Oxford cry. *Where do these people come from?*

□ □

At Eagle Lake in an old drainage from the great Mississippi River, out from Vicksburg where all the Union and Rebs had died for our sins already and now we were free to be boys and start again, we were in the trailer of Mr. Krebs. We'd bought some wine in Vicksburg and even Jerry Rankin, the future missionary, was there. It was me, Newman, Krebs, and Henry O'Neill and Art Lee, I think. At the end of the pier next to the boathouse and bait, with all those scrumptious snacks, we met Mr. Krebs. He was loaded on beer and smiling to have all of us lads over here at his humble resort. Thinking back, he couldn't have been much older than I am now. I really don't know why all the nice guys have to be so loaded, like my Uncle Troy. He was loaded but he made millions which all these widows suck around. I personally intend to leave nothing and let them quarrel about how thoughtless I was. We went into the trailer and got assorted and then went out on the lake with some lanterns and motored into a cove that was supposed to be haunted. Who was it? Krebs, Rankin, and me. We were sharing one bottle of wine, except Rankin, who was bound to be pure for the Lord, etc. That was all right. We had the minnows and we let them down. Big white perch got on the lines immediately. Maybe because Jerry Rankin had blessed us. Big things of two and almost three pounds were on the line so fast we were out of bait in forty-five minutes. The boat was heavy with fish and then my lantern shut down, cut off, for no reason. We just had the one tiny light to back up to the main lake and find our way home. The motor cut down as if somebody had turned it into a home mixer.

Eagle Lake is an immense lake at night with only a putting old Johnson, five hp, and a low beam. The moon was out and it had a beam right back to our dock, but we were afraid. Nobody else was around and when we backed out of the creek there was a loud laughing sound, a male's voice, off to the left. We usually had weapons but this time we'd just gone fishing and this voice scared me. They said there were a lot of dead Indians around here. A bobwhite went off next to the boat. A bobwhite is just a quail but this time I heard its voice amplified. It went through me and us like a shock. This bird was calling *darling darling!* Starts with a low C and then shrills out two octaves above.

We got back to the trailer and dressed the fish and put them in the fridge. Mr. Krebs's trailer was a great resort. It was capacious and we could wander back and forth. I got a shower and looked out the window while I was naked with the water still on me. In the moonlight I saw two baby armadillos play with their mother around the trunk of a tree. I had never seen an armadillo before. I thought they were Texas animals. But they were coming back here. The mother was feigning some little strokes and the babies were running up and colliding with her and rolling back, on their shells. She was teaching them how to be armadillos, bless her heart. They keep coming and they're so dumb they get run over by cars, but what the devil were they ever supposed to know about cars? Jayne Mansfield got killed on a road full of armadillos and she was human and once I saw her breasts in person at Gus Stevens's when I was young.

Brings up the issue of Camille Hykes. Smart as

next Tuesday, beautiful, so Sam Lawrence tells me, and now living with a painter. All these brilliant women live with painters. Painters are even more terrible than I am, and much more sissy. Even more conscienceless. They need like an acre of space, pretend to work for nine years, and then blame the world if they don't sell. They have a stoned vision where they walk through pussy and oyster shells with bare feet and never acknowledge what even was there. I have a friend who is a great painter and he still has no idea who he even married or what his kids are like. I saw one of his kids wandering around naked in Vicksburg with a dumb hungry look on his face. Do you know who your father is? I asked him. Your father is a great artist, I reminded him. The cops drove up. They were about to arrest him just for looking like a foaming idiot. I intervened. See here, I'm Hannah, the such and such, etc.

Camille and Jayne Mansfield. What wonders they are.

❑ ❑

What a hot number the old girl was before she was considered for the Nobel Prize. She was old, really old, but there was still some juice there. She'd pour me out a stiff drink and throw her cameras at me. It was deep and narrow, I tell you. We had libraries and weeks named for us. If I could just take you over there, I asked her, and she said yes, yes, her mouth full of my kisses. Capote when he was really drunk called me the maddest writer in the U.S.A. and I was continuing on this reputation. For writers you can never give enough praise. We are solid babies who have missed something and we want it written out in big magazines.

Over in the Old Chapel, we hoisted the last of the vodka and I kicked her down the aisle. Die, die! I shouted. But I had to drive her back home and cover her up and kiss her forehead, having sobered up, knowing she was a national treasure. Went by to see Brown, who has a Jaguar and we both need it every day. Brown the genius from high school and college. He was the only one who could talk to me *de mano a mano*. Brown had the courage of his beliefs but more, he was using the brain God gave him and the rest of us were sitting by saying, Yeah, what a brain but would you like to be given that weirdness? It occurs to me that at forty-six I want all the weirdness and the fellowship of pal Joe's brain.

Pal Joe quit the booze five or six years ago. He was into it like I was and he needed help and he called me. I was honored to give him my professional advice from California, Montana, though since I've been a failure by AA standards. Brown, Brown, how we used to argue over some passage in a radio song, whether it was a violin or a synthesizer. That was when electronic music was moving in and I knew it. I was right. But Brown was never attuned to the radio. His head was in the great symphonies and the Bach movements that sometimes go into a sort of calculus and Mozart when he moves into the clouds with his smart-assness challenging a god to strike him down he has gotten so impertinent.

Brown, in room 421 in Ratliff Dorm at Mississippi College, where we were talking about Freud and Marx and the room was crammed with all of Brown's books and sculptures, the metal stork, and the neighborhood of the room became zero when they threw in this zealot named Tom Rawlings who edited the school newspaper, in a room about fifteen by fifteen. We had a stereo and jazz and classics. Nobody had a chance to live. We were doomed at Mississippi College. We had an atheists' convention. We dreamed about opening up the roof and having ack-ack fire. Instruments all over the room. The Russians would never get us. We were not afraid. Rawlings wanted to fight with boxing gloves and show me what a real man was and I whipped his ass out in the hall, bloodied his nose. Don't mess with me, Christers. Gene Speed came in, busted from the Air Force Academy. Then there were complaints from the dorm counselor. Joe and I were doing the chloroform just to blank out. The teachers were almost uniformly wretched. We had a small civilization going before. Joe's parents came and dragged him out. Then my father came and dragged me out. I will never forgive my parents for not allowing me my life at college, never sticking up for me. They were spineless, discreet. I got home and then married to get away from home. Who needed all the lectures?

❑ ❑

Somewhere over the dying, '88.

Gene Speed is a doctor now. His father was a preacher from Meridian. Speed fell in love with Kell Gray and then wandered around her yard with a machete until Kell's mother let him in to have a drink of water. Kell was the drum majorette of the Provine High Band. She had a bikini very early. She apparently would let some men have some and then cut them off. Newcomb fell for her. Newman was into it. Older men like Charles Last came by to ply her charms. Speed was head over heels. I never cared for her personally because she was pale and had moles on her but other men found her fascinating. Speed was in 421 and was an atheist. I wasn't an atheist but I smoked and hated Jesus people. Jesus people were everywhere and loud.

But I was smoking my cigarette one day when a Christer came by and asked me, "Why do writers always smoke?" Speed was lighting one up near me and he said, "Why don't you run home and get yourself raped?" Speed was harsh. He fell head over heels in love with a girl named Eleanor and then when that didn't work out, he shot himself in the belly with a .22. Nicely. I was used to him because I'd knocked him out once when we were wrestling. He overweighed me by forty pounds but I slammed him down and he passed out. Speed was always wanting to pass out or be wounded. He loved me, though.

Give the guy a break. His father was a preacher who smiled at an organist or something. And got fired and discredited. It's happened. A preacher smiles and has the spirit and then a woman goes crazy. The preacher is a lousy man.

We're all all right. Speed, Brown, me.

❑ ❑

We had some dates at Millsaps, the smart school. Speed had his date and we were waiting in a sorority hall, with the Plymouth Fury convertible—white, blue leather seats—trembling outside. My date didn't show. We were waiting, maybe it could be my wife, I was all excited. Speed's date was two inches taller than I was and a great beauty. Speed was about six-one and his date was looking at him. Speed was a fine-looking man with a smart beak of a nose and big gray eyes in a ruddy skin. He was erect too, and he had told me about my posture and my diet. I thought I was pretty handsome, especially with my rich brother's Fury outside. Finally Speed's date, who was so good I wanted to lick her ankles, confessed that my date had gone off with another guy, a football player from Tulane. Speed told her to go to hell. He wasn't going to stand for his pal getting stood up. He let go of this wonderful girl and we walked back to the car, alone. She came out to tell him something. Go to hell, he said. My god, Speed was loyal. He actually loved me.

When Yelverston and I were talking he was plenty drunk but then he sobered up suddenly with a brandy and coffee. He and his wife came up to our house, with all my books and the horns and Bach on the stereo.

His wife Ruth sat on the bed and talked to Susan.

I wanted to take Yelverston out to the Grove at the Ole Miss campus and throw the boomerang. I had the new fiber-glass model, still in its plastic. But when I got to the Grove I was changed and I just listened to him and never got out of the car.

□ □

Back in the trailer at Eagle Lake nobody was smoking yet, the air was clear, and we had all these fish to clean. It was a miracle. Even the armadillos have children.

EVERY DAY

The birds are here in the morning and the dawn is coming into our lovely town. I've pledged to keep away from hostility with my wife. Sometimes propinquity is the thing. Marriage is a long-scale idea and you just can't live that close without having a fight.

I'm looking straight ahead to pussy and shelter and thirteen dollars. With that and a pencil, I can rule the world. The little sycophantesses in their tennis shoes will run and get the paper. I require the eight-dollar stuff at Square Books, heavy bond with ecru color. My god, all the pets are waking up and need food. We've got about eight cats and two dogs here. But that's all right. We'll move the rug out and have it cleaned and deodorized. Human babies get out of the womb looking shifty already. You ever notice that? Animals come out looking lively and ready for life. Maybe a case for original sin. I don't know.

What do I know, with my history of flying and cunning? All my seven wives wailing about my mistreatment.

I looked in the mirror and I saw that Susan really tagged me around the neck during our last battle. But I was a wild man and she was fighting for her life. She tried to kick the manhood but it was to no avail. I began strangling her and screaming out the ending of Poe's "Masque of the Red Death." I never knew I had memorized it. But then I left off her throat, and the vision, pure as a rhapsody from the weirs, trembled and yet stood her poise, against the green curtains and the smoke.

Top off the convertible and we're doing just twenty in an old forgotten place where the poplars are hanging over and we go into a tunnel of sudden shade, lost to the world, no horns no sirens no red light. Both of us hungry for a bite and only a half a Pepsi left. Out of cigarettes, no stimulants at all. At the end of the tunnel is a decayed barn, faded red and very picturesque. Just for the hell of it and for old Walt Whitman and Mark Twain and the boys who said themselves so well, I burn up a five-dollar bill while she sucks my person. This is the sort of squalor that Rev. Wildmon deplores. He is hot on the trail of such scenes as this. Never will it be allowed in our domain, he says, tossing another book into the fire like my last wife liked to do. She'd throw away anything that didn't go with the wallpaper. Wildmon is another homegrown idiot from the state of Mississippi. Now he's gone totally nuts, as most preachers with a political cause do. He has attacked Mighty Mouse for sniffing cocaine to get his strength. The cartoon Mighty Mouse was a loser anyway, like a flying Jimmy Bakker. He just glanced around. My wife beckons me back with her arms to our bed after all these nights away from her. I blame myself for being an artist and how awful it must be to miss me.

◻ ◻

Yelverston's boy was not a genius but he had his own way. He grew up and went to college and found the one he loved. The river pirates killed him for his tape deck. His wife was reaching toward his poor dying body to save him and they blew her hand off. He and his wife were camping under some willows with their twelve-foot boat pulled up on the bank. They had been catching a few fish in the Tennessee–Tombigbee waterway. The dope pirates were all black, but led by a white wino from Texas named Coresta Haim. The murder was so vicious and unreasonable it could only be compared to the wild murders of the Harp brothers back in the early days of the Natchez Trace. These blacks were a new ruthless breed in Mississippi and Alabama, who used crack and ran cocaine. Haim would sniff cocaine and direct them along the waterway as he drank his wine. He was a connoisseur of the vino. They would run a certain amount of powder and weed and then go back to Mobile and get more, and when they went back they were hungover and bored. That's when they saw the Yelverston couple.

Yelverston and his wife joined with the sheriffs along the river and brought the crew to justice. It was an amazing story of vengeance and righteous diligence in investigation. They rounded up every one of them. Now they're all in Parchman prison and Yelverston has remarried his first wife.

□ □

Yelverston took his wife down to Key West.

He was an old American, sixty-two, and Ruth was fifty. But she could still conceive and she was far away from her "change of life."

They had taken contraceptive measures.

Personally, I wish him well. I have too many children already. There is a quality of life when you listen to all of Bach and some jazz and you are out of cigarettes. Nobody is left but your pretty blond wife. Everything has been shut out.

They went to Key West and stayed in an apartment next to Louie's Backyard. They were astounded by the changes in Key West, with all the queers and the girls baring their breasts on the sailboats and the well-built gay men with their bathing suits like black jockstraps showing off all their butts. They waded in the water and swam toward the sailboats and they had punch system on the radio in case they had to work at the hospital or they had to rush in and suck a dick. Yelverston's wife held one of the punch buttons while a slim queer with a mustache went out swimming in his jockstrap.

Yelverston had been out to Big Pine Key fishing for bonefish and permit with Bill Schwicker. Bill had poled all over the bay and Yelverston had hung a five-foot lemon shark for fifteen seconds on a light Daiwa reel outfit with a floating crab. It was a thrill and he saw the fellow out there hung and resenting it. It snapped the line. The bay in the shallows of Big Pine Key was extremely clear and green-white right to the bottom. They ran up on a big nurse shark that was so big Yelverston didn't see it until the boat was almost over it and then it was there, purple-brown and about a foot across and it moved and Yelverston saw it. Why should this thing live when his son was dead? He watched it go out and struggle in the shallow water eating the little crustaceans out of the sand. Why should the niggers and the Texan still live in Parchman? They were all on death row now but Yelverston decided to change that. He decided to get them out of jail and own them. He no longer feared his own death. Death was nothing, death was the least of his worries. His son was dead but here was he with his handsome head of gray hair and his Pall Malls, five a day, and his habit of having five drinks a day, even though he had developed an ulcer. He realized he was an old fart and he and his wife had listened to old fart music coming down to Key West. His teeth needed fixing, his ulcer needed fixing. But just a swim in the crystal waters of Key West set him back on the track, and his mind cleared. He wanted to own one of the killers. He wanted to work him and train him until he was a close friend.

He saw the sun setting out in the Tortugas and realized that there was no revenge. There was never any revenge. He had been hitting them with a smile for years. Now his smile was tired and when he got home he saw his ex-wife, new wife, naked, lying on the couch innocently watching Wimbledon tennis. He was thinking about everything in the world. But he got naked too and the air conditioning rushing in felt wonderful after the hot trip with a sun around 97 degrees, and his head getting sunsick, so that he needed a couple of aspirins. He was wandering in his brain and wishing to die to be alongside his son in the grave. He was wishing to lie down with all the cool dead from all centuries. He was that tired. But his wife looked good and he wanted her. So she leaned over the bed and he gave her pleasure for ten minutes and he had his pleasure with her. He had almost forgotten how quiet and sweet her breasts with the big nipples were. He regarded the vagina where he had placed his son and saw it as a miracle of anatomy. He had never seen completely what a miracle the vagina was with his wife's white behind and her long tanned legs and brown toes spread on the floor. He wanted to do it again and now her hair was gray but she backed up on him and tossed her rump around like a girl. His heart was beating very fast and he lay on the couch, hoping he would have a heart attack that would take him off instantly to the town where his son lived. But he loved giving joy to his wife and she was lying in her robe taking a nap now too. What a thing it was to have a woman like this with his come in her and her being a woman around him, straightening the kitchen and bitching about small things. How he'd missed it!

Theories of women have gone around a while.

At one point Yelverston read all of them — Freud, Jung, and Miriam Fast, who conjoined all the information ever submitted about women on a computer and prescribed that most women want a glass of white wine on the rocks and a hard member underwater in a cool ocean inlet near the mangroves in Florida and a hundred thousand to shop with. He'd listened to the lesbians on teevee. They were mentioning how enlarged the world would be without men. If only they could just bite each other's carpet and think of releasing delinquent young women now in prison but soon to go out and kill men. His wife had a smile on her now as she slept. Women invent the special lovely things of the world, and have an elevated regard for the "mundane" and a deep driven sense like a seventh sense that they are the mama lions and they will protect all their cubs even if it means killing the papa. Okay?

His wife awoke grinning and told him she was dreaming of deer in a green meadow with high yellow flowers in it. She said she was running naked with the deer and she was as fast as they were, so fast that she began flying. She could feel the wind whipping by her bare feet and she put her legs behind her like a bird. She was leading the deer to a watering place. The big eyes of the does and the stags were watching me, she told Yelverston. Then we all came down and got in the water and the deer and I went underwater but it was just like a space full of diamonds and all we had to do was breathe in the blue air with diamonds twinkling around us. Then we got in a substance that was water and air and food all together. Then I woke up and I've just never felt better, honey, she told him.

Oh, Ruth.

He wanted her again and she obliged him. He knew he was a monster but he had to take her in the mouth this time and then come on her big generous breasts with the nipples dripping. Why do men need this? Yelverston asked himself. To make an elegant woman like her with her dreams of deer submit to this and degrade her? He thanked her. No, she said, thank you, darling. I've never done this for any other man, she said.

He was so amazed he slept.

He himself went into a dream where he was with his son and the lad was smiling as he walked on water.

I miss my sons now, one in Nashville, one in Tuscaloosa. I miss my daughter Lee too. They are all safe and I pray for them in their cars and traffic. Susan misses her son David every day. He is in Easley, South Carolina, with his pop and stepmother. He has more advantages up there in the foothills of the Blue Ridge Mountains. For the most part it is just my wife and I together in the gray house hating each other and then going into a coma when the television from Memphis takes over. She falls asleep and I try to slip out and get next to strange nooky but she always wakes up and tracks me down in her gown and bedroom slippers. I have had so much young nooky on my arm telling them about what a famous writer I am, but my wife shows up screaming in the alley like a fishwife, her blond hair flying around her face, and it's over. I try to get nooky at Square Books while the classical music is going and the doughheads with slumping shoulders wearing black socks with black hightop sneakers are standing around trying to remember their own names. Richard Howorth has the best bookstore in the South, but how come you never see any long-legged classical nooky in there? Does literature of fine quality only invite the ugly and the weird and the confident brilliant idiots who are writing things called The World As We Know It on endless legal pads? I go up there and have my cup of cappuccino, pretending to give a damn about *The New York Times Book Review,* but mainly wanting a lit-crazed nurse in white garter belt and white spike heels to light my cigarette and lick my face. You never see somebody like her to discuss feminism with. Three months ago I heard the rumor that women have feelings too, and I want to talk about it.

Women are the great new business to man every day. Every day. It goes without saying that a woman with good legs in sandals beats the hell out of a greasy breakfast with grits and comments about money. A woman who is not a swamp in a dress is a brilliant mystery, says I. And maybe Yelverston.

We *rely* on women the rest of our lives, said Yelverston. He was going down to see his daughter-in-law with her poor missing right hand. Then he told me some more.

❑ ❑

A terrible thing happened when Ron Shapiro's dog King got run over. King was always in the Hoka, wanting some petting. He was a black dog ten years old who leapt beautifully for a Frisbee. The guy who hit him near the railroad underpass called in and said he was to blame for the death of King. None of us wanted King ever to go. But he did. So canny about cars before, maybe he had got old and couldn't dart away anymore. Maybe he was tired of the same old trips back and forth to the Hoka, to Willie Morris's house. Down at Key West, Yelverston told me, they let the dogs swim in the ocean. He watched the dogs, all stripes and breeds, wade out and swim and walk on the sandbars. The noble sincere faces of dogs have always touched me deeply, as they have Yelverston. King would go out to the sandbars and ask, Are you coming along with me? Then he would stand up with his black hair all wet and ask us, What next, Masters? Every clod lost diminishes the continent, as John Donne said. David Holman is gone, an expert at literature, and King is gone, an expert at black dog. We are not the same without them.

⬚ ⬚

Yelverston and his wife drove through the Everglades and they went through the "Indian villages" and on the airboats through the brown glades in the swamps. Good thing to have a tank of gas going through the Everglades. For three hours there was nothing but the canals and the glades, and the Indian villages. His wife became amazingly bitter and angry out here in the sun-drenched nowhere with all the Indian history, Osceola and the boys. Even in the air-conditioned Jaguar sedan with the phone in it, she became bitter and began blaming Yelverston for the traits in their son which had come from Yelverston and led to the boy's murder. Your damned belief that people are kind and reasonable!

Your damned optimism about the earth being your friend! They stopped at an Indian village and Yelverston paid for an airboat ride. He'd never been on one of these contraptions, although he'd sold and bought boats of all sorts all over the world. The driver was a scrawny jerk who was maybe Seminole by way of a generation of petty thieves. He had a filthy gasoline-smelling aqua-blue blouse on him and deeply pitted skin. But his long black hair was handsome, tied behind him in a pigtail, screwing down his hunched back. The airboat got off faster than Yelverston thought it would, and he could see in the kid's eyes that he wanted to scare Yelverston and his wife and make one of them howl for a slower pace. But his wife said nothing and he said nothing, holding onto the gunnels for the ride and despising each other. Her dress flew up in her face and Yelverston saw her fine suntanned legs and her encouraging sandals. He wanted her, all in the speed and even as he hated her so much. They went over the weeds at 50 mph.

They went past alligators, who were just lying around, enormous, being prehistoric, sleepy, totally horny when the season came on, victims of tides and any asshole with a lantern and a high-powered rifle. All the wives and husbands and Texans waiting for the belts and the shoes. Yelverston looked at his wife's sandals and they were made of lizard skin. They dismounted the boat and went ahead in cold silence, despising each other, then went into the Indian hut where people sold everything that looked charmed and natural from the region. He saw his wife looking at a necklace of silver and stones and he saw the peace in her eyes suddenly and he knew all the ugliness was out of her. The speed on the airboat had caught up with her and the recriminations had flown away. The same thing had happened to him. His useless pity for all things killed and disgraced went through the hot air and down the white man's highway and on into St. Petersburg, through the hordes of stores and the billboards that Florida had become. A horror of "For Sale." You run through Florida from Key West to Point Clear, Alabama, and you don't even meet human Southern courtesy until you get to a gas station run by blacks in north St. Petersburg. The man who raises the hood has a toothache. The girl who owns the place is trying to make it congenial. Even when Yelverston's wife was bitchy, the black girl with her sincerity won her over. "Please have a safe journey," the girl said.

In upper Florida, where boiled peanuts were sold in a bar and the people were kind, the anger finally broke. They took an old motel with separate cottages as in the old days of the fifties and stayed in them till their anger was broken. Yelverston looked out through the folding glass and saw the rest of his neighbors around here. They were people who were there with wives and children in Chevy station wagons, people who could not afford to have a fight like this in the shade of the live oaks and under the Spanish moss, in a green oyster-shell-driveway kind of place. With a small swimming pool behind the restaurant, which was wood-paneled and had stuffed fish on the wall. Yelverston got naked and he began hating himself for being rich. He hated himself for running with his smart dreams and conquering everything. There was a time to turn over and be defeated, too, and be out of it and quit pretending to adore everybody he was in business with. There were so many weaselly little cowards he had commended because they gave him money and respect. He had quit smoking but he got a pack of salty old Pall Malls out of his kit. He had got them salty making love to his wife in the ocean five days ago. Sir Walter Raleigh, huh? he asked himself.

His wife was in the other cottage, and she told me later that she was distressed at what she had become, too. She had not armed her son with the canniness. She had not armed her son with the survivalness. He was too dumb and too smart. In the hospital, when she had seen her son's wife with her hand blown away, seen the lovely skinny girl with her missing hand bandaged and taken care of, she could not remember the girl's name. The girl started having a glow around her like a saint. Ruth's daughter-in-law's name was Grace Helen. She walked away, did Yelverston's wife. She was blinded by tears and so much wasted time that she had to see Yelverston immediately. He was in Oklahoma by that time, asking how to get back at the killers, how to find them all. Lloyd Helms was a sort of friend of his and he got all the Mississippi sheriffs on the line. Her womb was on fire to conceive another baby at the last of her time. She left her husband with a brief phone call and flew to Yelverston.

She finally found him at the funeral of their son. She addressed him and then she got nude. He did not want to make love but she got him out of his trousers and pressed her breasts against it. Come on, come on, she said. He couldn't but she persisted. Yes you can. I've read all the books about what you men want, she said.

□ □

At the best of my trumpet playing and my poetry writing there occurred a wonderful young lady named Tidy Armstrong from Rolling Fork, Mississippi. She had been taken by two athletes on the Choctaw team and I knew it. She had had her virginity taken away twice violently, but she was disappointed. We met there under the cedars near the Old Chapel where Grant had stabled his horses and attacked Vicksburg. She was smoking Salems and she handed me one but I'd quit for the last two months because I thought my future lay with my trumpet. I was still rather tiny but sincere. My limbs did not fill out my shirt or pants. Tidy told me: Please marry me. Don't marry her. Tears were coming out of her eyes.

We would have been divorced but we would have had respect for each other. Also she would have fought and died for our love. She would have never grown lazy and fat or mean. Where is Tidy now? Now that for me everything is as good as it will ever be. Like Yelverston and his wife—what was her name? Ruth—you can stumble ahead and bust through the next zone. Into the plenitude and into the horror. I look at all the movies and the teevee and the car wrecks and the explosions and the drugs and the antialcohol warnings from the rich hospitals and the ranks of phonies charging toward the old fart with a mere Gatling gun in the lighthouse, his mustache on fire. The old guys are me now, is the horror. I'll wander up and get registered and vote.

Jimmy Buffett came by the house the other day. He's lost some hair but he's looking great, very muscular and ready for his tour. Jimmy flies his plane to Belize with his sweetheart. Buffett is a sketch and we are all waiting on his next good tune. He has complete steel in his eyes. He can't spell and he has a café called Margaritaville in Key West on Duval Street. Almost all the waiters have sandy blond hair like Jimmy. Jimmy once gave me $7500 for a title on a song, and then wrote a happy Las Vegas tune beneath it. His tribe will increase. There is a happiness and sincerity in Jimmy's best tunes that has touched us all.

Jimmy Buffett gave me hope in Tuscaloosa. He is smart as a whip with his old songs and they make you carry on. Do you realize the millions of Southerners who are ready to drop out and go to the Caribbean and sail to Jimmy's parents' house? J. D. and Peets? What lovely people. She always sends me a note at Christmas. And Laurie and Tom McGuane, what people. I was never in any "extended family" around any of them, but Tom lent me money when I was low and he was surprised when I paid him back. He is a champion at everything. In Montana, I saw him knock three clay pigeons out of the air on Thanksgiving Day, hitting them from three directions with no long sweat. Laurie, beautiful brunette. She cooks and she exercises and she has gotten exalted, though people who mess around with horses over the years get strange on you. They amaze the little people like me. They spend immense sums to keep their keenness going. They have no demeaning job and so they buy jobs and hard problems. But they are the cavaliers, baby, and we need them. Tom McGuane was never from Michigan. He was a Virginia cavalier when he was born. God bless him and his books, and his brunette Laurie.

The fact, however, is: I have shelter, nooky, and respect. I have no complaints. I hate my wife, but she still keeps coming back. Even when she has the cramps and I'm out of money she cheers me. She says I am her hero. Even when she hates me she knows I'm her hero. I've fought in no wars, unlike the great calm Quisenberry who goes through his separation from Kathy in California like a piece of granite. I was out in the pasture fighting like hell as a tiny sincere guy but the Quisenberrys knew that to be cool and smart was the right way to be.

2000

The great publisher Sam Lawrence moves down to the South with his lovely lady Joan Williams. Sam was trying to keep up with McGuane and Jim Harrison for a while, according to his housekeeper Liz Lear. He was drinking and smoking and sniffing for a while. That's why Sam Lawrence is beloved to me. He is a golden man, flying to there and thither. All over the planet for his authors. He comes to see his authors and gives them spirit. Comes in a stretch limo to my humble house and makes the darkies at the icehouse stretch their necks. Nothing like that had ever occurred in Oxford, Mississippi. We've promised the moon to each other, Sam and I. We'll get the little ball down here sitting like a tame cool thing in our laps, domestic as a big flashlight. All the generations of wonderful dead guys behind us. All the Confederate dead and the Union dead planted in the soil near us. All of Faulkner the great. Christ, there's barely room for the living down here. We lost the war but we lost in such a wonderful way that even the blacks still look at us with awe. I'm free, boss, but would you give me a cigarette? I've personally been beaten so many times that death looks like a pussy to me. Come on, little dude, show me something. I've spoken my head off in nine books and have twenty lovers and friends behind me. Sam Lawrence will move next to me and be my Dutch uncle and we will cure each other of our diseases until the little bitch death shows up.

BOOMERANG

The last time I threw the boomerang was on the dirty beach of Biloxi, Mississippi. This time I had a black fiber-glass model that cost five dollars. The price hasn't gone up since 1952 that much I guess because there hasn't been a great demand and nobody except an aborigine in Australia knows how to use them. My wife and her children had got me a little terrier for Christmas. I'd named her Ruth, as *Ruth* married to Yelverston. Shannon and David were around the oak trees and they released the little dog to me, and she ran toward me with her white-and-black body coming forward like my old fox terrier Honey in the old days at this house, the home of my parents Bill and Elizabeth.

We took Ruth down to Biloxi and I threw the boomerang out in the gray cold late afternoon. We'd been having some fights and misunderstandings during the winter. There were no sea gulls to aim at or even harass. The weather was bad, the light was awful, the water was brown and rolling in reluctantly, the motel was cheap, the month was February. I just felt we had a need to be here by the ocean with our dog Ruth, the little black-and-white terrier got out of the Jackson Animal Rescue League.

My wife leaned on me, trying not to hate me. I threw the boomerang and this one acted amazingly. It took off seventy yards or so and then came back higher and much lazier. It was spinning in this beach grayness and taking its time, extremely patient to come back, hovering out there and seeming to inch toward us directly back to my hand.

I held my hand out as stunned as I was. It came in so easy and catchable I closed my fist.

Little Ruth, the dog, caught it behind me in her jaws. She just saw it and leapt up and there the big thing was in her happy mouth. She ran down the beach with it.

□ □

Went up to Square Books and got the *New York Times*, read about some poor Yugoslav bastard who was in Siberia for having a wrong thought or something. For twenty years. For twenty fucking years. For *twenty* years. Now he's come out with his statement that it was bad and that all he thought about was survival.

*

Yesterday was July Fourth. The Russians and their history. Vietnam and its history. They kill their mothers and fathers by the millions.

I love the land of the free. I'm standing on soil full of blood and I am still stealing from *me*. Even me, smart, and I've gotten away with it.

When I get tired of my wife I can dance.

I can work at the old Smith-Corona she gave me for Father's Day.

I can take my friends fishing and act like an important person. Blasting snakes out of the water with my pump twenty gauge. Catching bass from Mr. Latham King's farm pond. Bringing home the food, fresh from the waters of North Mississippi.

FURTHERANCE

When they got back to Mississippi, Yelverston could not even remember his wife's name, he was so drunk. She was so good-looking to him and they were in some Hilton or something in Jackson, Mississippi, a town which was really dumb. Yelverston chuckled. Even Larry Speakes can get over them here. Noteworthy about the Reagan administration was that even Larry Speakes, a man who was born to do judgments on the height of rodeo manure, could write a book. These are the awfullest of all times, thought Yelverston.

He could not remember his wife's name, but she was in her red silk pajamas. She was fifty but she wanted his baby. She took off her panties and assisted him. She was a lovely woman and he plunged into her.

Ruth!

All his wonderful memories of everything shot

into her womb and in nine months they had a new baby.

His name was Carl.

P.S.

Throughout the hate and the temporary madnesses, and the envies and the lack of regard and the calamities that have occurred and all the deaths that have happened as given to us by the mad U.S.A. and the mad god, Yelverston has kept on.

I visited him in Mobile for a while with his wife Ruth, but then he had to move up to Memphis because his heart was not doing well with that much heat and humidity in it. Personally, I know the difference. I visited Point Clear, Alabama, recently, with my brother Bobby and his wife Grace. Even at nine in the morning the breath was coming so heavy to my lungs it had already cut me down. Had to get in my air-conditioned Chrysler LeBaron with my wonderful wife, named Susan, who was born in 1946 but will not die yet, so as I can go on and be her tormentor and so that we will have our neighbors Stuart Cole and Bryan who provide speakers for the bingo and who meet with me at three A.M. and we share music. Tonight I'm listening to "Chariots of Fire" and the Christian in me goes on and goes on, even where the others let down, I get in training with my espresso, my Light Winstons, my friends.

Chariots of Fire was the last movie my mother and

I saw together. We got together, finally, on one point when we watched it together.

In this, my third marriage, there is a way to keep living. Work hard four days and cut off three. My wife takes the phone off the hook and I lie in bed in our new king-size bed with all the animals in bed around me. Nellie the cat since Iowa, Joseph the Lhasa apso from Arkansas, Missy the dog from the Jitney Jungle and Mr. Levi, whose daughter Alice was jubilant and kind to us.

Carl, the new manager at Kroger's, who was wearing his smart madras tie today in the Gin, is a good Alabama guy. I meet the good people from everywhere here in Oxford—the cream of the crop. I've got my madras coat.

Took my wife to the hospital tonight with a migraine. She's got PMS and took Cafergot with phenobarb in it, but it didn't obtain. Bryan, next-door neighbor, took us to the emergency room.

In the emergency room with her migraines and her PMS, we met with good people. An old guy with a cane and a good sweater whose wife had a brain hemorrhage. We prayed for his wife. He was a bootlegger and chief of police and worked with the FBI and was a veteran of the island fights in World War Two.

I and Bryan gave a prayer for the old man's wife. One day all of us will have to have a brain hemorrhage and be flown off to Baptist Hospital in Memphis in a helicopter. For all the bad I've said

———

about the Baptists, some of them have a good hospital.

Certain guys you cannot stop from being good even though they have zero money. Dr. Cooper establishes a mission in Mexico. Dr. Guy goes to Honduras to help the animals. The good love is flooding from this little town and we need the encouragement of Sam Lawrence's stretch limousine, we need all the encouragement we can get.

My wife was stoned on Nubane and the relief in her head was wonderful. She couldn't even stand up, and *then* she came into the living room where I work and wrote this note:

> I love you—thanks for being there—always. Please smile for me. Thanks for being my bestest friend. Would you still be my lover and knight in shiney armour. How terribly be withoutest I'd be without. Think of the lonliniss I'd much rather *(incomprehensible)* I'm your biggest fan *(totally unreadable)*.

On this drug she shouldn't have written anything at all but she wrote to say she loved me. Couldn't do without me.

Yelverston lives in a Memphis mansion very close to Shelby Foote, the great Civil War historian, and William Eggleston, the world-famous photographer. Which means he and I blast away at coins on a Sunday afternoon with our enormous collection of guns. Cowgirls are appearing to my mind. Somebody who would just graze me on the forehead with her handgun and then lift her skirts, showing thigh and boot.

Cut it down, babies. Cut it down all around the world. Quit shooting. Quit it, quit it, gallant Mississippians. Take time to write everybody a love note that you love. Take take take time to examine your own wife's anatomy and her clean clothes for you and take care of your children.

Yelverston brought young Carl on his arm to my little shack on Van Buren. His wife Ruth was very proud. Yelverston was wearing a beard now, very gray. He had on shorts and his legs were tanned. He was sixty-five years old now and Ruth was looking about forty, with her hair blond, but I knew she was much older. She must have had all the benefits.

Little Carl was running around the place.

My wife was in her best because we knew they were coming. She was in her high heels and the pink gown of immense expense. You get to be writer-in-residence at Ole Miss and you don't mess around anymore. Your wife has the best clothes and you meet only the best people.

There was a guy coming up the concrete stairs, a humble-looking man in a good brown suit. I had no idea what to say. He looked important but a little pale.

"Susan Hannah," my wife said.

"Coresta Haim," he said.

There was a big pause when I and my wife recognized the white man with sweat on his brow.

We had the best wine out and turkey and ham and mushroom salad. It was a hundred degrees and the air conditioners were on full blast.

"This is the man who killed my son," Yelverston said to me. "I think he'll want some wine."

Ruth and Susan got on very well. Little Carl was a horror, a loud running two-year-old.

Yelverston lent me $3000 on the condition that I quit smoking and Susan and I have a baby.

They left. We'd been talking about what the Civil War was about.

Yelverston got very drunk and lit one Pall Mall after the other. Coresta Haim sat on the other end of the couch with me.

"Barry, I had millions at one time, but I was nothing," Haim told me.

Yelverston looked around at me. He had a suit I'd never seen before. His belt was purple. His wife was in the next room, and she was beautiful, tanned. I had Bach on the stereo. Yelverston went and shut off the music. Then he cut all the lights off. All the air conditioning stopped and it was black and nobody said a word.

———

147

"I didn't die yet," Yelverston said. "None of us have died yet."

The medical news has come in.
It's all good.

After three years of trying my wife and I have a new baby coming too. What a lie. We have nothing coming.

We have Oxford and our friends, maybe, all in line, making a defense around Oxford so as to keep the carpetbaggers out.

November 10, '88.

Willie Morris's movie *Good Old Boy* premiered at the Hoka. We all had on tuxedos and the women were in their dresses and serious patrician shoes and splendid earwear. Yelverston and Ruth were there. He'd come back from his heart condition. He'd quit drinking and smoking altogether and told me he was miserable but now he was an old man and his wife liked him a lot better. It was a tender movie about youth in Yazoo City. When they played taps for the fallen man at the little cemetery, I started crying a little. Sitting next to me was Ruth Yelverston, with her smart white skirt and her wonderful legs reaching down to her black slim high heels. She was tearing up too and I lent her my handkerchief.

"You know, Barry," she whispered in my ear,

"Willie's movie's so wonderful, about when you were young and it was almost all fun, with nature and the friendly darkies all around you. I'm so sorry I'm sick."

They went away and when I was counting all the money for the Humane Society, Cor Haim, the man who murdered Yelverston's son, touched me on the elbow. He added five thousand-dollar bills to the fund. He smiled at me, in his tux. The Hoka, when the film was shown, was all around us — the plank walls, the tin roof, the reggae and blues posters on the wall, the endless nobility of females in their gowns and earrings.

"Ruth's gone with cancer. Got maybe seven months," he said.

"That's not possible," I just about shouted at him. Then I cut my voice down. "That's not possible. Look how she looks, look how she's — " I looked at her in the television lights. They were interviewing her under the lights and she, in her gray hair parted in the middle, was the belle of the ball.

Yelverston was there with his little son. He was smiling and handsome. A couple of black chauffeurs came in to handle them.

"Those are two of the guys who actually shot his son and his daughter-in-law."

I looked at Cor Haim.

"He rehabilitated them," said Haim. "Or thinks he did."

*

We, I and Yelverston, put Ruth in the ground this spring.

In a mansion in Memphis, he has the blacks and Cor Haim around him, taking care of Carl.

It's a lifetime deal, he tells me.

For Sam Lawrence
1927—1994
And my children Po, Teddy, and Lee

Back during the Civil War Kyle Nitburg was just twelve years old. The war was going badly around New Orleans, where he and his poor but beautiful mother lived. His father had gone off to fight in Virginia, near Richmond, they thought, but there was no communication and barely any chicken and peas. There might as well have been no father and barely any world.

Some ragged-looking people on horses came through the yard repeatedly and his mother would get on the back of a horse and ride off with them. Then some sheets of paper fell in the yard off a deep blue rushing cavalry that he knew was the Union.

He knew his mother was a spy. The next morning he ran over the paths to the blue people and turned her in. The reward was one hundred real dollars.

His mother was hanged on a railroad bridge.

Kyle Nitburg got the money and stood there with acne on his face, smiling, next to the rail where his mother stood poised on her bare feet before she hung. Somebody took a picture of this scene. An early cameraman got it perfectly in black and white. He was a student of Mathew Brady, the great Civil War photographer.

Later, when Nitburg moved west to escape the infamy, he made enough money to marry Nancy Beech, from an old distinguished but poor family in San Antonio. The marriage did not go well after she delivered herself of a daughter, Nandina, and Kyle Nitburg with his partner, James Ford, of the same stock who would shoot Jesse James in the back for money, rode out to West Texas with her to deal with a Comanche chief called Bad Cloud. They had just the three horses and met fifty Indians. Nitburg sold his wife into slavery as Ford watched, with his nervous hands around his Winchester rifle, sighing with a whining sound throughout this ignominy. He was looking over the plain toward the high mesa where Mexico started.

The Indians sold them a few blankets and soft boots while they bought Nitburg's wife for four thousand dollars in real gold. It was a bright red twilight and Ford wanted to move off. Nitburg wanted to sit there on his horse for a while.

One member of the Indians wasn't an Indian. He was a white photographer. He took a picture of Nitburg selling his wife and Ford, restless, trying to go home, wherever it might be.

Ten years later Nitburg had read the law thoroughly like a rabbi with a magnifying glass. His ally Ford had been shot in a saloon in Austin just for being a backbiting pest with high pretensions. He'd limped away with his penis shot off. But he had never much needed it anyway, and sailed to New York to nurse his real wounds.

Nitburg became a judge in a beige waste spot with the name of Dolores Springs. He married the blind millionaire widow Charlotte Dunning, whose son lived just fifty miles away, some rods down the road, as they said then. He was big and loved his mama. He would bop you on the snout quick if you mistreated the blind woman. Her full name was Charlotte Agnes Dunning. Nandina, who had become the local schoolteacher, sometimes called her Hagness. The old woman wore her hair to the floor and adored it.

Navy Remington, a sea captain who had known Nitburg in New Orleans after the war, settled in with the bounty of his old age at a sheep ranch forty miles east of the town now called Nitburg. He was an old bachelor with his memories, growing deafer and deafer, eventually buying a yellow automobile, a Winton Flyer. Nitburg continued to cheat, lie and steal, and pretty soon the town and much land around it was his.

The nephew of Navy Remington called himself Fernando Muré. He had a university education and was a gunfighter almost without intending to be. He had killed three men with his silver pistols in

Dallas. He played the game of seven-up and was a mediocre gambler, but that afternoon he won a fortune from three angry men with shotguns loaded for doves. They backed away from the table and when Fernando sensed what was happening he threw over the table, got behind it and received fire. With his left hand around his groin he ducked his head and fired through the table itself, took out the other pistol and did the same. When the smoke cleared, the table was shredded, but he had not suffered a scratch. All three of his adversaries lay dead.

★

— 'Member that good-looking lady had that German shepherd?
  — Yeah?
  — Hmmm, hmmm, heh heh.
  — What . . .
  — The woman with the dog?
  — Yeah.
  — Hyun hyun yhunuch.
  — Aw persist, Nitburger.
  — Hyun hyun.
  — My God. My God.
Neb Lewton and his deputy were talking. Lewton had killed a man thirty years ago. Lewton was the sheriff, along with his twin brother, Dantly. But he was old now, with cobwebs between his thumb and trigger finger, rust flaking out of his rectum. Leaves it there on the chair seat when he departs some-

4

where like to the other chair four and a half feet away where he scooches off, right now.

But Neb has dreams — hard physical things — those beasts, those mad hoydens, their quick feet in the gutter. He just pursues the old nastiness in his memories. He curses the light. He curses God. The world is really ugly and the people are sad, he thinks. Tom the Negro plays your favorite tune for a quarter. In his mind he goes back to that Mexican woman with hair on her arms. He still has a prodigious want for harlots. He knows he is crooked and fat and old, a daft old poisonous person, but something still calls him from a cool garden in his memory. Woman's voice with evil on her tongue. He is near rage every minute. I hate this town Nitburg, he thinks. I'm just a pitiful old creature who can't do a thing about it. He dreams of dead women underwater. They had brilliant futures, but now they were just slabs of flesh underwater. It gave Neb Lewton pleasure.

★

Fernando had his fedora and his long tan Mexican cigarettes, but he was worried. He was a creature of perfect idleness but he had projections about his coffin factory and, mainly, the way to buy one of the new motorcycles he had seen in New Orleans just recently. He had promised very loudly the other night that he would burn this town and he still meant to. It was bad enough, but now the Chinese had moved in and he had no use for the

5

race. He was thirty-eight years old and had the one constant girlfriend, Stella, a slut with tuberculosis. He had his friends at the pool hall and credit all over town. He was fine amigo with the preacher. Bankrupt almost, Fernando considered a lengthy suicide. That is, an extended debauch of fine wines until his speech slurred and he died in a fury of drums and small-caliber gossip.

But no, for he was merely thirty-eight and it would take too great a dedication. Again he delivered himself to the task at hand, which was a race through nullity and mere style. On third thought, he was tired, and humiliated. On fourth, he was a young man who had sworn to burn the town, which was mainly wooden. The town of Nitburg had rumors of Fernando's decline.

Fernando with his Mexican matches and his scarves and the small gelding he rode. His dancing testicles named Juan and Manuel. He was making progress through the *diem* quite finely. Nobody had been killed lately and the women were blossoming around him. Consider Nandina Nitburg with her curly long black hair. Consider the constant Stella, and his own singing voice, an exquisite instrument of wind and esophagus. But Stella was sick to the point of vomiting every other moment, though he attended to her with his handsome and devilish humor.

I must see everybody, I must do everything, he thought.

I must remember to buy or borrow some bullets.

I must stop becoming a totally newborn asshole every day.

I must make my mark on the dry soil; must live to say hello again without ugly thought or criticism. The bitterness is wearing me down, making me frown in my sleep, making my tits wilt and things of that nature. He was so sad he was turning androgynous.

Women watched, though, while Fernando was thinking this, and wished he would assault them like a shovel of passion pushed in the grave of their lusts.

Vicious tumbleweeds blew near and hit the alleys of the Nitburg Hotel. It was turning dark.

The sky was gray and the two trees on Main Street were rustling. Fernando swayed past the sheriff's office, being drunk. He connived, he wandered artfully beyond the new moon just now in the air. He wore filthy white pants with black stitching all tucked in big elegant cavalry boots. I remand myself to the custody of myself, he thought. He wore his last pistol but there were no bullets in it. Maybe he had gambled them away. My God, I remember when I was alive, he said to himself.

Fernando, soberer, walked down the alley next to the Chinese shelters and was promptly busted over the knee by a dwarf named Edwin Smoot, an associate of Judge Kyle Nitburg. The dwarf hit him on the knee with a baseball bat as hard as he could. Fernando howled and went down, raising a mad dust around his person. Smoot made himself scarce but could not erase the teensy bootprints. They looked exactly like an elf dancing around in flour.

So that night with his great swollen knee Fernando lay on a table in Doc Fingo's office staring up into Fingo's diagnostic eyes, listening for the rustle of little feet on the carpeted parlor above them where he knew the little tapper stayed. Doc Fingo kept his eyes dead on the knee and did not look at Fernando's eyes much at all, while Fernando listened, listened, sharpening his ears, pitying and yet stalking little Smoot, who might be above.

— It truly hurts, I'll say that, said Fernando.

— Certain it does. Most certainly, Mr. Muré.

— Christ of God! howled Fernando. Fingo had just touched the knee, lifting the calf and moving it back and forth, then wobbling the leg sideways.

— The pain, no? asked Fingo.

— Big as a melon and black and green. Yes it hurts, you goddamned fool!

— Easy. I'm the only doc you got. Researching for crackage.

— Holy fuckeroo. Stick some drugs in it, can't you?

— In good time. The kneecap and surrounding is a delicate matter.

— Tell me about it.

Fernando was not listening for little Smoot anymore. His eyes were flying over the vials in the locked glass cabinet, already thirsty for everything

8

there. Presently though not presently enough Doc Fingo neared him with a needle.

— This will give you some ease, said the old physician with almost no ears.

Fernando reached up and grabbed his arm. — And give me another one of those right after this one. Fingo blinked.

— That's a lot of drug. You allergic to anything?

Fernando held the free wrist of Fingo in a terrible grip, until the shot began taking him away. — Edwin Smoot, he giggled, though it mightily pained his kneecap. — And I want everybody who ever crossed me to come in here and kiss my ass, he said.

— Poor boy.

Fingo looked directly at his eyes, satisfied the drug was well in him. Fernando relaxed his grip and his eyes narrowed as in a happy conspiracy.

— You're asking a lot for someone of your . . . eh . . . vocation, said Fingo. He whispered through his short wet beard. — What do you finally want, Muré?

— Burn down the town and see the scum run, yawned Fernando. — I thought Evil was big but it's really a mighty, mighty . . . small thing.

★

Fernando was asleep, or so thought Fingo. He beheld the closed eyes and the easy-rising chest under the black scarf, the round red imprint of the hat still on his sweating head, just beneath the

9

flatted bangs with just now three drops of drug sweat racing down to Fernando's eyebrows and through them down to the eyelids, under which Fernando's big near-black eyes were yet awake, his ears coming back too, sharp for the tread of Edwin Smoot, a relative of Joe Snag, who would have killed Fernando in the alley and not just smashed him in the kneecap had he found himself in the vantage of small Edwin.

Now Fernando heard Smoot creeping down the carpeted stairs, the nick of a small heel on a plank as he missed the carpet by one inch. Fernando was alive behind his closed lids, with Fingo unseen holding the next hypo as if beckoned like a zombie by Fernando's request.

My holy ruler, thought Fingo. I'm in love with the man and my complete little vicious empire is threatened by him, but I adore this fool. Look at his freckles from the sun, his slim muscular leg, and the knife scars. He jammed the hypo in Fernando's thigh. Highly unmedical, he thought. This man needs a kiss.

Fingo sat on the floor spread-legged, despising the morbid fat of his inner thighs. He wanted to join the wrath of Fernando and so rose, waddled, and fixed himself a large shot, as Edwin Smoot eased himself down, in his hipwalk, hand around the floorpost of the baroque stairway.

Smoot wore a very large hat and did not think of himself as small. To himself, he cut a considerable figure: more dangerous, because ignored and ridiculed by drunkards, more special, because given an unwanted blessing by religious women he passed in the streets. There was a secret place for his own virtues and it would never be known to the regular folks. Up there it was ugly and vicious and he was working for himself in a deeper and vaster mileage than for instance the fool Doc Fingo and his mere several thousands. It was not the money, not the height, not the width, not the space or time, idiots, but the *depth*. He was like a great root that barely had a tree above, looking at another region entirely, down in the earth seven feet like a gleaming root, among small, elegant, lusty rootwomen with breasts round and hard-nippled. — Ooma, Ooma, he said, imagining some underground talk for himself.

But Fernando heard his polished little boots mincing toward the room. Doc Fingo had given himself a shot. His tolerance was very low.

Fernando raised the lid of his left eye, not the right, which Smoot would see from his underlingness, advancing nastily for the other knee with a spadelike razor in the dark to the right of Fernando, lying there, still, like a dummy abject on morphine. Fernando had tricks in wait, but what could he see with his left eye only — what was there to grab, what was there to jump up for and say? Worse, as he'd quit financing and courting her, he began hallucinating this gossipy woman from his *right* side, her picture thrown up in the air before him, a troll with her tongue on fire, spewing molten teeth from her mouth. She grew stronger with that right eye shut, and by so much that he couldn't bear it — had to open the eye — and there was the dwarf Edwin Smoot, with a naked chest and gold Saint Christopher medal on it. Lurking, peering at Fernando, he was dressed in black leather rider's pants and infantile black lustrous boots. Fernando had never seen Smoot full in the face before and neither had Smoot Fernando, head to head, first time betwixt opposable eyes.

— Hey, you're not a bad-looking man for late thirties, said Smoot.

Fernando could look but not speak.

— Stoned, thank God, said Smoot, glancing down at the snoring corpus of Doc Fingo. — I could cut your hamstrings, long partner. Then what would you do? My big Fernando. You're bound for catastrophe and too beautiful to die so young. Your speed. Maybe should crack the other knee. Who do you think you are, out in this whispering near-desert?

Fernando was taken by the second injection and could not even murmur by now. His cupped hands lay limp around his peter, a weak basket on the filthy white, dusty cloth of his crotch. Only his painful right knee was alive, and he fell dead asleep from fear of Smoot. Also, he was something of a rotter, a nasty man himself, and he invited the morphine in to forget this. He misted toward further calumnies and beyond into the revenges of the swamp and desert. He was from New Orleans and the water was coming up visibly around his boots, now that he was in the sand and dreaming. He hardly felt it when Smoot cracked his other knee with a baseball bat.

★

Judge Nitburg and his daughter, Nandina, the happy-lapped big spender with center-parted jet black tresses and intensely articulated legs (she had something of the evil eye too), were wrapped up kissing each other's teeth, fond of each other just an elf's step beyond common practice and her more so because of the judge's late rapid wealth.

Then Edwin Smoot knocked at the window, making circles of breath and drawing crosses in them, viewing them.

Judge Nitburg snapped away from Nandina, outraged.

— Can't you use the door like others, you little scrotum?

Nandina raced along a wing off in the back, both hands full of lucre. Her old stepmother was rich and blind and she almost tripped over the ancient thing there in the rocking chair in her long black coat and high-top lace-up granny shoes, gray hair down to the floor, slashing the air with her cane and nicking Nandina a light one on the breast.

— Creature! nagged the old woman.

— Hagness! whispered Nandina, dropping money.

Smoot opened the front door, veered in, and shambled. The waddling nub, thought Nitburg, into his handkerchief. But he is necessary. The

13

judge had sold many a decision from the bench and the dwarf had even once poisoned for him. The judge was the same age as Smoot, and he envied the dwarf's full tangled head of hair, whereas he was bald and only his sideburns were full, colored like speckled sarsaparilla.

— Our business? sought the judge.

— He's ailing with two cracked kneecaps, your worship. Smoot removed his hat and his curls fell out. The dwarf was solemn and the judge could have laughed in his face — for what you could buy with short cash.

Smoot brought his bandana out and wiped the sweat from the moon of his brow. He kept staring flatly and long at Judge Nitburg. He swallowed a gob of anxiety.

— What?

— Hitting a drugged man on the knee . . . takes it out of a fellow. It don't seem rightly . . . humane.

The judge's face expressed nothing, but he was enjoying a black glee in there. Fellow . . . humane . . . indeed, he considered.

— It's done all the time, Smoot. There's a whole continent of kneecrackers south of the border. I guess you've never been there, though.

— No sir. There was the matter of . . . an automobile.

— Oh yes, of course. Would you like a cordial?

The judge raised a tremendous cut-glass decanter, nearly as big as a wastepaper can, and touched two silver tumblers on the linen.

— I wish you'd remember it makes me sick, declared Smoot, though the offer seemed to relax him. — I'll take just ice water.

— I'd have to go get the ice, said the judge.

— The automobile would have to be . . . different, you understand. As for the rest, I prefer mainly stainless all over. Smoot took the plain water.

Prefer, thought the judge, howling joylessly inside. — You want a suit of armor to match?

— For your information, your worship, I'm not even here. Laughter at me don't scratch me one bit anymore.

— Automobiles like that are hard to find. Hard even to *discover*. You'd, eh, be *here* if you had one, wouldn't you?

— In a way, said Smoot.

— You're in south of the border trade and don't even know it, Smoot. Get you some medals and some filigree and those . . . what? . . . shoulder croppings, couple of speeches to make, no freedom of the press. You can borrow my sunglasses. You're not amused?

— Fernando's uncle has an automobile.

— Many, many rods away.

— Not too many. Forty miles. The eastern county.

— What do you expect from Fernando?

— He will go to places slower or have less places to go. I predict he will get back on the whiskey full time and stare at sparrows for an indeterminate period. Will collapse from spite and self-pity. Is what. Doc Fingo could also, with some ingeniousness . . . evolve a morphine habit in him. I see Mister Muré as an addictive type . . . like you, Your Honor.

— Me? The judge ventured toward outrage, then stepped back. — I can take this stuff or leave it. Set of slight nerves at this point is all I've got.

— Don't mean necessarily the spirits, said Smoot.

The judge glared down at Smoot but would not allow himself a sneer. — I'll work . . . on the automobile. In the meantime, how about combing old wife Agnes's hair? You get tender with that hair, small wheeler, and money falls right out of her ears.

— But, complained Smoot, hat in hands, — it's irksome.

— I've done it myself. Life is *duty* too, you understand.

— Yours, your worship. I defer.

★

Nandina, second story of the manse, was now through counting and ready to settle her options: a spell in Navy Remington's auto, a quail hunt on her pony, cards with the three sluts in town, or memorizing a Psalm.

> The Lord is my shepherd, I shall not want
> He makes me lie down in green pastures.
> He leads me beside still waters,
> He restores my soul.

Even though I walk through the
Valley of the shadow of death,
I fear no evil.
For thou art with me. Thy rod and thy
Staff, they comfort me.

Thou preparest a table before me
In the presence of my enemies.
Thou anointest my head with oil.
My cup overflows.

Surely goodness and mercy shall follow me
All the days of my life.
And I shall dwell in the house of the Lord
Forever.

That's a tidy dream, she thought.

Had the young unmarried preacher in town any prospects, she would throw another, chaster outfit into her trunk. The young preacher, McCorkindale, had once flown in an airplane, but his hand was chilly when she touched it and he was poor as sand. She could hardly imagine him naked, either. Thing was, she saw him on a hill shining, white and hairy with a few listless sheep on the slope below him. Curious he wore the long black coat and the immensely brimmed hat, as if to avoid the light he was sworn to deliver to his flock. Or perhaps it was an aviation coat and he owned no other. Some said he was studying for the law on the side. There was a career, but it seemed a very slow train coming to her. On the other hand, when he leaned in a saloon and drank his whiskey he had a faraway, fetching look . . . the look of . . . a valid aviator with a deed to the sky. His flying mate, "Python" Weems, was good with a bullwhip, but hardly ever in Nitburg.

Oh oh oh Fernando, gosh she wished Pop liked him. He was a contagious man, practically unswervable, though she had not yet made out his direction. What he did for a living was misty, but it had something to do with stealing from the poor and raiding the Indian reservation. He'd dispossessed a family of eleven Chinese from a shack. Hadn't he? These were tales told by Judge Nitburg. Her pop. And it was hard to believe when you saw the charitable twinkle in Fernando's black eyes, or the way he strode down the sidewalk planks, even with a full load of whiskey in him — like a ship's captain without a boat, in nature of his uncle Navy Remington, cavalier, imperial, yes, like in his head he bore a letter from the king.

He was nothing on the guitar, though, and did not ride well on a horse. Said he was waiting for a motorcycle. He was sort of friends with Reverend McCorkindale, wasn't he?

Nandina owned a number of dogs. They ran around her feet like avid geese, even following her into town across the desert. One of them, more songful and blacker than the rest, she named F. Muré. Fernando had learned to write songs in prison. This was a fact. He had a cunning and lonesome voice that touched down to her feet. Perhaps the Reverend was friends with him because he, too, liked the church piano, always better than that lambasted whore they had in the saloon. The canine Muré she would cuddle on her bed for hours. Then she would betray it.

There was a rumor that Fernando might one day have his own saloon and, furthermore, a factory of some sorts. Perhaps. Nandina had heard also that he might call a hiatus on the liquor. Nandina preferred wickedness that showed a profit, his gun hand to her lips, his tongue to her tongue, and no vomiting afterward.

She hoped the judge had got the dwarf to comb Agnes's detestable hair. The old thing would want to play badminton soon, before Nandina left for Nitburg, that was for sure. The judge urged it. The old woman would smile and come forth with any number of dollars. She would flail the racquet back and forth as you hit right into her. If she touched or smacked a birdie, she howled with ecstasy, but you were in for a whole tournament. Finally, she would perspire and fade, and then, get rolled back on her wheelchair, for a nap, most likely sleeping behind her sunglasses already. The volume of the woman was awful. From her blindness she had developed a stronger sense of screaming. "Child! Child! Smote *that* birdie, baby!"

What gruesome charity could really abide her?

The Reverend counted the old woman as one of his flock, and she had rewarded his attention. — In your blindness, Mother Agnes (her son, Robert, was fifty, two counties away; he was large and would beat the punk out of anyone not reverent toward his ma), the Reverend once asked her, — have you found stronger faith? What's it like in there, Mother Agnes? Tell it all.

— Naw. But God sure owes me one, said the woman. — Stroke my feathers, young man.

She held the Reverend's cold, pale, hair-backed hand in both of hers.

At the church she loved the trumpet, the cymbals and the piano foremost, lifting her greedy blind voice through the single stained-glass window. So there was church every Sunday to take her to. They could have an automobile if only the woman believed they existed.

— They do, they do! Nandina remonstrated.

— Can't prove it by me. Think you can trick me with that noise?

— But you've been in one.

— Guileful creature. That could've been anything.

More than almost anything Nandina wanted an automobile. And to be a member of some riding gang, though she was getting a little old for it. She did not sit well; she did not lounge well. She could not brood, meditate, or twit. The wind in her hair, a terrified javelina plunging before her, her heels given to everything but the sunset, clutching her horse. Oh gods, to rain unprovoked violence on something, someone! Certainly the judge would get her a secret automobile, though she had wrecked the bicycle and left it in the pine barrens in her spite. Nitburg feared for her life, and was frankly afraid of automobiles himself.

Oh but for the wind in my hair, the cock of a gun or whatever you call it in my hand, the thrashing putrid smoke around me!

And in town she would buy another hat, too, the one with Spanish doubloons around the crown in Nell's Finery.

★

Able-bodied, thought dismal Fernando. What a dream. What a pest of a word now. His crippled knees had just barely unswollen and he hadn't the energy or the footage to walk over to that woman Stella with the knife scar on her face he so admired. Little Stella, just down the row, was centuries away and his desire, worming out from his cruel knees, was a hunched nullity. The pain in his knees reached right up through his gut, and near broke his heart. Acute of the acute, he mourned. Too, all this wrath for a mere nub of a villain. Fernando could not remember having insulted the tiny man. He'd never even stared at Smoot like the others. He recalled that once, drunk, he'd gone so far as to lobby for the oppressed Smoot in the saloon. Or thought he recalled that late afternoon, sunset on the French doors. Sad, sad, he was deeply sad. He had forgotten what sadness intense physical pain brought on. What could he accomplish? Alone, he screamed out, "You think I can stand this? Thrown in here with my pointless mental life? God damn it." Must he become something on the telephone, pestering the Reverend and Doc Fingo for his ointments and dope? Who wrote in stone this guano about his fate? What was the way out? By God, these wild days don't allow for any convalescence — history is running outside the window like a rapid, thieving raccoon. Coon Soon Die, sounded like the late plague in China, and almost every Chinese was named something like that. Get me some Indian medicine, have me an old Indian in here that knows something. He rose, trembling. Look at this, a man on two canes and I can't bear that. Fernando had a slight lisp. — *Sfuck*, he said. Then fell back on the chairs. This tarpaper hovel with one window after all my travels? With the Chinese standing around and wanting it back, those poor yellow bastards — dispossessed because they think I have some bullets left. The rain snarling down and Main Street a swine wallow. He looked to his weapon in the black holster. It had been a long time since he'd thought of bullets. The thing used a forty-five caliber, as he remembered. It had been a hell of a long time since he'd shot anybody. Much more of this agony and there might be one to the brain, doubt you not, swore Fernando.

The nittering Chinese were sometimes louder than the rain. He had thrown them out of this shack, and now raved at them to fetch drink and Doc Fingo. The eggs and soda crackers were laboring too long in his stomach, and there was no satisfaction. The growling longitude of his intestines, the spit in the throat like a piece of iron, his eyes feeling like worn holes. In his health he could scheme, plunge through, grapple, pitch and desist, sleeping like a housecat afterwards. But now . . . ow, ow! There is no hell like the enforced idleness of a born idler. Run to ground with his haunted memories — prison in the bad territorial prison. The ignominy of sledging away naked and chained in the Louisiana salt dome, the disgrace of a rattler bite near Van Horn, Texas, when he was resting on the ground and the snake just came up and bit him on the mouth, and since then, the despised lisp. The afternoon he'd stolen the mail from Wells Fargo and then wept over the letters to loved ones he had deflected, all those pages around him in a dry blowing wind under a trestle. Little brook under it about the amount of his tears. Collected exactly twenty-three dollars out of one hundred letters.

Then there was his Irish Catholic mother who believed in him and wept beyond her rheumatism and neuralgia, with her letters so heartfelt when he was in prison. And to whom he barely wrote once a year.

His father crushed by the railroad car in Lafayette, murdered by his own work.

He studied his red hound in the corner. Even the dog he could give nothing but noodles left behind by the Chinese and an occasional egg boiled on the

Franklin stove. For himself, he mashed in a clove of garlic. There was some money in the barn on his uncle's place, but it was far away and he couldn't use a runner, not in this treacherous town. The man would be found lying under a cactus with his throat slit. The water in the jug was getting stale. The whiskey was growing disconsolate.

At college he could do a bottle a day, merry and bright, up in the morning and out to loaf at the crack of seven, the booze sweet and iniquitous in his gullet. Never let him down even through the rare lectures he attended. Fernando smiled weakly. In those days his home was a covered wagon in a grove banked by cedars, all next to two springs bursting with icy spume from a mass of marble. He recollected the shaded swimming hole, near fatal with chill, in which he swam naked with the first female graduate in biology in all vast Dixie, or said she was. No mighty looker, but a fortune in laughter and reason behind those spectacles. Her children were the plants and animals and she required no penetration. What a fool mistake to cock your hat and loins toward mere pulchritude, Fernando suddenly thought. Every beauty he'd ever known had an infinite selfishness to her, and my god the pissing and moaning as if constantly displaced from the Ritz.

Then he let go a howl for his knees. These things were too damned real. When he got to the dwarf, through tornado, typhoon, swine-wallow mud, red tape, whatever, when he . . .

A negro in rags and brogans came into the door out of the rain. He held a bottle and a syringe and a covered dish on a tray.

— Who are you? asked Fernando.

— Miss Stella sent the dish and Doc Fingo the rest. He say you be knowin' how to minister the painkiller. Say it work quicker in a arm vein.

— I don't even rate a visit from the old fraud himself? I had a few kneecap questions. Can't you get him down here?

— He be in research say tell you.

— He be in search of his own asshole.

— Où sont les neiges . . . ?

— What'd you say?

— I from New Orleans too. You know what I said, Mister Muré.

— I thought you were playing with me.

— Miss Stella coming down with her dominoes some time tonight.

— Lord bless her. You ever been bored, Nicholas?

— Only when I breathe, Fernando. Ennui be my middle name but I moves it from place to place.

— You see my dilemma, then.

The door opened wide to the yakking, nittering Chinese and the angry rain. It hit the roof and Fernando saw the negro Nicholas go out like a hunk of night lost at sea.

Downwind from the saloon Fernando could hear the piano and the shouts of a dozen rancid trailmen moving back and forth — getting, spending, losing and hooting, occasionally a woman's voice, perhaps Stella's.

Shrill and indignant — impetuous hand or mouth on an unwarmed slut. The crowd — he could hear — was joined by filthy longriders who, by their accents, were Swedes from Minnesota down for the last of the Pony Hunt. He was missing all this. Why, he could be low too. He favored walking into a covey of harmless alley-corner negroes and commanding them, "Break it up! Break it up! All right now!"

— What we done, boss Nando?

— Just *being* negroes, Rastus. We have laws here, heh heh.

Pity, his southern side sometimes, taking over like that, but men became mean when it was ninety-five in the shade. Boredom arose on stilts, sweaty with vitriol. Less and less lung, less and less heart. Big drop of sweat popping out on a Gila monster, that's how hot.

After the injection, Fernando dreamed of reptiles and armadillos born out of his thigh, more agony and throes. There was a woman on a stage, shivering with sweat, removing one garment after another, twitching like a zombie — heartlessly. — Isn't this enough? Aren't you tired, tired? she said in the nude. Then she began removing her skin and hair. All of this clouded with rain and Chinese nittering.

★

The hermit Nermer could see it all from the lip of his mountain hole. It had stopped raining, and the town of Nitburg spread out under him like the toys of a giant. The great black cloud was breaking up at his feet. The vanity of those little roofs poked out. He could not hate, though, the long rectangle of the saloon. They could have named the saloon Nermer for the amount of whiskey and dice money he had spent there, before he was a hermit with his mule and Bible, ascending the rocky path upward, as if somebody cared when he threw away worldly things. The zigzagged path of the incline was rugged, but there *was* a path, he'd noticed. It was dangerous, but somebody had been along before.

He had worn his burlap suit and cheap boots with no socks, mortifying the flesh, but did anyone even give him a passing glance except Nandina, the judge's daughter, whom he had lain with drunkenly thrice? She was at the clothier's, stomping out on the plank gangwalk in new high black boots, and a new black lambskin shirt, and pants with a kind of Paris skirt — rich gray — around her waist. Some kind of cowgirl of high fashion so far ahead of these parts that it looked damned silly. He preferred to turn away from her silliness and ascend with her concerned look on his back. It was awfully good, however, that *somebody* had paid attention when he made his statement, because to be a hermit meant you spent ninety percent and more of your time seeking *food* and water and resisting masturbation and staring at rocks and odd crawling high-elevation life.

He ate the mule, his pal, within two weeks. Then went into contrition for a week, not to mention violent indigestion, having to run away and poot so as not to skunk up his homestead. To the left, thirty yards away, was a more comfortable hole in the mountain, but he had achieved a sort of permanence here in the worse hole; even a child, though, would have chosen the larger hole with its chairs of natural stone, a rift at the top — practically a ready-made fireplace with drawing capacity, the natural kitchen of stalagmites with a fresh brook running through — which would also make a nice sewer, and a big den where a bear used to be before a former hermit, Raving Mick, had run it out previous to his suicide. He kept it as a dream and did not need it.

Over and over he read the Twenty-third Psalm from the Holy Bible. This was the only verse a man needed, really. He read aloud every morning at sunrise, with the magpies and two mountain goats, married to each other, standing almost preposterously on the incline together, faithful and not lecherous, not low, mean, bitching, crying, pissing or moaning, merely handsome man and wife goats together, hearing the Twenty-third Psalm and then when Nermer finished, leaving on their beautiful feet as the black and white magpies rose on their wings with the message. — David, David, my psalmist, Hermit Nermer said with tears falling down. — Keep me on this mountain with my true friends. Even unto the little mice and spiders.

The town was wide open — with the black cloud having rushed back to its fellows. It was vain, miniature, but profound to him, and he could forgive them for their little risen structures. Also he had had the best sexual favor in town, Nandina, and what was there after that but meditation, the song of the mountain air, and needing less and less until he shrank into a man the size of an eye — pure vision — with wings on it, like his envied magpie friends.

He loved Fernando. There was something in the man. He looked down at the tarpaper shack standing desolate, its own Chinese slum, so tiny and alone and with a moat of spangling rainwater around it now — but to hermit Nermer's flying eye it harbored a great meaning. Nermer had cognition. From Fernando there was something moving, something coming. Nermer was suddenly pigeon-toed from excitement. Fernando had promised to burn the town once when he was drunk, and Nermer wished it would be so, be so, be so. He hopped in the remainder of his cheap boots. Be so. Be so!

★

The twin sheriffs Neb and Dantly suddenly met each other. Neb Lewton still had memories and left a trail of rust from his pants in the chair seat and across the floor, where he had hobbled to feed

29

Quick, his Welsh spaniel. Some days Neb, who'd killed a man with a gun thirty years ago, thought about himself as a youth. But killing the one man had thrown him over like a surf wave on the coast of San Diego where the greasers jumped off the pier and were swept into a salty foam. His twin Dantly was a weak swaybacked man with a lot of attitudes, but the town was so busy in graft, gambling and whoring that they thought it was Neb doing his rounds. Dantly would shoot, just out of nervous habit. He would shoot a harmless dog on the corner just sleeping there, old Fido in the dust, tired of running. He drilled him, and then some ladies of the church came out and congratulated him for cleaning the streets. The person Neb Lewton, however, appeared to receive the reward.

Judge Nitburg, there with his riches and paranoia, came up trembling, growing balder and uglier by the minute. Truth serum had been invented recently and the judge was so nervous he even forgot to get fellatio from his old wife Agnes. In the old days he could just ram it in and be forgotten, all his lies and secrecy behind him like the diarrhea of a millionaire. Some afternoons the judge was so exquisitely friendless that he rolled over and over in a hot tub of water trying to suck himself. Threw water out of the tub. He had another vicious migraine and had summoned the sheriffs. Dantly and Neb came in the house, rust falling out of Neb's gun and the old bullets close to his butt. The judge wanted to be shot. He couldn't stand the pain anymore. The judge was in his robe, all wet and wrung out, as if having swum from Galveston.

The sheriffs refused to shoot him, though neither of them cared for the man. Neb might be a useless, ancient man with gruesome corpulence, but he would not shoot a man with a migraine, whatever that was. It must be some pain in the head. There was a problem of shooting him in the head since so many jobs and so much graft depended on him, for one thing. Nitburg seemed able to buy away everything. At Christmas and Easter he would deliver a bunch of foodstuffs to orphans and Chinese, hence possessing them, in a way, further.

Well, it was always Neb Lewton's talent to turn away and go home for a good meal, hanging the gun up with a gasp on a hook. He was near suicide himself and often thought of getting a chair and hooking himself to the brain and falling off dead with his eye strung out and what gut there was from the eye to the brain prolonging some vision until he got to heaven and had that *really good* meal — with his one friend, the old boy he'd shot thirty years ago. He had in mind a trough of lobsters and fried yams.

★

The Reverend was giving his last speech to himself, here in the church and nearly alone. He was about to die from horniness and love of Christ, together.

31

For Nandina, who would not give him a serious look. For Christ, who was his own age when He died and forgave them all. The Reverend did not have enough energy or vigilance to pursue the wrong things anymore; lately, too, he'd gotten a raw deal on his skin and increasing bodily hair. My God, what am I supposed to be, a *skunk* with black hair piling off me, a godforsaken *wereman*? Give me release, Old Master, from this vale of tears. My vale of late and growing hair where there is no relief. I've been exceptional in my business as a big fish in a small pond here, Great Fisherman. Yes, cut back my arrogance, but I've gone around for five years with an erection the like of which must be hidden by some exorbitantly long coat — and my head won't even stay steady anymore without a hat. Holiness, however, does fill my head when the trumpet and the piano and the cymbals and the voice of Bernice lift the hymns — Fernando standing right outside the stained-glass window, adding his very extra-sweet voice, lonely and brave, even in what must be his terrible hangover and guilt. My God uses so many of us as instruments to bring His love home, home. Where is home when I get paler, uglier, hairier and more breathless every day? Where is the place, Lord?

Please, I don't want to meet every hideous fool I've ever met, don't say we'll all have to be there in heaven like that. I could not bear mine own self at a heavenly convention. You must not give us that supreme music too often, Lord. I am begging to not be accepted into heaven now. I am begging you to stop this eruption of hair and rash. Is Satan the master here? Is the laughing Fiend the master of our streets? I shall not allow this. Perhaps the death of Judge Nitburg, our rear-pew benefactor. What can I offer, what more rules can I announce, before your Grace falls into church like a sequoia?

Reverend McCorkindale had earlier officiated at a service; but Fernando was not at his usual place, outside the stained-glass window singing off his hangover. What was wrong?

The sun had come up sharply after the rains of the last three days. Old Mrs. Nitburg was continuing the hymn behind him. Nobody had come through the mud for her yet. They were given a hard crust to walk on with a three-foot-deep world of mud with hogs in it beneath them.

When he strode out of the church, there was a family ahead in a buckboard, only their heads visible, inching along. Their young were disguised as children. There was no expression at all on these Mormon young.

This is a foul town in all regards, thought the Reverend. And I daily fouler in it. He was wading in the crust as a hog erupted. His sexual guilt was about to overcome him when he saw dry land in front of the saloon. There was another dry path toward the tarpaper shack with the Chinese off in mud knee deep, protesting around the doorway where Fernando was sewing a poncho out of canvas with a large needle while smoking a Mexican cigarette.

Reverend McCorkindale stumbled as a great wind came up. His face was red and welted, angry over his new hair. He called in, "Could I have a look at you, my friend?"

Fernando brightened toward the voice.

— If you can stand this broken-down society, Reverend.

— I can, I can. I believe we are twins in misery.

The Reverend sat on the cot, a board with a quilt fixed on two sawhorses. Little Stella moaned and rolled to the side with a sigh. McCorkindale had not noticed her sleeping. She was still in her shoes, her lavender pumps shot with silvery thread. The girl stayed dead in her dreams. The preacher, filthy with mud from the thighs down, shoved to one side and caught up the whiskey bottle held out by Fernando. He gave himself a rough and sudden splash. Instantly he felt the vastness of his own dreams, a sort of smiling lust for heaving nude angels.

— You seen Smoot? asked Fernando.

— He wasn't at the service.

— He will need consolation, soon.

— They say he's out of the county, searching for something, most likely an automobile. The man seeks internal combustion.

— Which would set him around my Uncle Navy's spread. I don't like that. Here with my cursed knees. Say . . . He peered closer in to the cheeks of McCorkindale. — Are you raising a beard?

It seemed the Reverend's forehead wanted to participate, too, a scatter of black hairlings racing for the scalp from the eyebrows. The man was reading for the law nights and seemed to be letting himself go. McCorkindale blanched and poured more whiskey into his red mouth.

— God hates me, Muré. An animal thing is happening to me. Tears rolled out of his eyes.

— Hold on. Thought you and the Lord were thick.

— There must be something deep down queer and wrong.

Fernando looked back to his roughly stitched poncho. Outside the sky was darkening again. The four-hour blazing sun in the morning seemed a perverse demonstration. Like the poncho he was working on while his legs were useless. What did he know of stitching? The muck outdoors frightened him. His unbathed body seemed dangerous as well, all of a sudden. Be damned, the drug was running out and he could feel it leaving like a Kansas City train with a last hoot round the bend into the alien hills. He had the Fear. You didn't want a preacher to talk like that. He needed more of the drug and he did not hesitate to awaken little Stella. He gave her almost all the rest of his money. He asked her if she could bring a fried chicken back for the Reverend and him, though he had no appetite at all. He made her a cup of black coffee off the stove and kissed her without passion full on the mouth.

She was tubercular and brittle. She could be snapped right in two. He dearly loved the gasping naughtiness left to Stella now that the final hours

35

seemed upon her. They made a pair, didn't they? Barely a spare part of motility left to either of them. This old friendship left from the hot vigors of yesteryear with the hound sleeping in the bed afterwards. Give us your little cough and apologetic smile, my toy pet. But please be prompt with Fingo and the drug. He put the poncho on her. For gloves she was wearing a fresh pair of Fernando's wool socks. The preacher paid for another bottle. Fernando was curious about himself. He could not bear whiskey any longer.

The Reverend said when she'd left:

— How about producing the guitar and let's try to sing one?

Fernando looked at his own chest. — I don't think there's anything there, McCorkindale.

— "I Walk in the Garden Alone"?

— That's for them that can walk. I can hardly tumble toward the outhouse.

Outside, the Chinese moaned and remonstrated.

★

It was raining where Smoot sat his enormous ashy horse. Persimmons were on the ground all around him, and the tree partly hid him from the house, a U of speckled, varnished blond logs. He moved his telescope from the house to the barn door, through which he could see the automobile. Inside the house Fernando's uncle was playing with something that moved. That ain't right, there ain't nothing supposed to be like that, white and black and upright, he

36

thought behind the round vision in the glass. Navy was prancing in the window with the creature, first caressing, then kissing it. The creature ran out of sight before Smoot realized it was a monkey. He was stunned, heartstruck. His little feet curled in their boots, almost something like lust in him. Some elves' magic told him the being was female.

What a promise to have that thing beside me in Navy Remington's automobile! The driving apparatus could be cut down, dwarfized, and you could melt steel onto it, with a prow for roaming, great and dangerous! Natural law should yank that automobile right out from under him and put that monkey square on the seat beside me. The three of us — auto, monkey, and me — would be *beyond, then.*

Nobody could say anything, just like you can't say much about a cyclone — it's just there and it ain't up to your opinion. Or it *was* there, and even if you move a word or two out of your puny mouth like "What a hell of a thing!" it ain't never no real part of nothing, because the cyclone is what was.

Them others wouldn't even know Smoot was in view — like now, astride his giant ashy steed. He was growing tall underground, toward the center of the earth amongst everything marvelous that was never seen. His brow was cooled by underground springs and his legs were white as a mushroom and it didn't hurt at all. The hell with the sun and the tallards with their shifty crotches, about all he normally saw of them. He had that perpetual crack in the neck from looking upwards. But nah, it didn't hurt at all underground.

He had spied on Remington a great deal before — five times, indeed — and was used to his movements. So he was patient, especially with the new monkey. Navy Remington was a man of the ocean.

★

Sometimes he would book ship in Galveston, steaming to Brazil. Whence the monkey. He was an old man now, sixty-two, like Judge Nitburg, a contemporary in too many ways. The judge wanted to take care of that. Remington had the pictures and knew the things. At any second he could drive into Nitburg and the judge's court itself and blow the town wide open, the judge and his blind patroness out on a buckboard at night toward Mexico before the smoldering town overflowed itself out to his manse and reviled him. There were still plenty of old Rebels here and others with honor, though they were cowardly nowadays.

Smoot clicked his tongue on the roof of his mouth, as he did most of the day, so a little nickering sound popped out of his realm while he dreamed of the picture, the things, the revulsion of the town, the rambling buckboard, the smoke of South Texas dust, himself ramming through it in the long steely automobile, beyond it all, circling it, the monkey in goggles sitting next to him. He would mount two steel barrels of gasoline in the back seat so he would never run out of fuel. He could drive to Brazil and meet that monkey's relatives if he wanted to.

There wasn't going to be no passengers in *this* automobile — only two earnest pilots. Eat our dust, caballeros.

Remington left the house much later this time. It was three in the afternoon. All that daylight automobile time wasted. Smoot could not understand it. But sure enough he came out with the monkey sitting trained on his shoulder without a rope or chain on it. It looked permanent and wise on his shoulder, more like the monkey was conducting the old man than the contrary. Remington was stepping around some peafowl droppings and barking at the big lustrous birds, who hustled away as in Brazil, Smoot guessed. The monkey must be telling Remington to scold them useless hussies. There ain't much else in the world now I'm here, you could bet she was saying. Smoot's eyes watered thinking of her gentle monkey directions. The sun caught the brilliant white fur of her stomach and at her hands and feet, with the pink big-eyed face solemn, the rest coal black like a deep blanket. Smoot near perished with tender feelings for the little beast. What a cunning little pal she'd be! The wind whipping by, her little eyes in goggles, a dustcoat matching his, the smoky wake of the machine behind them!

Then Smoot became sullen in his duty. The automobile leapt out of the barn with smoke like a disaster pouring on the ground. Remington and the monkey were left to vision. Smoot put the telescope viciously back in its case, almost knocking himself over with ire. The car raced off to the west. Toward Nitburg, Smoot guessed. Remington could afford the hideously inflated prices of the grocery over there. Smoot poisoned his garden every solstice. Navy Remington might have been a big man on the sea, but he was a fool moving his garden from place to place in a sublime watered meadow. Probably looking up at the sky toward God and asking what the deuce were these last two years, Papa? Smoot smiled, but not very much.

He would have to ride down to the house and look for the pictures again. The only bright spot was if he found them, the judge was practically *his*. But he had gone over the premises before. They were neat in a military way, with all the moveables nailed down as in quarters full ahead on the high seas. Neither plush nor mean, the house had a quality of collected bachelor habit. There was a Bible, an insect collection, a telescope on a tripod at the bay window overlooking a plat with a little river curling through banks of purple sage and buttercups. The old man liked his flora. Tulips bloomed around the whole house. Next to the kitchen door were two great banana plants. Smoot judged that there was too much damned sissy prettiness around the place, like some spic's flower wagon had blown up. Or like some imported woman was around here. He touched his little pistol in case somebody else was in the house.

Whoa, here was something new. In the study, in

a locked glass case, was a thick moroccan-bound logbook with a piece of white tape running across it, printing on it: *The History of My Life and Times by Capt. A. Navy Remington.*

Smoot was no locksmith, nor could he leave a loose clue about his searchings in these rooms, else the old man would barricade the premises and impact somebody with that old Winchester over there. The afternoon would be over. But what kind of pompous scrivener would leave this thing locked under glass, title up? He must have an enormous strutting idea of his life and times. That log was just gloating there without a speck of dust on it, insulting the trespasser. The judge would worry. There were droves of eastern press men covering the Wild West for such as this, Smoot knew.

He sifted through what was loose or stacked for a while, but there was nothing of the pictures. Also not a speck of money, hard or soft. The old man had buried it or carried it with him, what he didn't have in that New Orleans bank.

Then Smoot came to the room he suspected he would come to, and he was burned down by jealousy. The monkey had a room to itself. Remington had crafted it a small bed, an elegant crib with a pillow and fringed Mexican bedspread on it. There were rubber rats and frogs on the floor. Bananas and nuts were in a canister. The room smelled a little sour but there were no droppings around. Suddenly he was infuriated, and raced out of the home to the outhouse, expecting that wonderful and queer thing, and there it was when he yanked open the door: a new blond plank, a double-holer. One large for a human and the other miniature for a monkey, with a box of tissues between them. This was so *cute!* He could hardly stand it. The monkey should be his and that was all there was to it.

That old rich man has . . . everything and more, and me, me! Turd of the gods. Smoot began weeping. All philosophy had run out of him. He took off his great hat. His curls tumbled down to his wet eyes, and he wept with big shudders.

At the last he saw to his nose with his bandana.

If he *lives* to have it, brooded Smoot. Or something don't happen to him.

★

Nandina could not figure it out, quite. The wretched Smoot, even more the insect from this distance to her bare eye, stood for half an hour outside the outhouse door, hat in hands, barely moving except for here and there a kick at the soil. He seemed to be going through some temper and priss. She'd ridden up to the persimmon tree exactly in time — blast it! — to see the auto depart to the west in front of a cone of dust, sunset bound. She had called in sick to the schoolhouse, freeing herself of the children for a day. True, it was her time of the month, but more, she direly needed a ride in Remington's auto. She had speculated even romancing the man, if the old bachelor required it.

She was wearing her new black hat with the

Spanish doubloons circling the crown. She knew she was fetching, though this hat and band of coins was heavy and she took it off her sweating forehead while the palomino munched the persimmons behind her. The auto removing to the horizon gave her a pang square in the lair of love and she was hit by a powerful cramp. She was not used to a horse this long in the hills and her back hurt too. But here was Smoot, fretting himself.

She smiled, because under her her wonderful legs were in no trouble at all, straining to run quick into iniquity or wherever adventure demanded. My word, I must be good, she grinned, I ran Nermer clear up in the mountain to a hermithood. He was a handsome brawny lover, too. But here was Smoot, frozen to weird space, ignoring the great roan who moped around the tulips of the blond place.

She wanted him out of there and she must not be seen, now that Remington and the automobile were gone.

Nermer, once a bosom buddy of Fernando's, had one night come on to her so charged with whiskey and spunk that he had grown quite a tongue on him. He had whispered the secret of Fernando's "something" in the "barn" just before urging his sperm into her the third time, then hanging aside like a morose rag doll. He wished to hell he hadn't spoken, and she could see the hate for her striking from his eyes. But there would always be a bit of barter when a man had his delight with you, even when you enjoyed the thrusting yourself. The secret was misty anyway. Something hidden and important to a man might just be a box of old love letters — as from that bespectacled, scientific drab Fernando was so fond of knowing back at "college."

Nandina once heard a song about this woman from below the saloon window — wondering whose sweet voice it was, until she heard the inept guitar and knew it was the drunken Fernando himself, her wanted one, perhaps her intended.

At last Smoot left, almost never climbing the saddle of the big roan, a bent puppet completely ignored by the horse, who took the auto road and finally got out of eyesight.

Why am I so bound and determined to get things? Nandina asked before the thought could be prevented. The palomino was lowering gracefully toward the barn and she moved, a glorious woman with tangled hair, down with it. In *McGuffey's Reader* it said the wind was tempered to the shorn lamb. But the same advice from the deity, should it go to the pirate and his cutlass on the hopeless virgin with her multiple petticoats and little slippers, her father the Captain, both of them soon dead despite his elegance? Oh, how Nandina imagined. Maybe these thoughts came from her unknown and gone mother, because she couldn't remember ever not thinking them. But there was not even a picture of her mother to be seen. What was her mama like? She must have been a whirlwind. Accidentally, during one of his migraine attacks, Nandina had seen the immense naked member of Judge Nitburg, and that condemned her, she reckoned, maybe even biblically. She could not stop the wonder about who in hell she *was* — the fury of that thing in her mother, already dreaming of life among the vicious Comanches, as her father had confessed. The next day he'd walked calmly to the Dolores Springs signs east and west, torn them down, and nailed up two new signs with the name *Nitburg* on them.

His old blind wife had cackled with glee and her giant son had come over to protect the signs before the rigged vote for the new changed name was in. That brute so tall, muscular and ugly he was a gender unto himself. You wouldn't provide intercourse for that thing with heaven in the bargain.

Nandina was in the barn now, afoot and stroking the noses of Remington's stock. So, she thought, apparently I can't bear children. Otherwise, I would be swarmed under by Nermer's brood. And so I must bring forth things and adventures. Things and adventures are the fruit of my womb and there is nothing I can do about it. — Is there, girl? She spoke to the mare in the barn. — Thank God horses can't talk. But I wish, pretty thing, you could tell me where the goodies are.

She looked in the stalls and kicked around in the familiar aroma of manure and sweet hay and dusty oats. Not to dirty her swell black boots and sterling tips, though.

You really needed a man out here with a pickax. For surely it was underground. She went up the ladder and kicked at the bales but there was nothing there, as imagined. She let herself down and began staring, hoping her gaze would collect some fortune to it. God, give the best of your Comanche stargazers, their priest roaming out from some butte, give me some talkative astronomy all above them and my mother, too, calling out to me from the Indians. Give me your best.

She saw the slick of oil where the car had been. It pooled in hard clay, a bowl, where about an inch of the stuff glistened like a dark rainbow. Walking to it and kneeling, she noticed a boxy depression of soil and kicked away the straw and pea gravel until she was sure, then stood across the boxy depression with the pool of motor oil right in the middle of it. There was something down there all right. She could not know the beauty of her widened raiding eyes. Dark-balled and hot like an Indian's.

She knelt and put her fingers in the oil, right down to the clay. Then she put a finger in her mouth. This was a first for her. So this was what made the New World run. There was something awfully familiar about the taste, something from way back there in the swamps, the gas, the rotten roots, the scaly alive things heaving mud around. She put her finger in again and sucked the oil off.

Actually, she thought, this tastes better than men.

★

In the night when she passed the shack, which the Chinese called "House of the Afflicted" — still crouched around it, wanting back in — she heard the ailing voices of Muré and McCorkindale, puny with drug and drink, struggle toward harmony around a wretched commotion on the guitar. The songs spoke of loss in vast spaces and moony crouching near rocks and sinkholes; woe, terror and defeat. "How yellow the heart!" she heard distinctly. The men were blind with chemicals.

Someone told her that Fernando had had his knees broken some weeks back. You could hear it in his voice — a coward's pouting at the universe. The sickness in McCorkindale's voice was remarkable, too, though this man could never sing squat anyway. What disgrace she heard from Muré. It was said that the man had dancing testicles named Manuel and Juan, but there was no believing it in this sorry crooning. "The yellow lizard lurketh nigh! Color of my sigh!" McCorkindale sang backup — "My God! My God!" over and over.

She stepped back into alley shadows as Doc Fingo hurried past her from the door of the shack, a kit in his hand. The Chinese parted. A morose wind came down the street with tumbleweeds and the smell of whiskey from the saloon. Nandina was nevertheless happy, though nervous in her thighs. The alley, the Chinese, even the bad music — they were hers, they bore her name. The soil of it was all over her and her hands smelled like oil. She clasped the handle of the great dagger she wore with her riding gear. How sublime it felt.

"Yellow mucus was her name!" moaned from the window. Inside, she could see that little tubercular

47

slut sitting on a cot, blowing bass notes in the neck of a quart bottle. You'd best keep the air you've got, thought Nandina. Shadows of the trio flickered from the coal oil, flame of catastrophe.

★

1911
— There used to be gunplay here. There's hardly any now, you notice.
— Yes, your worship.
— Actually there wasn't much . . . play. People shot each other, from the back at close range, preferably. One true pistolero came in the territory, you wouldn't hear a peep for weeks. You could say I was the first to introduce . . . an unpistoled dwarf as . . . regulator. You can't just have Law, Smoot. You've got to have something *of the night,* you understand?
— Yes sir.
— Well, take pride. But still nothing from Remington's place?
— Nothing. Smoot lied in a way. There was the monkey, dear captive of Remington.
— Remington came in this afternoon with a damned monkey riding in the seat next to him in that car you covet.
Smoot's eyes watered.
— Lonely bachelor fool. Pitiful simian for company. He'll be full over the loon farm come nigh. People won't believe a damned thing from him . . . Nothing at all. Not the slightest suggestion . . . A monkey.

48

— There ain't intrinsically nothing wrong with a monkey, your worship, really.

— What?

— A man . . . a person could have a monkey.

— Are you hurt? Why're you wet?

— Out at his house. Something hurt me.

— Does it hurt, by the way, Smoot, to be . . . short?

Smoot was enraged. — That old man's writing the story of his life and times. He ain't cuckoo.

Judge Nitburg narrowed his eyes and blanched. The blood of migraine roared from some gland and bumped his noggin. His right eye drooped and his right nostril filled with slime. It was as if a wire heated from his eye to his gut, came back, and blew off the right side of his head. Stars burst in his vision. Nausea gripped him. His upper lip shone and curled.

Smoot knew what was happening. He dried up immediately, cuff to eyes.

— His house is neat as a pin. The barn, you could eat in it. He's an ace carpenter and an autopilot, drives that automobile. He planted out them tulips. Must be patient as a monk.

— Christ, stop it!

— Course if you'd rather hear he's out there tuppin' his sheep with his seacap on backward, I . . .

— Cursed man sailed all around the world, all over the world, and wound up in *my own* backyard.

— Something could happen if I had the automobile . . . and the monkey. Something could happen.

— Ow! Ow!

— The vehicle would have to be cut down.

— See to it! Don't just hang around being . . .
Ow! Whoa!

The judge thrust away to the dark rear shadows
of the manse.

— Get Fingo! the tiny voice called out to Smoot,
like a cat in a well.

Back on his transportation, Smoot barely kicked
the horse. It moved out like an inchworm. Smoot's
mind was hot with cunning and any speed would
destroy this rapture.

★

The magpies flocked around Nermer the hermit, too
many of them. Mountain goats nibbled among the
crevasses while magpies rode their backs. Mountain
mice shot back and forth, rustling. Magpies were on
his feet and shoulders. Great mountain armadillos
shouldered out of the cave, as if it were theirs. Others,
hitherto unknown relatives, rocked by him without a
nod. Word of his gentleness had traveled to all the
wee and big folk of the timberline.

Nermer strolled the precipice.

He should be looking everywhere else, but he
gazed down at Nitburg. The town was ugly and
sad, but he could not keep his eyes off it. He had
not achieved real hermithood and he knew it, yet
there was no book written for this occupation. He
had abandoned women, whiskey, smoke, his soft

bed, his soft wool socks. All for vision, rapture, solitude. But look where he was looking. Right at the miserable anthill itself. It was not so much the sin but the paltry times there that disgusted him. He had been high, wide and handsome down there, but to what avail? With the goons of make-do staring at him over their dominoes? Skinny coyotes of the spirit.

Even Nandina, very deliberate in her "surrender." Her father might be a monster, as they said, but was there even the possibility of a monster in a town of mountain mice? Nandina and her cupidity. He'd been with her over and over. Something was knocked down in him. An exhausted depression followed that never snapped up for him. A refractory gloom, a morbid disaster in the belly. Nermer wondered whether there was always, in the heart of an arsonist, a woman on fire in the middle of the buildings. A gorgeous devastator with now her comeuppance from the aggrieved. Or if men — Christians especially — loved that vision of the flaming earth at the End because their bad loves and bad mothers were burned up.

He would not have to look at that town anymore when Fernando burned it down. It would burn the woman, his own sins, his own paltriness. He could then return his gaze to the mountains and the heavens and be about his hermithood. He could go about "his father's business," as the Carpenter said. He of the whip and the sword as well as the humble donkey and the meek lamb.

Nermer considered his own mother, a vicious, callous pioneer who could neither read nor write nor barely talk. Nor eat, with only her gums left toward the end. The concept of either humility or pride would never have occurred to her mind. Mind? Mind? All she had was mean habits — a protesting hunk of dust in motion. There was a "party" once in the squalid huts near the red stream where they lived. Someone was "having a party." One person had a jug, brought from far away in Kentucky. Another had a Jew's harp. They cleaned their clothes in the stream, combed their hair, and some ancient thing with an Irish memory rose and squatted as the harp plucked away, a "dance," although the old man wasn't raising dust. His mother stood out front from the hut for a while, spat on the ground, and went back in to tear apart a chicken. She did not know what a party was, nor what Kentucky was, nor what the man was doing with the fart-sounding iron thing in his mouth. As for the cooking, it was fast, vicious and terrible. For fifteen years they did not have a vegetable. She had scurvy, tuberculosis, piles, and never noticed anything until the stroke lamed and blinded her. Some man of the cloth, or formerly of the cloth, presided at the funeral, but after opening the Book several times, he couldn't find anything to read or say. So they just named the settlement for her: Dead. Later on a poet came through the place and they changed the name to We The Living, New Mexico.

For years after his mother died, Nermer would

have a colorful dream in his sleep and awake with horrid guilt, as if he'd somehow violated the rules. Later on, he shot an Apache child in a wide desert for getting in his way. Along with his gun, he sported a maroon leather outfit that burned him up in the sun. What was he to do, leave the outfit on that Mexican found dead of thirst in the other desert two weeks ago? Leave the long silver pistol and all those bullets in the fancy bandolier? He was very tired of hitting nothing with it on the byways, too. So he just shot the child.

Another thing about that outfit and pistol was that they had bought him an instant career in Nitburg with Fernando, who saw Nermer at the horse trough — buried in it, really — new in Nitburg and nearly dead of thirst. He drank and drank, staggered back to the ruts and the sun, and vomited water, which felt almost as good coming up as it did going down. A wet munificence spread through his stomach to his blood, and by the time Fernando saw him, walking his horse toward that tall, narrow, curious church at the end of the street, he might *have* revived to the hero that Fernando mistook him for.

— By damn, I always wanted to look like that. That's some suit and pistol.

Fernando was taller than he, with a merry white-toothed mouth under a long mustache, Mexican style, but he was obviously a tanned white man. Those hidalgos down there wore mustaches to differentiate themselves from mere Indians, who couldn't have mustaches. Nermer, unable to reply at first, just smiled.

— Ain't barely a point to the West if you can't have a beet-colored pistolero outfit like that, is there? With that silver hand-rifle.

Nermer noticed then that Fernando was drunk. He looked for a short-gun somewhere on him, expecting it now, in fact, because of his remorse about the Apache child. No gun on the man. He had a colorless serge coat on him and held a guitar in his gun hand like it was a negligent, small child. Still, the man had an alacrity about him when you thought he might suddenly produce a short-gun from the top of those old Sears Roebuck boots with the other hand. Bang. You are dead.

— What kind of church is that? asked Nermer.

— Kind of straight and narrow, isn't it?

— And tall. Four stories. Wood. With a bell.

— That's Reverend McCorkindale. Like he's daring a high wind, lightning, or fire, said Fernando. You can't ever tell. Something might happen. Jesus Himself turn up in a leather beet-colored pistolero suit.

The guitar flew from his right hand and Fernando did a backflip on the soil flat off the ground in front of Nermer. Next thing Nermer knew, his hat had flown backward and the barrel of a short-gun was in his mouth, Fernando smiling over him and himself thrown rearward with the man's other arm under his back, his own pistol cast away with his hand making a claw in the empty air for it.

— Jesus, even I couldn't miss you like this, could I? grinned Fernando.

— Please. Were you kin . . . to the child?

— What? Fernando threw the gun somewhere back in his coat and brought Nermer up straight.

— Hello, man, just polishing my practice. You get into weird steps with your idle time, like me. It doesn't mean a damned thing. Out West, you got all the time in the world to practice.

— I'm very glad, said Nermer, going to fetch his gun.

— We've got a pool table now. Old Judge Nitburg's bought a table and some cuesticks for the hotel. Muse is running it. Have a rack with me?

— What?

— A game. It's with sticks and balls, pockets in a table.

— Why not? If I could get a meal first?

Fernando bought him the beefsteak, potatoes and beans, with some kind of tasteless mushroom botany on the side.

They were chums thereafter. There was always the glossy and impossible glow around Fernando. Though he never pulled that insane feat with the pistol again, there was a constant dread that he might. Nermer was always a bit wary until the out-fit rotted off him and the pistol was at Nitburg's pawnshop, gathering specks of rust. Then he was simply mild, high, wide and handsome, winning pool games from Mormons and that huge crowd of dusty idiots from Minnesota, who knew next to nothing about the marvelous game of eight-ball pool, elegant on a sweet rectangle of green felt, whisked clean by Muse and a smiling whiskered Chinee, Uncle Hsu.

The money is real, learned Nermer.

There is certainly something out there in Remington's barn. A lot else, Fernando told him. The guns and the money and pornography. Old Captain Remington, the wealthy, winking eccentric with the Winton Flyer. The old man had promised Fernando a motorcycle when he sobered up, too. Told him, though, he wasn't old enough to see the pictures yet.

Now Nermer could see almost to another county, to the east where Remington lived.

He'd come in Nandina and betrayed Fernando to her.

He was a sorry soul.

Here on the mountain with his cuestick as a crutch and helper, peering grimly at the odd church — a mere finger on a rise from his vantage with a cloud of magpies between. More his synagogue, the billiards room of the hotel twinkled now as night came near, and he could imagine the balls clicking with wrath. Certainly some Minnesotan newly out of the tub, his hair slicked back with water and lilac, was picking his teeth, wide smile of a sucker on him. To be taken by the best in Texas, Randy Black. Now that he wasn't the shark in town, Black was.

★

Weeks later the man — who *was* that man? — was on his crutches beneath the lone stained-glass window of the church. He had dropped his mother's locket in the mud and was lowering himself to scrabble for it. His skin was yellow where it wasn't gray. On his back was a ragged orange shirt. His hair was long and black, with white streaks in it. As for his speech, he muttered as if he'd fallen into a stream of involuntary profanity. Church members heard him outside the window, a steady low raving and to the right of McCorkindale's sermon, which was incoherent itself. Something about larceny and revulsion. The preacher was in black, a black robber's kerchief on him, preaching under it, sucking in and blowing out. You could see nothing much but his eyes, hot and suffering.

— The Lord giveth and the Lord taketh away. Rotten Indian-giver, eh? McCorkindale was saying.
— There is no mercy. Things can turn on you like a stomped snake.

Old Agnes Nitburg was smiling. Yes, yes. Preach on, beloved lad! The others, worn out by greed and bad diets, harked along sleepily.

Nandina sat by Agnes, drawing the long glances of her older male pupils, Highboy Warner and Clem Hook. These lads were devastated by Nandina. When they were out carp-fishing together, they never quit imagining her. They would save her from cannibals and then eat her themselves.

They would cut her loose from Geronimo, and then she would owe them something. Or they

57

would catch her bathing in the Red Breaks — she was naked, and they would wear her clothes. She was very stern in the classroom, practically a kaiser. How they hated and wanted her, especially now in church with her bonnet on.

When McCorkindale would pause, you might hear the low mutter of Fernando outdoors. He had found his mother's locket and licked the mud off it. It was the last thing of value he possessed. Now he wore it, hung low from its thin gold necklace, and swung himself into a rut back to town. He made a sorry sight to the churchgoers exiting at noon, offering them this effeminate locket for sale. Pleading and cursing at the same time. Who *was* this man? What depths were necessary for him? Why didn't he drop his crutches and just wallow? This shabby orange rug of a man.

Old Agnes heard him. She, with her ankle-length hair, on the arm of a petulant Nandina. — Who is that man? she called. Nandina looked past Fernando at the splendid automobile of Navy Remington, parked on dry soil near the Nitburg Hotel.

There was fine coffee in the hotel, and Remington would travel a great distance for good coffee and a cheroot. Her astonished eyes retreated. Gosh, it was Fernando, all yellow and gray, a nasty stubble on his cheeks, the wind blowing him like a nasty kite. Crutches tormenting him.

— Take me to that man. I know him. In my mind I've known him somewhere.

— No, Agnes.

— Take me to him, horrid child.

She led the old woman near to Fernando, who was saying, "Ten? Ten dollars? Last of the estate." Then he went into his low muttering.

— I'll buy, my good man, said Agnes.

— N—

— Hand over this twenty, the old woman said, going at her purse. She could feel denominations with the tips of her fingers.

Fernando raised the locket, touching Agnes's hair. She purred. Another bill flashed toward him. It was doubtful Fernando recognized Nandina at all. Or rather, she saw, that he felt entirely hidden by his recent awfulness. A stale funk came off him, not alcoholic but awful nonetheless. He licked his lips and took to his crutches. Even his hat had been sold. His black-and-white hair streamed in the wind.

— Much obliged, much obliged.

— Who was he? asked Agnes.

— An old cripple. Something else is wrong with him, too.

— I've heard that voice . . . singing somewhere. You can't tell me.

★

Doc Fingo, out of church, saw Remington with his coffee and cheroot at a rear polished table of the hotel dining room. He had a punch at the bar, his hands shaking a bit. Fingo was a potbellied man with small weak legs. His feet were tiny too, in the natty laced ankle shoes of the day, but they had a thrill of fear in them. It ran up his thighs to his back. Remington was not conscious that the man was in the room. Other thirsty churchgoers had penetrated, calling for coffee or punch. He could not know he was haunting Fingo. Fingo was awfully glad for the crowd. His stethoscope was in his pocket. His watch chain was in place across his stomach. Was he not a respected man? Had he not kept watch over the smallpox plague a few years back? Had he not the pits of the scourge himself on his cheeks? Caught from that little orphan boy. In the mirror behind the bar was a proper man with the deep bagged eyes of experience — himself. The six weeks of medical study still told on him, he calculated. That was thirty-five years ago. There were proper aspects of him to cheer. He ordered another punch, and was near the last swallow when a hand grasped his shoulder. He saw in the mirror who the man was and quailed. It was Remington, smiling, with . . . some placid beast on his shoulder with its arms crossed like a schoolmarm. A monkey. Fingo's ivory-handled cane fell to the floor.

— Oops! Not to frighten, old sawbones, said Remington, stooping for the cane. The monkey mounted his head, perched on the white waves of hair. Even his hair seemed naval, in motion. The monkey then perched on Fingo's cane, outstretched in Remington's hand.

— That's quite a piece of business, said Fingo.
— My little imp. Look at her.

— Is it dyed?

— Nah. Came out of its habitat like that.

— Don't it pee and poot on the floor?

— Seems like you the one leaking, Fingo.

It was true. His right shoe was wet, and the tip of his returned cane sat in his urine. Fingo was mortified.

— A resultant of the old pox, he said.

— No distress. You have a moment?

— Here?

— No. On the veranda, if you would.

Fingo bought another quick punch and followed the old captain to the veranda, where the wind was still stout. Up on the hill the church bell was clunking and rocking, an elevated and demoralizing *dong*. In the shadow of the tall church was the tarpaper shack, Fernando leaning at the door on his crutches, peering distinctly at Fingo and now more animated, raising one crutch and shaking it over the huddled Chinese.

— They say he's not drinking, said Remington.

— He won't visit me, so I have to listen to the talk about him.

— Broke knees. Bring a strapping man down.

— They say he can't stand water on his skin. The boy used to have a hot tub once a day. He loved it better than anything.

— A fellow that's down on himself'll change. I've studied many a depressed case . . .

— Why is he holding money up in the air, beckoning you?

— Maybe square his bill a bit. Been sort of carrying him. I ain't impatient. Man down on his luck, well . . .

— If you don't cure him, I'll kill you, said Navy Remington.

The monkey leapt from Remington's shoulder and was sitting in the passenger seat of the automobile before Fingo could open his dreading eyes. Several times he'd been threatened while sawing off a limb or yanking a molar. Even Judge Nitburg, amidst a migraine, had threatened him once. Poured near a quart of laudanum down the man, his patron, who had owned him for years since buying his degree and exonerating him from the matter of . . . eh . . . tenderness with an unhappy dying cowboy. But that was years, centuries ago, the Civil War still hot in the heads of the citizens and still some gray jackets on moochers and grifters. Remington spoke of new death — his. It was said Remington had beat off a whole pack of coyotes with nothing but a belaying pin.

— I think I'd better . . . need a punch, said Fingo, backing into the lobby of the hotel.

— He's still calling to you, holding up the money. That's my sister's boy, Fingo.

— I *have* to see a man about a horse.

Fernando suddenly spotted the automobile and his uncle on the veranda. He turned directly around and crutched back to the hovel.

My poor lad, stricken boy, thought Remington, though Fernando must be near forty by now. The wind's near blowing him over. Used to, the boy would dive off a cliff into the quarry pool and pretend drowning. Stay underwater a couple of entire minutes. Bobbing up a quarter of a mile away. Used to, he'd run down a tumbleweed in a full gale, jump over it. Slice it to bits with his bowie. Bring it home for kindling.

★

Smoot chose this range, all flat with a few joshuas and cactuses, to apply himself. He lay in the gulch with the enormous rifle, a Creedmore of the old buffalo school. He had shot it twice earlier. His shoulder was still numb and blue from the kickback. But it had not knocked him over or embarrassed him, and the second shot took the head off a cactus fifty yards away. These legends like Buffalo Bill, he spat. Who could miss a beast with one of these cannons? This thing would stop an automobile. He wanted a still shot and not a mite scratched on the auto. So he had stolen a dress from Agnes Nitburg, some shoes, and a mannequin from Nell's Finery. It was a child mannequin that went with a mother mannequin, but they did not use it anymore as people thought it had false airs. So the mannequin child had lived in Smoot's fastidious room at the Nitburg Hotel, not out where the rabble could see, but in a closet, sometimes brought out when he took his supper upstairs and imagined an interesting guest from the East chuckling with him over the foibles of the herd. She had no name.

63

He was not insane or moon-lonesome. But he had written proverbs and epigrams all over her body in permanent black ink with a quill pen. She'd stood in his second pair of boots in the closet.

Before dawn she'd ridden with him through the dark and now stood out in the road in the dress, shoes and veil. That was correct, that was necessary. The road here crossed on top of a double arroyo. You had to move her or drive over her.

Smoot knew old Remington was close to deaf, which would aid Smoot in case the first blast did not take him. When he heard the car, however, he was painfully excited and moved fifty yards farther up the gulch. He trembled, the Creedmore becoming a ponderous thing. The monkey would be in the seat. What would it do? He was wild with tenderness for the animal. He could imagine nothing worse than her racing off across the plain without him. Wiping moisture from his eyes, he crept back farther into the gulch, losing most of his savvy. The automobile was really coming up and this would be no dream.

The car eased to, with a deep clicking. Half of it — Remington, the monkey and the yellow nose of the car with the white grille — was clear in his sights. Navy Remington (pompous, stuffed, unfortunate man, thought Smoot. Mr. Captain Navy Remington, grown so tall nobody could hardly miss him, Mister Seafarer with his buttons and pomp) and the Story of His Life and Times got a good ending to it now. This piece of work *evaporate* that

64

thick book. He cleaned the front sight of the Creedmore with a wet finger. His tongue remained out in
flat, mean concentration.

But he was shaken. Murder would put him onto
another road entirely. That and the automobile
and the monkey. They would be driving past a
nature he had never seen before, nature coming at
him fast in different shapes as never seen before.
The wind and the wonderful eruption of the engine and the living things parting in front of you.

Remington walked to the mannequin in the road.
He did not study it long before his seacap blew off.
Curious, this, with little wind around. He fetched
his cap some feet away, then came back to regard
the dummy with the veil. He lifted the veil and
there were things written all over its face. This was
no ordinary scarecrow. "I highly agree!" read one
of the lines. The dummy did a violent twist and fell
to earth. This wasn't reasonable. Remington felt
there was some oddness about. Why, the thing's
foot had been powdered. This place was not right.
He touched the stump of plaster. The shoe was
nowhere to be seen. There was dreadful medicine
going on here, perhaps voodoo. Kneeling in the
road, he picked up the powder of the blown foot
and read another line: "Fools rush in, ha ha!" Then
the *head* of the thing was gone suddenly and he had
sensed a popping of the air around him, something
changed in the barometric. No head, no veil. Remington was frightened, in that part of him that had
hardly ever been frightened before. Dust was in the

air in front of him, just risen up like something spat from underground. He gathered the mannequin to him and rose with it. Then he walked slowly back to the automobile, looking all over the plain of joshuas and cactuses. But there was nothing. Maybe he was having an attack, a stroke, something cerebral. But he wanted the mannequin with him to prove he was not mad or fanciful.

Smoot was out of shells. His shoulder was broken. The monkey was leaping up and down in the auto seat, pointing Smoot's way and screaming. Smoot had sweat so much his hat had slipped down to his eyebrows, dragging his curls with it. He was furious at Remington, furthermore — if he could stand any more wrath — for taking the mannequin with him. *His* mannequin, his supper guest. This was terrible. This was unbearable. The thing had Smoot and Nitburg written all over it. Low . . . woesome . . . ignominious. Another new road indeed.

The automobile, the monkey, everything was gone. His whole right arm was gone. When he found the immense roan stallion, the thing peed on him. What else? He put his Saint Christopher medal in his mouth and wished he were already in hell. But provide me, Saint Man, with smooth travel there, he thought. Then prayed.

★

Obed Woods had tried to be a criminal in Nitburg for the last three months, but he was an addict of morphine and laudanum and the gang he was working with threw him out. They were petty thieves, but sometimes there was cash at Nell's Finery or Pete's Leather, and they would move in on it. They would not touch the Bank of Nitburg because of the time-lock safe. None of them had ever stolen more than sixty dollars at one time. There was only one little gun between them, and they were scared of that, because even Neb Lewton could shoot, and they couldn't. Dantly Lewton would shoot a dog just for practice, forty yards away. But even they kicked Obed out because he was such a mucker at his simple job, watching out for the Law — Neb and Dantly. Neb who barely got out of his chair but had killed a man thirty years before, and Dantly, his twin brother, who after nine o'clock at night shot first and asked questions *about where the bullet went.*

Obed would keel over on the ground from chemical fatigue, with coffee grounds all over his face. He ate coffee to kick him up but it didn't work. He would fall over yawning in the dust and Dantly would discover the break-in, every time, coming in with his pistol and noose. Judge Nitburg would send them to a lonely territorial prison so hideous and unreformed that the very structure collapsed periodically, releasing felons in all directions with bitter attitudes. Some came back to Nitburg and started the same thing all over again. But Obed was not among them. He was fired, even as a puny watch-out.

Fingo finally thought of him in light of Fernando, since Obed was now every day in his face, in his office, begging for morphine. He had brought his own syringe, but the doc was still standing off. The man was Black Irish from New York City and still had good-looking teeth and a wicked Irish grin that encouraged Fingo, the fairy, to give him five or six shots, though even in his comas Obed would never come across. He would curse Fingo and never even give him a niggardly toe to suck.

— Have you ever been *off* this stuff? Fingo asked him.

— Yeah. I been.

— What do you do?

— Woods reached for the doctor's throat and got only his shirt, dragging him forward to his own face with Fingo smelling of coffee and his last meal.

— Ya hoit, ya bastid! What else?

— But what do you do after that?

— Spanish-American War. For godsake, gimme da shot. Ain't you seen the wound in me balls?

— No. Could I?

— Shot foist.

— Now that you're fixed, I suppose there's no . . . testicle-showing?

— Lump it, goofer. Fill my jar, I be on my way.

— But it was mere water, Obed.

— Ya knowed if I had da strent I'd tear yer open.

— Settle down. I'm getting someone else over here. You'll like him. It's Fernando himself.

— Fernando Muré da hoofer and da boid?

68

— I can't understand this New York Irish gibberish.

— Gimme da injectionuh.

— Let me tie you in the seat with this little rope here . . .

Fingo went across the street and down to the wretched shack. The Chinese did not acknowledge him. Fernando was lying on the cot while little Stella, near death herself, stroked his forehead. She had tears in her eyes and was so concentrated on love for the man that she never heard the doctor enter. The place was lit by four sperm whale candles, and had the character of an enforced twilight.

— Is he eating anything? asked Fingo.

Stella looked up. — No. Nor I. We can't seem to need food.

He drew near the cot and placed his hand on Stella's shoulder. These people were so ill it touched even Fingo. An orchestra went off in his heart. Sympathy for the man with beautiful black-and-white hair spread out on the rotten pillow. Sympathy for the skinny hand of the woman who was stroking him. She couldn't even be a whore anymore. Since he could not touch Fernando he touched the woman. You could smell death itself coming off her, but his hand remained on her bony shoulder. It was the first time Fingo had really touched a woman. Another kind of music went through his hand. He had not expected the softness and mortality of her. Why, even *he* could break her in two and suck her face off as he would a crawfish.

Fernando smiled up at Fingo. — You brought me the relief, my man.

— Not this time, Fernando. We're getting you well.

Little Stella whispered up to Fingo:

— Me too?

— You too, Miss Stella, he lied.

— You goddamned pest. Get me a shot. I'll get some more money.

— Come along with me. Both of you.

When they left the hovel the Chinese were up and excited, seeing Fernando crutch along in a final way, Stella supporting him, coughing deeply, the doctor following with his hands behind his back.

The Chinese occupied the shack immediately. They had new relatives just come over for the bounty of America. There was a lot of cleaning up to do.

Obed Woods sat there withered and trembling, tied to his chair.

— What's going on here? asked Fernando.

— Mister Muré, would you take the other chair? I'm going to tie you up too, said Fingo.

He fetched a rope. Stella had drawn up the other chair in the office, sitting beside Fernando.

— Tie me up too, Doc, she said. — We'll get through this, Fernando. We'll get healthy, my man.

— Well . . . Fingo got a length of twine and tied her up.

They all sat around and looked at each other for

a while. Fingo was in a sort of paradise. He even desired this tubercular little *woman.*

— Er. Has anybody ever died ... *without* this stuff? asked Fingo.

Fernando looked at him dully.

Obed Woods spoke up:

— I don't know. I been on it since the Spanish-American War.

★

Shapiro, the solitary Jew in Nitburg, owned the other automobile and an eatery to the west side of the hotel. He was a clean man who eschewed almost everything, as far as the citizenry knew, except for his business and his Cuban woman. He ran his car just under the window of Smoot, black and blue and moaning with agony.

★

McCorkindale bought a fish at Shapiro's delicatessen. Fernando had been several days in Fingo's office room in the Nitburg Hotel. McCorkindale thought the man might like a toasted fish and some of that dark bread. Some radishes, too. Those were peppy-looking ones Shapiro had in there, big white ones that cheered the belly. Things were a bit relieved now for Reverend McCorkindale. He had never ceased praying, even in the narrowest valley of the shadow, when hair erupted in painful volleys. The hair had begun falling out, though, last week, with the warmer weather. He shed like a housecat, and his wereface reappeared as that of a stern Scotsman, blue eyes twinkling more than ever and his lips very red. The long black hair left his wrists and back, and he could feel more looseness in his thighs, which had really piled up with fur. His hips could now swing in his pants with a wonderful manly liberation, and he recalled his glorious days in that airplane. Shapiro did not know quite what the man was doing, standing around in the deli this long, approving of the food, sniffing and licking his lips.

— You need something else, Reverend?

— Just enjoying your store and my health, if you don't mind.

— Not at all.

— I like your automobile. What kind is that?

— That's a Ford. An open, plain Ford.

— I suppose you know ... McCorkindale blushed, as he always did when he bragged, — I have flight experience.

— You can fly? asked Shapiro.

— I can. An old friend of mine has his own craft.

— How fast? How high?

— It's hard to remember, said McCorkindale.

Shapiro looked at him with a hard recollection. He'd seen only three aircraft in his life, and the men in them did not look like real human beings. He was certain that transmogrification occurred to those who were airborne. They were tiny friends with grins on them. McCorkindale, with his foolish gaze, did not look quite regular himself right now.

72

He was stunned by something way up there.

— Can I get you another mackerel, Reverend? asked Shapiro.

— Indeed, Mister Shapiro. My good man. Another.

★

She'd taught the children well. She rode straight into the hills that Friday with a pickax in the rifle scabbard, thinking about her one-room school, her pupils, all the littlest to the biggest. She was a good teacher and knew it fully. When she taught them reading, writing and arithmetic, she did it without a book for the most part because the Reader was beginning to bore her. The badminton with Agnes was an agony, the dominoes with the sluts was downright morbid, and clothes themselves were growing a bit tedious with nowhere really to go in them. Her father asked her to attend his trials, but the man was such a stiff little bitch in his judgments, which were long and room-emptying in their pedantry, illustrating hardly more than the tedium of Nature Itself outside the window, and he lost her. He liked to grab her and kiss her down to her teeth, however, at home.

— Step away, pony, she said to her horse.

There was something ruthless and circumspect at the same time about the judge — like a coyote on the lope. She held the locket once owned by Fernando's mother in her left hand, lifted it to her lips, and prayed for him. He had disappeared utterly.

Even McCorkindale would not say where he was. He might be at his old uncle's. The old man had not been to Nitburg lately. There must be something going on.

Nandina was smitten by nausea: she suddenly remembered neither where she was nor what she was doing. Her head's compass seemed to have fallen off. She was out in the wild counties and she could not remember what she'd lusted for. Her hands were unfamiliar and sweaty. Her throat and stomach wandered on her, pricked by a hot syrup of something like jalapeños. The weather itself seemed to have become curious. A blue norther coming in while the sun still shone. Over the ridge of the next hill something blue in the air like federal cavalry. And here it was Saint Patrick's Day. Moving in, with a blue dust above them, the snorting horses and sabers popping up like stars. Her mama's face formed from the blue dust and the silver above the cavalry.

Her lungs were full of hurtful dust. The cavalry had passed through her, over her, and here came the direct torment of the cold. The storm knocked her off the horse. Then the pickax in its scabbard whistled around and struck her in the back. She went black, and her head felt like it was crawling away on its own, lengthening her neck by yards and yards.

When she awoke she was hot. The sun was boiling her, and she raised up on all fours, spitting sand. Her long black hair was in her face. The big mesa to the east had a kind of fence on the top of it. Then she saw it was Indians, Indian horsemen, just staring at her in full feathers. The cavalry had run away from the Indians, and the Comanches had come up this close to her, just to stare and have their rifles, lances and purpose. She could hardly believe the skinny dark loneliness of the men on their horses. The war paint crossing and barring them, living in the air with wild purpose. Then wave after wave of men on horseback with the sharp edge of steel running through her head.

She was on her horse again, her back painful from the ax blow. She was having her first migraine and then she knew it — caught straight from the judge, her father, my damn! This was what they were like.

Randy Black, the very best pool player in Nitburg, was on a puny nag in front of her. He was scrubby in the cheeks and sunburnt after looking for a little gold along the creek. His pool cue and filter were tied on his back. This man could beat even Nermer, who was on the mountain now, the only man who'd ever possessed her.

Randy looked down at her with a sheepish grin. She was lying on the neck of her horse. Her head was now impossible with pain. Her right eye was shut. Tears were pouring from it. She cursed in a whisper. Was Randy all there was after the cavalry and the Indians and her mother appeared?

— You having trouble, Miss Nandina?

— Help me, please.

Randy got off the horse and stood beside her. He did not know whether he should touch her. She was one gorgeous thing, now she'd fallen off the horse again. She was on all fours weeping. Red ants were all over her arms.

— The ants are hurting you, he said and knelt beside her, handkerchief out. He flicked it at her sleeves. — You've fallen off on an anthill. Can you get up?

— I can't stand this, she said.

— You're covered with them.

There is absolutely no point to this pain, she thought, rising. Ants all over her, too, and a pickax bruise on her back. I haven't even done anything yet.

Randy gave her some water and she tried to look around the country. Even looking was painful. Her head began pounding with pain again while the rough man looked at her. She did not like to be seen hurting. But then, there was some relief to her head. The mesa beyond Randy was shivering, red and black, vacant. Now nothing was moving at all. The man with the pool cuestick on his back was smiling and offering an outstretched hand.

Nandina went frigid. Nothing was out here and the two of them were alone. It was not the right place to be, even with Black's hospitality. The pain had left her with the feeling of having been *occupied*. She was cold and empty.

— You been going through something, Miss Nandina, said Randy. — Like seen a lucination. It affected me and you and we come to a ground of common understanding.

— What are you talking about, Randy?

She dusted her knees with her hat, like a man.

— Seems some point me and you's alone on the golden plain. Like the onliest ones left on the earth and in my dreams of carrying on the race.

— You . . .

— I din't know how come I rode the lonesome plain so far from the streets, the roads, the houses, the crowd, everything I knowed as life except for a little gold in the creeks, and come upon your quietude like this, 'cept in a dream. Have you saw us together once before?

— You babbling ass.

— . . . fill our needs.

— You want me to *commit* something with you?

He got down on his knees.

She spat on him.

Then she got on her horse and urged it over the hill so Randy could not see her anymore. She rode past the great alkali lake. It was not much, but she owned *this* too, she thought. Out West, your eyes owned everything nobody wanted to possess. All these clouds and colors and distances, thank God. Nobody could get close to you. Not too close, like Nermer. She was glad he was up on the mountain, suffering. But eventually she would be in Austin, New Orleans, or Memphis, maybe San Antonio, where more people could look at her.

The Remington place was hers, too, she gloated

in the late afternoon. It lay down below her, a blond-logged U facing her, with the old man (his hair seemed longer and wilder, whiter) out dancing by himself. Not by himself but with a monkey that leapt straight off the earth when he came near, screeching, delighting him. Was he drunk? He was having too glorious a time here by himself with a mere animal.

She was a little envious.

I can change this, thought Nandina.

She rode her horse behind the barn and hid the pickax behind two bales next to the magnificent Winton Flyer, yellow and lusty with petroleum smells. The whole barn was a heaven of odor to her. She knelt and looked between the front tires where the earthen recession gleamed with oil. She put a finger underneath the car and sucked on it again. This was it, that lovely taste beyond everything. Her own sex tasted something like it, she thought. She'd always tasted like petroleum and the color of it was in her hair. Her brow was dripping with its taste.

Now. Now.

She soothed herself and went into straight, guileful avarice with her sex, her legs, her long youth, her brain, all she called her own.

Remington was holding the monkey and watching her with a wide smile when she rode down to him. He knew the schoolteacher very well. She'd come out once before, admiring his auto.

He had seen her dawdling in the door of the

schoolhouse with some hangdog older student who
had some last remark to make before he could
begin his dreams again. Remington was an old deaf
connoisseur of women, though he had never married. His dreams were long, calm, expansive, very
appreciative, what with the constant religious silence in between his ears. He'd never dreamt that
he would be a dreamer, but now he was a good one.
The pleasant harbors and the women, the lemurs
and pumas hanging off limbs of the trees bordering
uncharted small ports, smooth drums of the natives
and the accordion under a pounding moon all
orange at the equator.

★

Fernando, man, he said to himself. You with the
broken knees, but now you can walk a little. Stella
had improved with food and they sat out in the
sun together near the old shack in a couple of
hardbacked chairs among the busy Chinese. The
Chinese were afraid he would want the shack back
but he didn't, and had told them so. But he could
not speak Chinese, and they looked at the pistol he
wore now and they were troubled. But Fernando
and Stella had a free room in the Nitburg Hotel by
Doc Fingo and they were being mild. Fernando's
legs seemed to have come to a better life around his
kneecaps. They were surging with spark. He hardly
needed anything but a cheroot and a meal now —
and to polish his gun.

Stella still coughed, but she had put some more

flesh on her bones. She adored Fernando beyond earthly loves. They held hands in the sunshine. One of the Chinese would play the xylophone, and they listened to the pleasant wobbling chords falling from the window of the shack. Fernando would smile fondly and lick a bullet while the music hovered around them. Then they would go back to the hotel, hold hands, and fall asleep, clear in the head.

Fernando was dreaming of his factory, with the Chinese. He was among them and he had his factory, turning lead to gold, noisy and laboring, cursing, yelling with glee. He could not identify, quite, the real product yet, but it was wonderful and direly needed. His ambulation was intact. He rode a motorcycle, and overhead biplanes flew low and high celebrating his enterprise. Then he saw what it was — what the factory was. It was a coffin factory, the very finest of coffins of the best teak and mahogany, and he and the Chinese were shipping them out to New Orleans, San Antone, Austin, San Francisco, Seattle, New York, Chicago, Montana, Mobile. These coffins were prettier than new grand pianos. They were so beautiful that an elegy or sermon would be unnecessary. The people would see the coffins, and then McCorkindale and his planes would swoop down, and he would load one coffin onto a bigger plane and simply leave, delivering it to high heaven and then coming down, the big plane releasing the beautiful coffin like a pretty peaceful bomb into the blue ocean where his Uncle Remington had traveled. It would zoom like

lead to the bottom and come up flush among the
sea creatures.

★

Fernando saw Stella walk to Nell's Finery with fresh
dollars in her hand. This was part of his stake from
Navy Remington, who had posted the money to the
hotel. She wanted a hat and a dress, another size
now that she had gained weight. It was a sweet
thing with her well from consumption, oxygen in
her lungs and pink in her cheeks.

He remembered himself and his rifle in the City
of Mexico and his brain about the size of a shelled
walnut, out of fear. The air buzzed with bullets like
hornets. So many of them it was almost funny.

After that he had taken up the guitar just to have
something on his belly that would be hard to shoot
through. He knew he could not find the strings like
the greasers with the big hats did, and he knew he
could never be passionate on the instrument like
the violinist in Juarez, but he liked the big thing
around. It was something to hold on to.

★

The air was smart for enterprise. Nandina saw the
photographs of her father.

After making extreme love with old Navy Remington, with her washed hair down and her breasts
to his mouth and his surprising old thruster wanting more and more, with the monkey sitting there
calmly on the chiffarobe chewing on cashews and

81

silent as a tiny black and white god, the both of them went out to the barn and he backed up the Winton Flyer.

Nandina didn't speak for the rest of the day.

The monkey did not amuse her. She wouldn't eat. Old Remington, seduced and in ardor, felt altogether miserable himself. When he had collected himself from lust, he felt a puny man. Not even Fernando had seen the pictures. They really were too nasty to be witnessed and there seemed no great point to them now, except to break the heart of a daughter he had ravished. The judge's daughter, then the judge's pictures. It was a mean thing he was in, and he was not a mean man. But she had demanded and demanded to see his "secrets" and it was the first any woman had ever demanded anything at all from him. He loved the girl and her voice owned him. But this was wicked and small. Their sex had carried him over to unconscionable lewdness. This was life, this was blood, this was her.

The pictures had given him a bit of power, even rule, in the town of Nitburg. An aggrieved Confederate widow had thrust them on him before she died on his ship out of Galveston to Brazil. All that old honor, the Old Cause — it had been gone almost entirely a long time now. Remington looked out at his sheep near the river with the Mexican shepherds moving around in them. His life had been heavy with honor and duty, and he had never suspected that one afternoon with a naked woman

82

could hurl him to depravity so quickly, within the day.

A man like him should never have had any such "secrets" at all, was the thing.

Broke a young schoolteacher's heart. He sincerely believed he had.

★

Fernando got drunk again. He didn't mean to, but he was sitting there on the hotel bed with a bottle on the dresser, looking between his knees. Stella wanted him to take coffee and food, but he wouldn't. He was not interested in the guitar either.

— Something in me ain't no captain of industry, Stella. Those coffins, that idea ain't me. I ain't got the cut for that. That was a damned moron thought. Fact is, I ain't been nothing at all and I been feeling too damned wonderful to do anything about it.

— But you've been nice, Nando. Real nice.

— Nice don't cut it for all of us. Nice could be a captured ape in a zoo.

— You could be a lot of things. Anything. Your uncle would help.

— Comes to the point where you ain't nothing but a couple of stories blowing around like a weed. You can't even keep none of your promises. And you're not even none of those stories anymore.

— But your testicles can really dance. I drew those little faces on them and you made them dance.

— That was just a relay from the guitar strings, Stella. Hardly any future in it either.

— Your hair is getting nice and silvery places, darling.

— Well I guess you just said it all to me pretty as a poem. A man has to stand up and do. I can't be just sitting here. Voices are calling me, dear Stella. Let's move.

★

Fernando set fire to the courthouse with a bottle of kerosene and then walked away with Stella in hand. It went up like a box of matches. Nermer saw it from the mountain and he stood up. He walked down the mountain very softly, seeing the fire, having nothing but his bare feet left. The fire came very close to the hotel, but an east wind blew it away. The magpies sat on Nermer's shoulders, and his little goats and armadillos wanted him, but he had to descend to the town, as he saw the black cloud of rain run by his left shoulder, onward and then down as if on a mission to extinguish the fire. He traveled more rapidly and his horny feet hurt when he reached the timber line, his little friends leaving him and loving him even after he'd eaten several of them. There against his hand was the big mama goat he'd always loved. She had lost her children and slept near him in the better cave that he finally went to when winter hit.

Nermer stepped more carefully. His feet were bleeding as he left his animal and bird friends.

behind. He was going back to a hell, but he wanted to see what happened and dwell with the fire.

And the minions that Nitburg had ... Which building was it on fire? Which one was it that flamed so eloquently, popping the sky orange, crawled about by roving insect citizenry? He witnessed a storm roam right down in front of him — and what was this, coming practically over his ears? A biplane, with Reverend McCorkindale in the front seat and somebody else in the back. They were following the storm toward the fire. The storm was wandering down the mountain with rain above the fire and the hearkening folks. This must be what war is like, reckoned Nermer. Oh my feet, my feet. My dissolving rags. Be a raw nude John the Baptist sort of fellow when I finally make the town. As for the terror of those women of Lesbos in the back of the hotel in their well-known opium den, it must be intense by now, with the fire that close. Scrambling from the sin that knows no name, from the flames themselves, perhaps of hell, for kissing desperate others of their own kind.

Before the fire Nermer had never seen a lesbian up close, only heard they were there. He was anxious, though, to see one. Maybe assist one of the curious females to safer quarters. Maybe try some opium himself. Help, if he could, these forlorn sisters of the lesbianhood.

Nermer was hungry now for the town and all its sin. He was very homesick for sin. How he'd missed it, through his health and hermitness.

Did he hear shooting already?

Where was Fernando, who could really shoot and burn?

Nermer came down off the mountain and walked across a rocky meadow, near naked when the rotten cloth departed from him. He held his head up toward the dimmer orange of Nitburg with its sparks jumping at the moon. Only a belt of mule leather was left on him, and underwear made from his last bandana. He was a sunburnt thin man when he looked down at himself.

He walked past a high forest of cactuses, and then raced toward the smoldering buildings; Reverend McCorkindale flew overhead in the biplane, hollering down, "Nermer! Nermer! Back in town! Nermer is back in town!"

The plane came low and landed in the main street of Nitburg. The street was solid with four feet of dried mud, and the contraption put down violently with some serious leaning back and forth. It rolled earnestly toward the high and narrow church, wobbled, and stopped right in front of the smoking hotel. McCorkindale jumped out in his leather coat and goggles and long white scarf, another pilot following him.

They came toward Nermer and behind them ran out the tribe of distressed women in their frocks from the back of the hotel. Nermer shook McCorkindale's hand and received a great hug before recollecting his near nakedness, and bleeding. But smoke covered him, and after the Reverend hugged him, he looked into the billiards parlor where he had played eight-ball and acquitted himself well.

Then he saw Fernando dancing in the street. He was doing it with Stella as the piano went on, with the fiddles and cornet, along the crusted Main Street mud. Nermer thought she'd have passed on, but little Stella seemed healthy now. Nermer could barely believe it.

After the fire brigade formed, Nermer joined in the smoke, and helped the chain of townspeople hoist heavy buckets of water — mainly to save the pool hall and the hotel where he'd received his earthly reputation. He wore a long leather coat and a white scarf to block the smoke, a gift from McCorkindale, who was alongside him with the other pilot partner, trying to keep the fire away from the church.

But Fernando was dancing with Stella and laughing, eyes happy with reflected flames. It was rumored that the man could not only see behind his back but around corners.

★

Smoot hit the telegraph repeatedly to hire those that would shoot Fernando. Two weeks later, nine hired gunshooters came to Nitburg, and Smoot was armed with the same big Creedmore he had when he missed Navy Remington.

When Fernando burned the courthouse, he had made a great smoke in Smoot's room. Smoot had run from the hotel, horrified for his littleness. He was so low he almost ran underground, but he'd managed to get somebody else's horse, and race it into the desert, where a strange orange moon with smoke along its bottom edge trailed above him. Coyotes, seven of them, picked up his hot fear and ran after him and the horse for many miles. Smoot was practically elegant in his terror. He rode straight up and slowly so as not to fall off. The Creedmore was about to overturn him every second, and he was not used to the bay mare. One of these days soon, he swore as he rode slowly with the voracious beasts near his heels, the joke ain't going to be on me. An eternity rolled by before he came at last to the judge's house. The judge was on his front porch watching the orange sky to the east.

Even from this distance, two and a half miles away, they heard something extraordinary coming over the plat, echoes dying in the sand and the joshuas and the willows on the river behind the house.

It was the sound of a whole band, with drums and — what was this tinkling over the dunes? A xylophone. The band was not too wonderful but at the time, with the east wind taking it, the sound seemed to be coming up on the right and left very close to the house. The men on the porch armed themselves with what they had and the judge walked back inside.

Nitburg considered the fact that his daughter now had pictures of his treachery. She had seen her grandmother and her mother, both going away, though Nitburg had not thought of it in that fashion. Was he not on the great Lincoln's side in the first instance? It was a terrible war, brother against brother, hence child against mother. He was in the main sweep of an awesome history, and he could not help it. The wife Nancy Beech? You released wild things for their own good and yours too, didn't you? Wasn't it done? They "put away" wives in the Old Testament — it was ordained of the ancients. Nancy Beech had heard the rumor about his mother and laughed at him. She'd brought Nitburg no eminence, no lucre, no connection. Did not even know what an opera was, did not know what opera glasses were, yet had to fall in heat for the first tenor of the first opera through the first society binoculars she'd . . . had to fall in heat, a rabid despondency of lust over a florid pompadoured dago keening over a dead woman on the floor of a stage in New Orleans. Just about ate up the flowers between herself and the strutting fool in the dressing room. Wanted the privileges later and she lifted up her skirt, spread herself all cockeyed with champagne, all moist for another man, called out to him "Sing for your supper!" Sure, she was trash, and he'd have let that one go because of the champagne and the sudden high society, but there was the other matter of, well, it was the final punch on her ticket to Indianland, that thing, that habit of poverty she had that morti-fied his . . . that, just . . . was *it*. She poured honey on ham fat and ate it, right in front of the governor. She liked animals too well, even chickens. She'd had that provoking far-off gaze out the window ever since the opera wetness, spying out some repulsive dream land, some ungrateful foreign wretchedness. Well, there was a land for her, all right, and contacts were made all right, and she fetched a bit of gold when her dreams came true all right. Though the singing and the hooting might be a little rawer than what her damned loony eyes were looking for. Sing for my supper, sure.

He got in the bathtub running the cold water over his hot feet. Finally, he could not hear the music anymore, and knew no infantry or cavalry had come to attack him. From his tub of Vermont marble he could hear the new hired men stepping around the grounds, talking mildly, and he was more at ease. The pain never even came close to his temples.

But then his wife Agnes opened the bathroom door and stood there with her cane, her long white dress, and her hair to the floor around her bare feet. Charlotte Agnes Dunning, a stunning square-jawed society millionaire in San Antonio with her newly dead husband when Nitburg met her — some hair left on his head and with a stealthy charm, also with a river of silver-tongued words flowing from the pool of law around him: the torts, the precedents, the clean law, as a rabbi might have bathed in. When Nitburg took her for his bride, the yellow fever was on and he collected a great many cheap army barracks near Austin with help from the governor. Partitioned, they rented well to the likes of impoverished Confederate widows, amputees and itinerants, half of them alcoholics and addicts whose needs were attended to at the "town" store, which sold whiskey and army morphine with a few beans and some salt pork up front. Nitburg became deft at attaching pensions and inheritances through credit and carrying charges, and there was a happy rotation of the dead and the mad hauled off the premises by healthier alcoholics who worked for him. All of it executed by crystalline law. The remaining orphans he sold outright to various gold rushers heading west. These were "apprenticeships" with finder's fee, clear as a bell. Of the wife seventeen years his senior, what could be better? Who was the fool who prescribed passion for marriage, with its drool and jealousies? Why, even his stiff chilliness seemed to attract this woman, whose husband had died crazed and syphilitic.

There was the one matter of the large son in the carriage with them that Sunday afternoon as Nitburg rode the precincts in his single demonstration of Rollingwood Barracks to Agnes. An old morphined haint of a vet leaned out of a window and vomited.

— Something's not right here, somehow, said Agnes.

— Duly noted from the henhouse, Nitburg said before he knew it.

The big son stopped the carriage. — Just a min-

91

ute. Come around here, Mister Nitburg. They went behind the carriage. — See here, spoke the son, and popped him square in the face. He sprawled and sat up dusty-backed.

— That wasn't pleasant, that 'henhouse' thing. I believe we are looking largely at my mother's money.

— Duly noted, muttered the ringing Nitburg. (His head had not been right since.)

That and that damned meddling fool Charles Dickens, who came to Austin, read in the theater, and denounced Rollingwood from the stage. Snot-bearded limey poking around our America. Brought to shore in Galveston by Navy Remington himself, they said. With those damned photographs.

Two months later Agnes had a stroke that took her eyes away and crippled her on the left.

He promised her her own whole town. With his earnest, knitted brow he traced the Colorado River to a hamlet far west and harvested the dot with his eyes. There would be no operas and no theaters there. Even the map seemed barely interested in the place, blurring out. There could be certain strokes welcome there. He had heard rumors of enterprise there, real enterprise.

By then his daughter Nandina was budding. He was thrown into an entranced felicity with the young beauty, in whom he believed he saw the lineaments of a grace denied him by rough western history.

Their Mexican woman taught old Agnes to hit

the birdie and play it back in a game called badminton while Nitburg calculated the map and began populating it. The first arrivals were Doc Fingo and Edwin Smoot, who had become handy at Rollingwood Barracks. There were others who came along solely because of the morphine, a rolling young fortune unto itself. While he was at the map, he touched himself and exuded a pleasant sweat. Here was real creation. Here was enterprise.

But here was Agnes standing in his own bathroom with her cane and her long hair, tamping on the ground, saying:

— Kyle, I hear such fortunate music. There were sounds in the air more lovely than a bird's singing. It was a band, a whole band. Dear Kyle, what, God damn it, does the world look like? Tell me.

— Go away, Agnes, I'm naked. There could be violence. There could be strangers with guns nearby.

— I smell something wild, something burning.

— From here? What you smell is the hitch. The knot in things. Seems like there always has to be one.

He was wishing his daughter was here right now, so he could kiss her, right down to the teeth. Outside his window, in the east, the sky was lowering from orange to yellow.

— Actually, it's rather pretty out there, he said. It makes me sleepy somehow.

Nitburg saw three hats and faces on a ridge, several guns with them.

— We have us a land here, really, where no heroes are required.

— I used to be somebody, said Agnes. — I was something with a smile. I liked smooth things, sarsaparilla ice cream, my spring carriage, raw cotton. Now I've got this block of dark to walk around in. He put out my light and . . . I've truly loved only the music of the church and the voice of that young man . . . Fernando.

— He's really not required. They have the radio now, Agnes. I doubt the man is anything. Doubt he has one dream that'd square with the earth. Best go on now and get a haircomb from Juanita.

Edwin Smoot stood all dusty and haggard out in the hall behind Agnes.

She could smell his gamy presence and moved backward to her large windy room with the curtains whipping out blond with lilac flowers printed on them. She knew the house very well now. Smoot was a piece of low smoke in it. She found her bed and the cool air and strained her ears for the music.

Smoot came in while the judge was wrapping up in his robe. The judge was sweating all over again. He knew the dwarf's mouth was full of trouble and for a brief moment he had a superfluous urge to hang Smoot. The man did not go with the room they were in now, the study, crowded with law books black and gold and red. Nitburg had saved robes from presiding at the bench over the years, and they hung stiff with officious sweat on the walls. The bought men, either swaybacked, potbel-

lied or consumptive, milled into the study. There
were two real sharpshooters, gumming away about
Tom Horn and Geronimo, but Nitburg blanched
when he saw them. They were as old as Agnes.
Among them, the group had been shot one hundred and nine times. One came in late and meek-
ly, trailing dog excrement.

— You have a lot of dogs, your worship. Could I
possess one?

Nitburg looked at him blankly. A pre-senile boy
of some sort.

— They're my daughter's.

— I'm Snuffy. Could I possess your daughter?
The boy was squirrelly, about exactly the size of the
ten-gauge he carried.

Somebody cuffed him.

— Could we get a designated leader here? asked
Nitburg. — I'll be using English. Perhaps an *inter-
preter*, then?

— Pet's the meanest, came a voice from the back.
— He hollowed out a Spaniard and wore him to
escape.

— I been in every modern war, said a tall man in
a coyote parka. — Spanish-American, World War
One, World War Two.

— That ain't been held yet, clicked Smoot. They
looked down toward the front. — What's wrong
with *me*? I know the layout.

— Old friend, smiled Nitburg. — I was . . . praying for a bit more . . . no, *less* subtle —

— I can listen, I can lead, I can shoot, spoke out

95

a jowly man in an old cavalry jacket with chevrons on the sleeve. He was in the middle of the group but his low barbed growl made a path. He stepped forward and took a long pipe from his mouth. White hairs were on his chest where his longjohns parted.

— Done. We have here . . . men . . . a pest. Nitburg held the giant decanter on the desk and at last splashed himself a vast toddy as he spoke. The group hearkened to him with blind thirst. — The effect of my life, this struggle on the darkling plain, has been creation, quite from practically nothing, I might add. Men, like me or not, you are staring at civilization. Fate has prepared me, and I am a special kind. When there was nothing and then there is something, whatever that is, is right. When there is nothing to eat and then there is something to eat, that is good. Gentlemen, I am the last water in the well. Not so tasty, perhaps, but water, and it is right.

The judge yanked on the decanter and served himself another tall one.

— I deputize you, he said.

— Kneel, kneel! cried the man of all wars.

— This ain't the goddamn middle ages, clicked Smoot.

Nitburg, enchanted by whiskey and the moment, opened his desk drawer and withdrew a four-barreled thirty-eight derringer, a thing of hand-some golden snouts pulled off a bankrupt drunken

gambler by Neb Lewton years ago. He raised the
weapon above his head.

— I shall not be moved!

★

The rest had gone out. Smoot remained, chewing a
soda cracker. Luther Nix, the chevroned deserter,
herded the men toward the hitching post and
refilled his pipe, looking at the peppered moon.

— This ain't much, he said. — Really, there's too
many of us. Meaner, leaner's what we need. Come
here, Snuffy, that your name?

Snuffy came up with his giant ten-gauge. He was
a very dirty little man with raw red gums like a
wound amongst hair. The crowd knew something
was up and stepped away.

— Kill yourself, said Luther Nix, without taking
the pipe out of his mouth.

Snuffy stared at him and grinned.

— Say? I ain't possessing your sense.

— I said put that goosegun in your mouth and
blow your head off. We got a population problem
here.

— You mean . . . Snuffy brought up the gun,
shifting as if he didn't want it anymore.

Luther Nix raised the forty-four Colt from his
belt and shot him in the stomach. The pipe stayed
clenched in his teeth. Snuffy staggered back with
huge eyes and reached behind him where his colon
was blown out the back. Then he spiraled and fell.

The others made a great clatter receding from the explosion and the body.

— This man have any friends? asked Luther around.

Nobody said a word. They were paralyzed with awe, and saw Snuffy standing and alive a second before, saw him over and over, then saw him on the ground moaning.

— Why, I think little darling is still alive. Are we now, little darling? Well . . .

Luther Nix brought out a long flash of steel from his hip and knelt, seeming to wrestle vaguely a bit and then snapping something as the man on the ground gurgled. Nix's hand chopped down, and then he arose with the head held high and streaming against the moon. The men could not believe it and roamed close to take stock. It was as if a man had performed magic on a stage somewhere. He was so busy with the head they felt safer.

The ponderous thing was that they knew he had done this *before*.

— We'll let darling Snuffy be lookout, then, said Nix.

He jammed the head on a picket of the fence near the hitching post.

— You. He hardly paused, beckoning the man called Pet, who was scared white. — Ride into town and witness, my angel.

— Witness, sir?

— Just relay what you've seen Mister Muré's way.

Nitburg and Smoot had come out when they

heard the muffled gun blast. Nitburg was trans-
fixed to the head on his fence. He did not know
what it was and sent Smoot ahead. Everybody was
just standing quietly by then. Luther Nix was relighting his pipe. Smoot came back after a long
minute. He was beaming with admiration.

— Nix is your man, sir. He has foresight. They
watched the single rider trot his horse east toward
the town. That would be Pet, the supposed hard
one, and he was merely a messenger.

★

— Smoot, asked Nitburg, trembling, — am I truly
corrupt?

— Of course, sir. The Meecham bribe, the Holst
bribe, the Chancellor blackmail, the Chinese deeds
fraud.

— Yet Nitburg *is*, is it not?

— The town?

— Am I seeing a little gray in your hair? What
did we have when we first came twenty years ago?

— Nothing. A man selling water.

— And what happened to him?

— I poisoned him, per your instructions.

— But slowly, wasn't it?

— Yeah. Slowly, with Fingo's stuff.

— You know something, friend Smoot?

— What, sir?

— It's Christmas Eve.

★

One of the hired gunmen at the Nitburg house wasn't a hired gunman. In the study he mingled toward the back, staring ahead fiercely through wire-framed glasses. He had a scholarly look and whispered about the long ride from Colorado, but in fact he was Obed Woods, reformed morphine addict and a friend of Fernando's. His disguise required bare stealth, because the dwarf had never seen him healthy and Nitburg had never seen him at all. He was sweating terribly, however, and he had not thought even to bring a gun, any weapon at all. Woods had not shot a gun since Cuba, and to his memory had never done one good thing in his life. This was his maiden good thing, and the terror was awful. It surpassed the wound in Cuba when he was eighteen. He did not have love of his country then. He had love of Fernando, but this was a sweaty thing. His clothes were drenched and his veins were way out on his head.

Outside, with Nix and the explosion and the head, he was already on his horse and near fainted. The horse caught his fear, smelled the blood of Snuffy, and headed back to town while Nix was instructing the man called Pet. Woods was down the road, expecting a shout or a slug from Nix the whole first mile. Then he expected to be ridden down by Pet, who was a vicious hero in the very war in which he himself was a coward, pissing and moaning about his butt wound.

But he reached Fernando a good thirty minutes before Pet appeared, just after dawn in the hotel dining room. The place was acrid from the nearby fire. Only Stella, then, was sitting there at a table, drinking water, staring out at the sleeping hogs in the ruts of the street.

Pet walked over to her. By now he had reestablished his dignity and highly resented being Nix's mere envoy. He intended to kill Fernando himself and then Nix too if it came to it. He had almost forgotten for a while what a fierce and vicious person he was.

Stella had become almost plump. Though her lungs were still very weak, her bosom had swelled, and she was a remarkable creature in the gray dawn, drinking water in the smoky hotel.

Pet Rankin was hungry, violent and sexually aroused. Only a farm woman or a whore would be up at this hour and this wasn't a farm woman.

— You know a Mister Muré? Rankin said, seating himself right before her face.

— Somewhat.

— I hear the man likes a fire. I hear he's got the Chinee with him.

— I hear he's very sick. After the fire he got very sick. Went up to the mountain, very scared and sick.

— Not much of a finisher, huh. When'll he be back, reckon?

— I never seen him sick like that.

— You know him fairly well? I believe he will be sicker when you tell him that Luther N— He stopped and considered. — Some nonadmirers of

Fernando Muré got restless last night, shot and tore a hillbilly's head off. And he was on *their* side.

Stella looked down at her water and bit her lip.

— That's a dreadful rough crowd you run with, mister.

— Pet Rankin. Lately of Matamoros and the Glick Riders. 'Ninety-eight, I myself while in Cuba was obliged to gut a Spaniard and drape him across me, walked right out of their lines.

— Oh no.

— The man was alive, I hesitate to say before a morning blossom of your charms. I'd like to gut the person put a knife scar to your face, though it ain't really that bad.

— You're so extra rough.

— I've been a long time on the trail, if you catch my drift. He flared his nostrils and cocked his hairy eyebrows.

— I'm duty-bound to tell you I got the clap, sir.

— Well then . . . A pity. Looks like back to the ranch. You remember me and the headless man to Mister Muré. I'll bet he likes a good story. I'll be gettin' my feed and water from the Chinee and telling them too. This ain't somethin' they'd want to miss out on.

— How you hold yourself, it'd take a tiger to tame you, sir.

— Shh — He lit up, near to explode with worth and danger. Then he left.

Within an hour he was back on the rideway to the judge's, whistling bits of a hopeless love tune. "Oh, sir, my big, big tiger! Oh my, sir! Oh my horseman, dear sir, on! on!" he began saying suddenly in a little girl's voice.

He'd gone half a mile on the flats when he heard someone calling. He turned in the saddle and saw some blamed fool running out of the buildings and down into a dip, then up onto the flats again, veering into the rideway, like a deeply sincere and anguished sprinter. The man was really churning, as if something were behind him, but Rankin could see nobody following.

Fifty yards away he saw the man had closed eyes. The man seemed in great pain and urgency.

— Wait, wait!

— Wh— His horse stood quiet. This lunatic was near sprawling, kicking dust behind. His hat was in his hand. He staggered in the last wretched yards, panting and weaving ghastly. When he got near Rankin's horse he lowered his head and leaned on his legs, seeming close to vomiting.

— I thought, never, almost, near . . . to. The terror. The stark fear. It doesn't seem fair. My awful God.

He raised up and Rankin saw something wrong in his face. He was speaking smoothly and didn't seem that blown.

The man threw his hat down. He began stomping on it and raving.

— These old hats is so heavy, so heavy! The man thrashed his black and ashy hair.

Then he pulled something from the back of his

pants and shot Rankin swiftly in both shoulders. By the time Rankin's arms were blown back, palms up, the man had grabbed the bridle and pushed the muzzle of the gun deep in Rankin's stomach. He followed the panicked horse around as if glued to Rankin's belly.

— Please stop the horse. I'm scared to death and I might kill you. The man was not pretending now. Rankin kneed the horse in.

— I guess you'd be Fernando, damn you, said Rankin.

— I didn't want to be this much Fernando. You know, you start with little things, they grow, pretty soon there's something grown beside you looks like you. Get on, I'm damned crazy in the head.

The horse turned toward the Nitburg house. Fernando watched them a while, until the rideway lowered them — Rankin wobbling like a dummy atop — and his eyes blanked out on a spooky heat shimmer.

Then Fernando fell to his knees and wept, wild grieving sobs, right in the hot rideway.

★

Rankin held on with his desperate knees and bridled punily with his hands. You weren't supposed to have a man run out of a town like that and plug you, there wasn't any reason in that. And he had just sat there like waiting for a letter. Monstrous poor luck. But the man hadn't killed him. He didn't understand that. That was better luck. Fernando should've killed him. Only he sort of acted like a man dead already, that Fernando. In a way he was odder than Nix. The nerves were coming back now and he was in a grievous state. The horse could not step softly enough for his shoulders.

The entire morning had been odd, too odd, and you put that with his lack of sleep and it was nigh a dream. The woman alone in the hotel dining room where a whore shouldn't be, the smell of smoke and the charred courthouse with the cage of the jail still standing unburnt in the rear. Nobody else. Not a sign of Chinee, though their shanties connected by clotheslines were there. He might have shot a Chinee just for sport. Those sleeping hogs in the ruts were not right either. Something damned sickening in that.

It's taking a year, he thought, and I'm going the wrong way. They all knew about the fortune in morphine in the bank vault. The dwarf had bragged about it. Maybe there was some at the house.

Finally the house came into view; men were gathered around outside, and his heart went down suddenly when he saw something hanging from the tree. He felt very old and dry and gray. Both of his arms were liquid. The amount of blood on his stomach and saddle was enormous. Then he saw they had slaughtered a steer. They were having breakfast. Some old Mexican thing was helping them with a great pot of coffee over a fire and it did smell fine. Rankin was violently thirsty. He had not been able to raise his canteen. The men parted and there was Luther Nix, kneeling with a stick and a piece of hot meat on a knife half a yard long, it seemed.

— Ho, man! Oh it's my angel. You ride weird, old lonesome.

— I've been shot-up bad, Mister Nix.

— Why, the boys and me're just having Christmas, ain't we, boys?

— Yes sir, they all said.

— This is Christmas? asked Pet Rankin.

— Somebody plucked you right on Christmas day. Who was this person?

— Fernando Muré himself. If I could have some help getting off. One of the ancient scouts and a man with a sad walrus mustache and bald head edged toward the horse.

— Wait, wait. Hold on. We need more testimony here. We need some reconnaisance. What of the town, my angel?

The dread in Rankin had swarmed him like a coat of ice. His heart fell deep and nowhere. He looked over at the picket fence with the corner of his eye. The head was still there, swarming with flies. He was extremely cold. He was in his own personal weather, looking out of a hard terrible fog at the rest of the men. He looked around for helpful eyes but couldn't find them.

— There were just the hogs and the one woman. A whore drinking water. I delivered the news. This Muré run out and shot me. I thought he was crazy.

— I heard the man was hardly anything but a
drunk and an acrobat with a good singing voice,
spoke Nix. He was still chewing on the beef and the
smoke from it came out of his mouth.

— He tricked me.

— Eh. Figure that.

Nix flared his coat with his elbow while the knife
with the meat flew up in the air. His right arm
seemed to be very much longer for a second, but it
was the Colt and he blew Rankin out of the saddle
with three rapid shots, the last one through the top
of his forehead. Rankin turned a slow back somer-
sault off the horse's withers and plopped flat supine
on the ground.

— Trick is, said Nix as if he'd just escaped a huge
jeopardy, — your eye picks out those fingers inching toward the butt of that short-gun a good piece
of time before that even ever happens. Sometimes,
an *hour* before. Nix let blow a roaring broken giggle.

— God rest ye, merry gentleman. He made a *poot*
sound with his lips and stooped for his knife.

The men crouched back down. One had fallen in
the fire and knocked over the coffee. He tried to set
the pot back up as if this mattered. His hands were
burned but he could not emit a noise. He just tried
and tried again to get the pot right on the grill.

Then there was a long, long silence.

There were very careful murmurs then. Things
like "ain't remainding many of us left, this keeps
on." Or so Nix thought he heard. He looked over

107

at the ancient scout, the man from Geronimo and Horn adventures. ". . . thinned out," the old man finished.

— Not at all, Gabby. We ain't thin *enough.*

— I didn't say nothin'.

— You bet you didn't. Say, Gabby, you're an old man. You don't look like nought but a stick with a mouth-hole. It ain't even apparent where you shit.

The leathery old fellow was shaking and gulping, about to relieve himself unwillingly.

— That Geronimo, he couldn't even see you coming, could he? But . . . Maybe you're too old. Ever consider that? You ever of a morning, say like this fresh Christmas morning, with the judge inside sucking his turkey and that old lady farting cranberries, think about blowing your head off? Just so there wouldn't be so much upright shit on the world?

— I been nicked, nicked, nicked twelve times, sir, tried Gabby. — I am old, but I'm mean, mean, mean, too.

— You just a smelly old echo, coot. But I seem to like you.

Gabby smiled broadly. They all relaxed. Some remembered they had never noticed Nix replace the Colt, but it was gone. It was very chilly and they loved it when Nix buttoned his coat. Something blue and northern was blowing in.

— Now, Gabby. You and some of the muckers cook his fingers up and eat them. That's right, Rankin's. Just about one apiece. Tasty.

— Rankin, Rankin, Rankin? asked Gabby.

— No quitters, said Nix.

He walked to the tree, threw a blanket over himself, and slept the entire day.

Smoot had observed it all from the shadow of the buggy shed. Two men got silently on horses and rode away, just disappeared without a word. The others hacked off, fried, and ate Rankin's fingers very quietly at the end of the day when the sun fell down.

What a man, Nix, Smoot thought. He's done this *before*.

★

The plane lifted and strolled in the air. It was exceedingly cold up there. They blew around in the wind as if direction of any sort was out of the question, then the propeller seemed to chop into something a little more solid and certain. They wavered off to the eastern counties and Fernando was thrown hard against the right fuselage. He felt very modern, too modern, loony. He was not there, he was so modern. Somebody else alongside him had occupied this big raccoon coat and was there. The man in back flying was named Python or Tiger, he couldn't remember. Pilot friend of the Reverend's. Flew for oilmen. What could an oilman be like, climbing down in a hole until he fell in it? Never saw the sun, stayed pitch black and sullen like a tar baby forever? How could an airplane help him?

Fernando was stricken terribly by an awful thing, beyond the chattering of his teeth: he was dumb. He was immutably stupid. The terrible loneliness of this knocking cold craft proved it. His college did not mean anything — it was another cold airplane in the sky wobbling toward nothing. A blessed man might go through life assured that he was everything but stupid, maybe scrambling for quarters in a saloon but not stupid. This low revelation brought tears to his eyes. The prison days, the Mexican adventures, the accident of the three shotgunners, the murdered drunken hours, months, years. His imprecations and his sulks, his painful kneecaps, the dwarf Smoot still running free and with a nest egg, no doubt. But Fernando had no stash, no hump, no scratch, no booty, no cache, no hand. His singing voice went out, his stupid dream of a coffin factory went out — why, it was just no better than the dirtdumb song of all Mexico. Some fornicator without even a bicycle crooning away about why the queen don't adore him. The Chinese liked him, sure, because he was idle and cruel, while they scrabbled for belly lint. Must remind them of some old tyrant back home. Bunch of them dumped off the end of a railroad spur, nobody told them. Nitburg taxed them for their hog space. That and the opium. (Those Chinese got pregnant quiet and quick. Seemed like there was a new nub in a bundle every three weeks.) Nitburg tossed some drifter in the jail for nothing, thirty days, introduced him to opium, had a lifetime customer and slave. (Why did Nitburg *need* so much? Why was there a moat-wide hunk of business all around him? Because it was there for the taking and nobody else saw it and he was smart? Because he was queer for a buck? Because he relished people like Fernando paying Nitburg to be Fernando so Nitburg could be Nitburg? he thought dumbly.)

He could not make the Chinese understand his feelings about the airplane, but he knew they'd seen him frightened. They did not realize it was fear of the plane, abject and pure. Smiling at his gestures, they had probably thought he was going hunting.

The pilot called up to him. — Look down!

— I don't really want to! he shouted back, hunched.

— No! I mean look down! Is that it!?

Fernando peered over the edge. A vast herd of sheep with tiny Mexicans in it. Then the barn with the Winton Flyer in it, curled spangling river to the right.

— That's it! Yes! Fernando was near sick and then the craft goosed up suddenly, banked right in a lost motion full of woe, it seemed to him, everything groaning and near collapse, wires popping.

★

"They're still there," said Remington. Nandina was holding the monkey and acting familiar around the quarters. Fernando did not quite comprehend the air here. She had good legs on her and they were propped on an ottoman rather smugly, a little cheroot smoking in a tray beside her on the couch. Yet she looked grim and weary.

And the old man looked shy. He looked fresh. He had the slight jitters.

— With ammunition too, yes. Not a lot. They're old Navy Spencers I got a deal on. Practically historical now.

— They could save my life.

— Why don't you just leave, my boy? Keep flying and flying. You've the contraption that was made for it.

— Certain . . . things are committed. Men have gathered.

The old fellow twisted his mouth. He himself felt he had gone over the bridge in showing the pictures to Nandina. He was an old, seduced fool. It was low business. It was unworthy. It was nasty as Nitburg himself. He was a vile fool on the rut. The last wild horses of himself had dragged photographed muck from him.

— Give him the guns, Navy, said Nandina. — My grandmama and my mama say so.

Fernando did not know what this could mean. He considered Nandina again, out here cozy and queenly, stroking the monkey. It was stroking the monkey most of all. She was a lengthy regent in her chamois riding habit, and his stomach stirred despite his despair.

— Who would shoot them?

— Some friends . . . with some Chinese.

— Chinese? Why would the Chinese shoot?

— They adore me. And they're starving. And I will pay, I hope. That money you said was mine in the barn.

— My boy. True. But I had hoped for some, say, enterprise.

— I ain't a boy, Uncle Navy. I'm near a dead idiot.

— I'll go to the barn with him, said Nandina.

Old Remington blushed.

At the barn Nandina backed out the Winton Flyer and showed Fernando the pickax. The soil was already loose, and he stared at her. She had come alive again. Her eyes were bright and mean.

— There's lots down there. Guns, money, pictures.

She closed a door of the barn. He began digging. The sweat and the fear leapt on him. He could not remember physical labor. It was a hateful thing. Pounding away at your own slot in the ground, some god behind the door busting his ribs to keep in the laugh.

— You came out of the air. You smell like the air and gas, said Nandina.

He could not help it, he began crying, mildly at first but then with disguised heaves as he went into the ground. He kept his head down. His hair fell forward.

— Men complicate a little thing like this, she said.

He heard a rustling between the falls of the pickax. Next, he looked right and saw her bare from the waist down, sitting on a bale of hay. Her feet with boots off were white as the moon.

— You take a look at those pictures. Then you kill my father. You leave me enough for an automobile. Navy promised me that.

— But Stella . . .

— No, you're just *with* Stella. Ever since you saw me, it's me you want. You might as well know I'm something of an alley cat and I don't care.

After the airplane was still, the propeller idled, in Nitburg, Fernando spoke to the pilot, Python Weems.

— What was the World War like?

— Loud, said Weems.

— You don't mind old gold, do you?

— Anything that spends. You seen that nitro blow them sheep up?

— Yes I did.

— It was old but it worked.

★

Luther Nix was gone in the night. Gabby spied over and he wasn't there anymore, just his blanket. He did not need them at all and he was in Nitburg doing the task of Fernando by himself, is what Gabby and the others thought for a long while. They were frozen and they ganged near the fire and commenced squabbling. Nothing was proven except a general weak anger, which they lobbed back and forth for over an hour. The man of all wars asserted himself, but they knew he was a lunatic. He wore himself out and soon all of them cursed, fell around the fire, and dove into a profane sleep.

Somebody put a hand on Gabby's shoulder and drew him up, then pushed his head down, snatching his rump up in the air. Then it was cold on his privates. Something had slashed his pants and he was butt-up, eating dirt. Then a fantastic pain entered his rear. Before that, he had felt spitting and blowing on his nethers, but now the pain indescribable.

— Wawwwww! he spoke. His head was pushed down, lips flat in thin garlicky grass.

— Shhhh! old Gab. Told you I liked you. It was the low whisper of Luther Nix.

Smoot was sleeping with the hirelings by now, and he raised his head, groggy and alarmed. In the twilight edge of the fire, he saw the shadow of Nix moving back and forth over Gabby.

Nix might have seen him watching. Smoot was the only one awake. The whisper was louder, and carried over to him.

— Guess that's about all there is. Money and sex. And grit, said Nix.

Nix never stopped hunching, bleakly and almost sorrowfully, Smoot thought.

— Piece of history here, old Gab.

Smoot closed his eyes, straining at the lids, but opened them helplessly again.

— Them fellows were riding off with some un-earned money. He was idly yanking Gabby back and forth now. — But there was a part of them that wanted to come back.

Smoot understood something hard and possible at the very edge of the fire closest to him. It was quite possible that those were the heads of the two who had ridden off earlier.

— Nothin's really that strange, whispered Nix, who was near his crisis. — I heard that someplace niggers have their own newspaper.

Earlier in the night, Agnes heard something at the cracked window beside her bed. It was a singing, weeping sound. It came in with an awful odor from the yard, something dead and rudely decaying. The little singing and weeping sound seemed to come in on a frowning breath of human rot, sweet and keen. The notes and sobs, on the other hand, were pathetic. A trapped voice in an odor.

She recognized it.

Somebody was just under her window, huddled, mewling. Yet there was haunting goodness in the voice.

— Fernando Muré?

— Quiet, Mrs. Nitburg. I'm stark raving. I'm not even here. God help me.

— Nor I here, my child. What is the world like? What's happening?

But he was already gone.

Nitburg was sitting with his knees on the couch

in the front receiving room, holding a curtain to the side and peering at the head on the fence between him and the fire of the bought men. He did not have the courage to ask Nix to take it down.

Nix could make nothing from something so quick, as he could make something from nothing in not much time. Perhaps they were bound to meet.

Having announced this symmetry, he lay down and slept like a baby.

★

— I seen a coolie with a gun, said Dantly Lewton. — He darted right back in his shack, but he had a gun all right.

— I was in the building when it burnt up, you know, said Neb, the other sheriff. They were standing in the charcoal in front of the cage of the jail. — My damned old hat caught fire, and before you knew it, why, I was concerned.

— The Chinee is a interesting nation. Before they was discovered it's purported they weren't yellow at all. But being discovered made them mad and sick.

— I required just three things from a woman: her hair combed, her mouth shut, and her legs spread. Wish I'd ever had one. I've never even had a pal, except you, who was my twin, and that was more like just two of the same liking nothing.

— Every Chinee is a twin.

— My eyes water when I think of having one

whopping huge meal and then cutting my throat.
The good Lord above give so many golden oppor-
tunities for suicide, and what'd I do? Wasn't up to
'em, let 'em pass. Sorry, shh. They ought to hang
me.

— Marco Polo knocked a hole in that wall and
they come spilling out madder'n hornets. Don't
believe in eating. Confusionism.

— Thing is, I never *worked* toward suicide. Fernando, how I admire that man, God give him a few
talents and he didn't hide them under a bushel like
me, not at all. He went after it. The rest of us just
shuffle and wait, and before you know it, what, shit,
natural causes, another dumb casualty, with so
much promise.

— I seen Fernando swimming naked in the cold
river this morning.

— Glorious.

— He's not right. Weeping and singing sometimes.

— He's perfect. Just at the age when there's
nothing really left. The lumination comes early to a
lucky few.

— Ain't even drunk. That whore, she was sad
and swimming too.

— A woman receives the hopeless sorrow of a
man between her loins. He can't bear it by himself.

— Seems the case. He's getting married this
morning.

— Together cross that happy river.

A photographer from the East walked into the

charcoal. He was chewing tobacco and lugging a folded tripod.

— Philip Hine. Verisimilitude and illusionism is my game. I hear something is up. You'd be doing the sheriffing here?

— Har. Eh.

— Give me a chance, fellows. I'm broke.

— You dressed more western than anybody here.

— Like to blend in. This is a town of how many souls?

— Four hundred. Or that and forty if you count the hogs and Chinee.

★

Reverend McCorkindale looked at the cornet player and the pianist. The music was thin, a sort of sacred rumor of retreat. Both of the musicians were alcoholic, like almost everybody else in town. The whole American West, McCorkindale reflected, might be drunken eruption and hangover. He himself was drunk and horrified. Fernando was drunk and horrified. Nermer was conked on opium, he and the lesbian with him. Python Weems was drinking even now in the rear of the church. The two Chinese at the door with Spencer repeaters, who knew? They came out of such smoke and distress. Fernando had promised them the hotel.

Perhaps only Stella was full sober, and the preacher noted she looked better than ever in her life. In fact, as he married them, McCorkindale made a sort of pass at her, shocking himself so that his knee buckled and he dipped, then up again, smiling grimly.

— . . . tender ministrations in an existence too often nasty, brutish and short, he continued.

Python Weems disappeared to the airplane, looking neither left nor right.

The wedding party came out on the church steps, led by Fernando and Stella, a beacon in her rose dress with the morning sun straight on her.

— Very well my imp, said Luther Nix one hundred fifty yards down the street. He was off his horse now, and looked at Smoot kneeling in the road with his long Creedmore out front. Smoot seemed to be asleep on the thing — Occasionally I prefer the sanitation of a long-ranger, said Nix.

The weapon made a long startling *hoooom!* and flew up, but Smoot retained it, sitting flat on his haunches. On the church steps the woman in rose reeled back, disappearing into the dark slot of the door.

— The wrong mark. But hello, said Nix calmly. The other hirelings spread out into the town. The citizenry scattered at the noise and scuttled here and there for a safer view. More people than usual were about, combed out of the county by rumors. Main Street was clear except for the town idiot, who stood straight up near the Chinese shanties, taking a frank look about and discussing it with the hogs, who had looked up from the ruts.

Philip Hine, the photographer, dashed for the church and had just entered when he was knocked back by Reverend McCorkindale, who ran from the church in the direction of the river. Nix could hear Fernando or somebody howling now. The church steps were bare. Nix walked straight at the church, Smoot wobbling alongside with both the Creedmore and Snuffy's ten-gauge.

They were delayed by the yellow Winton Flyer turning into Main Street. Old Remington's conscience had attacked him and he wanted to stop the hostilities. A woman was driving the auto — Nandina, wearing goggles and a bandana over her hair like a Haitian woman. The ruts were narrow and crisp and the auto went down so that the passengers were at head level to Nix when the thing stopped in front of him. He and the dwarf were on higher ground. The dwarf was looking straight-on at the grille.

It was all an unnecessary dream to Nix. The old captain stood up in the car in an old white diplomatic suit run about with filigree. Nix was impressed by neither the uniform nor the automobile. Another burst of irrelevance was the handsome quiet black and white monkey leaping from the seat behind onto Remington's shoulder. The monkey and the man stared at each other with no interest for a moment. Nix had never seen a monkey but he gave it no more study than he would have an insect. Smoot could see the captain and the monkey above the windshield. The old lump came in his throat.

— You, sir. I'm requesting the offices of Judge Nitburg.

— He ain't here yet and there's his offices. Nix flicked his eyes over at the great heap of charcoal and the far cage of the jail. — In fact we're doing some arsonist-hunting right now, if your commodoreship don't mind.

— I have certain documents of interest. I'm surrendering . . .

— Like to see me miss from here, said the dwarf. He raised the ten-gauge and blew off Remington's forearm, the one that was waving the papers, the one that was away from the monkey. Shreds of blood, flesh, bone and paper flew fifty feet beyond the automobile. Nix had jumped to the side. Nandina stood in the car and shrieked down at the dwarf, whom she had never seen.

— Damn deafened me, Smoot! Nix raged at him. But he changed face. — I like you anyhow. You going to retire me. Go back to smoking cigarettes and being bored. Shut up, he called at Nandina. — We got bridegroom business.

They walked around the car and bleeding, quiet Remington, half out of the car with his head in mud.

— For our kind, the die is cast, said Smoot.

They were about even with the shanties, closing in on the church, when they turned to a racket behind them. Nandina had turned the car around and it was wallowing toward them without a grip for good speed yet.

— Why don't you put a slug from that howitzer in that grille there, Smoot?

— I can't. Not the car.

— Well I can. Give me the piece. Nix reached down just as the automobile got purchase and lurched fast at them, thirty yards or so away. Nandina got the vehicle to twenty miles per hour, and was bearing on them. But there was a spatting, just a spatting, noise from out front of the hardware store, smoke puffing out from the boardwalk. Nandina fell over and then a rain of heavier slugs popped the car from heavier guns at the mouth of the saloon. The car stopped and rocked. Nix narrowed his eyes. The sun was in them.

Four men were lifting their rifles, one his pistol.

— Got you covered, Mister Nix! shouted out one of the hirelings, maybe Rupert, the man of all wars.

Nix looked grim. — Perfect scum.

— That's the judge's daughter, Mister Nix, said Smoot. He seemed very sick.

— Wasn't any war required. Count those men, Smoot.

— Sir?

— You're counting the dead. C'mon, boys! C'mon down here with us! he yelled suddenly. Good work! Bravely committed!

— You're going to kill them all?

★

The biplane came over the street, leaving town with a pecking disregard for the earthlings, Weems and McCorkindale peering down as it banked and went *peckapeckapeckapecka*. The craft shadowed Nix and

Smoot, and the dwarf did not like it, not even for the quick second of blacked-out sun. That thing had been around during the fire.

— We got the navy, the air force, dead women. Shit, let's have foreign too, said Nix.

There was a Chinaman with a rifle at the door of the church. Nix reached, drew, fired at him negligently, and missed. The Chinaman went back inside.

— Come here, oh my angels! Nix shouted at the men. — Prayer meeting! The die is cast! Gawd, you're a skit, harfed Nix to Smoot. — I sure like you. The die is cast!

The tall and strong lesbian prostitute who got opium for Nermer had guided him around back of the livery stable and found the back door of the hardware store some minutes before. Nermer crouched terrified behind the counter, looking square into the face of the store owner, who was shutting his eyes, because there was loud shooting suddenly on the boardwalk just outside. Opium was bursting out of Nermer in big drops that fell on the oiled floor. He had a gun in his belt but he had not even thought about it. Tall Jane, in her high heels and blue wedding smock, came back from the door where she had watched the shooting. She squatted down, running her hand into Nermer's crotch, pulled on his manliness briefly, that wasn't it, and finally plucked out the gun. Then Tall Jane smacked hard on the wood with her high heels and walked out between the shooters and their dangling Winchesters. One was Rupert, man of all wars. The other was Tim Room, contemporary of Gabby's and a veteran old woman-shooter from the Indian campaigns. They were gazing at their handiwork in the Winton Flyer and hearkening to the boom of Nix up at the church. Tall and plain Jane, with a million abandoned male grunts in her ears, faced right and shot one in the ear, then turned left and shot the other in the ear. They fell spewing from the head as if cut down from wires.

She clattered back in, handed the gun back to Nermer.

— They killed two of my domino partners, she said, white-faced but not alarmed.

— Why you . . . , began Nermer, creeping up.

— I ain't even started yet. Light me those lanterns.

— But . . .

— It's you that liked fire so much.

— Not in this place, pleaded the owner.

— The place come to me.

The woman walked out on the boardwalk and dashed a lantern on the head of each body, which lit up amazingly black and yellow. Then she took off her shoes and danced back and forth over the bodies and the flames, in and out and sometimes leaping very high.

— What the . . . ? Nix was viewing it all from fifty yards.

So was Smoot. — Hadn't ought one of us to shoot her?

— Still, Smoot, be still. He was smiling. Was he making the motions of applause with his hands? — You don't argue with art, man.

Then he seemed sad as the remainder of the hirelings gathered around him, looking over their shoulders at the flames and the harlot with the raised dress, yellow stockings.

— Fact, I've got in a rut here, dog it. Get in the church door, Gabby. You're special. I'm letting you.

— But I . . .

— I said *special*! he howled.

Was he going to cry? wondered Smoot. Or kill?

Luther Nix kicked Gabby viciously in the pants. The thin old man did a crippled length of aiming and headed to the church steps, holding his butt.

In the church the Chinaman, tallest of all of them and named Lin Hsu — though Fernando knew none of their names — walked away from the splatter of the bullet in the door, hurried down the aisle, and knelt. He said something. Fernando could not comprehend. But the man, with a scared, gentle face, repeated it and Stella, who knew a little from the maids, opened her mouth. Nothing came out for a minute, with Fernando holding her there behind the lectern.

— Well I'm kilt but I'm sorry for you. She's a fine gal and I'm thinking bad thoughts, Nando. But don't let me be glad, that ain't right. They've shot Nandina for some reason.

— Don't talk, try to save . . .

— You ain't ever been shot. You don't know what.
I imagined you have loved her intense and long,
though you never touched her, so you swore.

Tears fell from her big tubercular eyes.

— I always had a kind of tender jealousy of her.
Why me and you ain't natural, she was the natural.
I got the old knife scar from that rough man in
Baton Rouge. It ain't looking too bad, is it?

Fernando shook his head.

— I had the grim lungs. For a while I had a envy
bordering on insanity, wishing that elegant bitch
would get older faster like the Cajun girls in south
Louisiana, but Nandina would not oblige. She
taught the school and she rode into town with her
legs covered by her dogs, nipping at her fine sorrel.
She'd gone to Miss Winnie's Finishing School in
Galveston for the whole course. How she held herself. She had a genteel snoot to her, them flushed
white cheeks after she rode, and she spanked
that dust from her calves so fine with her hat. She
dressed so well, darn it, and you was in thrall, I
seen it.

— Nah . . .

— Shush it, my darlin' husband. I seen your
imagination like a flickered magic lantern on a
white sheet. I dreamt she was holding you in with a
extr'ordinary number of arms and legs.

From her poor lungs Stella spat a line of blood
and sputum bright on her rose dress.

— They've shot her and I'm still jealous, God
forgive me. But tender jealous, I swear. The minis-

127

ter he said *tender,* dear Fernando. Darn it, I was something just for a little bitty short while and now I am dead, forgive me. I wanted her black hair.

— And all my fault. I'm dreadfuller than nothin, I . . .

Then he saw that she was dead.

Fernando looked up at a white man bending over the lectern with a camera in his hand. The man was looking at his new Quaker wedding hat.

— Are you a hired killer?

— No, sir. Philip Hine. A kindly verisimilitudinist. I believe I am witnessing a quite mournful actionist, Mister Fernando Muré. The hat threw me for a few minutes.

— You better git.

When Gabby leapt in the door mournfully, already shooting, the photographer ran wide, and then high. He did not stop until he was in the belfry house itself.

There was a great amount of gunfire in the church beneath him.

There was quite a wait as Nix and the others looked on the doors. Then Gabby came stumbling out, next waddling and kneeling. There was blood all over his legs.

— Now by Jim I'm all shot up, it ain't fair! He sat on the steps and began throwing his boots off.

— You look done for, Gab, said Nix, stepping up.

Old Gabby came down from his luckless rage and quietened like a sucking infant, hopeless bright blue scout's eyes fetched up from red sockets.

— It ain't so bad. Just the legs. And I bet I kilt the Chinaman. The Chinamen shot me first, then Muré popped up from behind that ... shit ... *preacher* thing at the front. Was in there with that dead woman.

— You're a goner, seems, darlin', said Nix. — Ain't a mighty scout like Gab a pathetic angel when he's all done for. Done rode out of history. Nix opened the flap of his coat and then did nothing. He just howled, that roaring prolonged giggle again that touched a man in the last chamber of the heart. Acoustically, it was impossible, lapping both sexes.

— I'll do her then. You boys cover me. Ho! Nix was on the steps in one leap, then through the door with drawn gun. They heard a few bootsteps and then a long quiet.

— How good was Muré? the bald man with lugubrious mustache asked Gabby.

— Wasn't so much good as all over the place. Something, I don't know. He should have shot me dead.

— That wouldn't be him there, would it?

The men looked idly to the right window and there came a man charging around the side of the church toward the Chinese shanties. He wore a Quaker hat and he was gone through a fire in the door of one of them before hands ever hit a holster.

— That was a preacher, wasn't it?

— Naw. That was Muré, said Gabby.

129

All of them pronounced it Mur*ee*, as did all Fernando's world except for his uncle, who was at the Winton Flyer now, in shock and touching the corpse of Nandina with his remaining hand. He was crooning something about not being able to swim, and it spooked the hirelings on the steps.

— Look who's up and about, Stump.

— Gives me the geechies.

Smoot was at the door, calling in.

— He's not here, Mister Nix! He's run to the shanties!

— I know he ain't here. Bring 'em all in. Man's a rabbit. We got something wondrous on our hands.

The hirelings filed by Gabby, sitting on the steps. They looked right and left, the five of them remaining, vigilant to the point of idiocy. Up on the dais, Nix was kneeling over the body of Stella. He was pulling at her dress, gently and fastidiously, like some solemn priss in the window of Nell's finery.

— Oh, darlin' Missus Muré, my old army doggies is so tired, my old cavalry jacket so out of fashion, darlin' seraph. I been running for things, you know, I know you're listening, and I'm ready for things to run to *me*. These old tired feets. Look at them tender feet on her, Smoot. Look what you shot.

Nix had undressed the woman and flung the gown out to the side. Then he removed his filthy blue jacket, blood gone brown at the cuffs.

Smoot and the rest could barely be amazed by him anymore. He was going to possess the woman right in front of them. Right in the middle of pursuit, Fernando in the shanties and where else by now? They gathered close, however, though most looked back at the pews. Smoot, only Smoot, was able to cast himself into a zone of pure religious trance. It mattered and it did not matter, and both of the situations were enormous.

— There now. Let's be handing over that dear long Creedmore, Smoot.

— Sir?

— The lofty device, great little man.

— Sure, well. He handed the cruel rifle over to Nix.

Nix had already got the head off the woman and now he lifted it up, streaming, and rammed it neck-down on the muzzle of the Creedmore.

— Hold this. Don't let it fall for nothing, he told Smoot. Nix reached down and picked up the dress, knocking his hat back so the string caught his neck. Then he pulled the dress over his head and was suddenly wearing it, with bare white hairy arms and sunbrowned hands. The rose garment glowed, almost laughed you might say, under his dark jowls when his head popped out. He spat out his pipe and didn't even look where it fell.

— I ain't *in* this, the man with sad mustaches blurted before he thought. The dress was over Nix's gun and knife, but the men still hung there frozen.

But Nix was mild. A staggeringly mild comment came from his mouth.

— Maybe you weren't even invited, Cousin Smut.

Nix walked off the dais and up the aisle and out of the church without another gesture, holding the Creedmore with the head of Stella on it, her pale red hair wet around the barrel and her eyes closed.

— Imagine where he *is?* said Smut of the sad mustaches. — Shit, let's revolt. Fuck, or just hide.

— Can't you . . . *locate* a act of genius? rebuked Smoot. — Mister Nix has gone to smoke out Fernando Muré.

They heard Nix beginning to howl outdoors.

★

A man stepped through the men on fire outside the hardware store. He was an Indian, no doubt of that. They never found out who he was attached to. He stepped right through the fire, hair long and silver but with a Rough Rider hat on, and deerskin holsters for two pistols turned hammer-in at his navel. He looked at Tall Jane, then at the grieving owner, then Nermer.

— Not you, he said to Tall Jane. — *You.*

He was very old but he had spring to him.

Nermer ducked back behind the counter and pitched himself out the back door. He flung himself around to the alley, broke out into the main street, went down the alley east of the hotel, and panted into the backyard at the end of the railroad spur. There was no real cover but a tree with an unlucky man in it. A great fat coward unrewarded in life, a dealer in hams and sawdust, he had arrived on a buckboard unwittingly into crashing gunfire on the main street. He had whipped his horse around, spilling hams and sawdust, only to arrive under the tree, where he kicked away and strove up perfectly high among the branches, so he thought, to escape harm. But the Indian behind Nermer came up in the alley and let go one shot, almost by way of cleaning his action. The bullet struck the poor man through the hand. He fell down from the tree and broke his neck, right in the tough roots around Nermer. Everything was awful. Nermer had quick and thorough pity for the man, but he rolled behind his corpse. Eventually he owed him damned near everything. He could see smoke run in front of the sun and here came the Indian, who took to the rear steps of the hotel kitchen when he saw Nermer's gun. He was on the porch, really without much haste now, and began shooting down at Nermer.

Nermer sorely missed the cave and his animal family. The convivial magpies. He thought of Nandina, too, and her thrown-out schoolteacher's body, the hot galaxy of sperm he had urged into her, helpless as surf. Something popped the heel of his boot and he thought almost with unwanted largess of the imagination about Nandina, already powerful in death. He thought of the smoky parlors of sin, delicious idleness, the click of the pool balls and the most violent blasphemies over nothing at all. The great sweet warm wrath of climax in Nandina, again. She was a world, a whole merry dangerous gasping planet, and he had traveled her like a pilgrim, clouds trailing behind him. But he had been sapped entirely, naught remaining to the backbone hardly. Up the mountain without another choice, that was it.

There was an angry gathering of bullets into the corpse of the innocent bystander. This Indian was very mean. A slug passed through the toe of his boot this time. Why was he, Nermer, so necessary to someone? Why so ruthlessly after him? He turned over, prone, and spied past the dead man's hair. The Indian was busy reloading. But who *was* the man? How could he find such lone vendetta in this confusion?

It was a person grim as a surgeon over the task of reloading here on the rear stoop of the hotel, just standing there straddle-legged and it seemed now almost sleepily. The long silver hair of him, the narrow bleak face? Some burnt leftover, tougher than the desert, not even friends to himself? Nermer fired at the man, some sixty yards away, making no impression at all. The man did not even budge and blew a tight quad of lead at him, followed by a more careful blast that near tore the head off the unfortunate climber and made Nermer scoot back. Nermer was spattered and cried out against God.

Then he remembered the Indian child, the one he had shot in the desert years ago, simply because he had a new gun. He was overtaken by a vision of despair and vengeance. A grown Indian corpse was firing at him, plucked out of that desert and time, gripped down on the stoop, blowing hell out of him patiently — else the man made no sense. Nermer was a mere chicken, a yellow belly. There were plenty others to shoot. Nermer's animal and bird friends shrieked and took leave of his soul. The Indian would have him and he would be correctly in hell. Yet he fired once again, hiding behind the brains of the climber. It seemed something afflicted his pistol. He was positive he saw the bullet loop out and bump on the stoop railing. This horrid miracle brought tears of awe that seemed to flow *inside* his face.

The Indian was not even annoyed.

Then two Chinese came out on the stoop with rifles and shot the Indian in the back several times. They had been in the kitchen. The battle had been so curious it had taken them a full minute to choose sides. Finally they noted Nermer's singular abjectness and recognized the Fool of the Mountain. Also the Chinese boys were formally occupying the hotel, as per Fernando's promise. They were, too, slightly racist. They looked away with scorn when two negroes ran out of the alley and began raiding the corpse for cigarettes.

Nermer stood and realized that he had been hit four or five times by slugs passing through the body of the climber. Some of the bullets were hanging out of him half entered in sucking craters of flesh. They rattled off him when he shook himself. It was a miracle from Satan himself and it sickened him.

This was too much sin. He had not meant to return this far, this deep.

He had wanted only an enormous fire.

★

This particular affair had transpired just yards outside the window of Doc Fingo's office, where he had locked himself when the first report of gunfire was heard. Really it did not seem to matter much, for he was heavy onto the opium pipe with a little nick of morphine in the wrist vein too. Obed Woods was locked in with him. Woods was blackmailing him for three monstrous square meals a day in the hotel kitchen lately. His mode was not subtle. He promised to stand in front of the office and scream that Fingo was a queer if he was not elaborately nourished. They were table partners, in fact, and Fingo did not find this disagreeable. The town could see the man that Fingo had brought off morphine. It gave substance to his trade. He thought the Woods boy was striving, even, to act more politely all the time. He was not ungrateful and Fingo sometimes gave him money. Woods sat on the floor and stared at him, flinching with each shot down the street, then holding his ears and raising his eyes as the Indian on the stoop let off nearly right by them. The doctor sat down on the floor as well. It seemed the thing to do, though nothing was really that urgent. He went under his desk and dwelled on the pipe, long streams of sweet smoke fleeing to the ceiling. There was a nice soft

136

kick in the back of his brain. A ricochet from Nermer broke the window and whacked the wall. Fingo was taken by pleasant inner visions of manly gunfire outdoors, the crackling and the booms. War has its romance, too, he mused. Rather cozy here, as men burst back and forth at each other, snapping metal. He heard something like a salvo just feet away. He was there, in the manly world of men and armed conflict! He pushed a finger above the desk top as a wistful target, feeling he was full in the fray, actually leading a sort of opiated assault on the army of his own shame. He was in it, he was off into it! He had a sort of cavalry in his ears, his own craven blood pouting away. Fingo once mended a broken dog and dwelled with the heroism of that act. Now the main fight seemed to be down the street, mooting away until there was an awesome boom and clattering of lumber. But all he could see when he looked out the front window was old Remington ranting away. The poor fellow seemed to have thrown his own arm off, looking for it down the street. Fingo looked back at Woods, still squatting, chubby and healthy on the floor.

— Chee. Somebody brought in da thunder!

★

The airplane, *peckapeckapecka*, made them look up again. The hirelings were all around the church door above Gabby, who still sat on the steps nursing himself. Smoot was out in the street, lagging a bit behind Luther Nix, who was ranting at the shanties.

Three Chinamen with rifles stood at one shanty door now, beholding the man in the dress.

Smoot did not care for the airplane. They did not need all this visiting. The street was not right either. Old Navy Remington, though silenced by the vision of Nix and the horror of the Creedmore, stood by the Winton Flyer as if it were still his, the monkey cuddled by his good arm, as if it were still his. The town idiot had not moved from the swine ruts, and he was glaring down. Some other officious fool was poking out of the door of the billiard room. You should not have these gawkers just standing around during your high adventure. Neither did Luther Nix like the plane. The rose dress flicked up behind, his Colt was out, and he banged away at it as it came low up the street, shadow in front again. He moved the Creedmore up and down, bawling, as the plane disappeared over the top of the church. You can't have tourists about. This thing was beyond and they would never know, even when they thought they saw.

The hirelings did not like the plane either. They backed farther into the church with a few imprecations.

What they saw from fifty feet above in the airplane was ghastly, and McCorkindale, who was piloting, had an instant, terrible sickness, and barely got them over the steeple and belfry.

Luther Nix walked forward to the Chinese, shaking the Creedmore and the head and railing for

Fernando. Then he changed into a little woman's voice, pumping the head more gently.

— Come out, dear Fernando, my husband. We never seem to talk anymore! Har!

Nix raised his gun and blew down one of the Chinamen.

So sudden, thought Smoot. The dress had them going like a cobra in a basket.

— Damned coolies, will you!? Shoot me, shoot me! Here I am, shoot me!

One man adjusted his rifle up and Nix walked right at him. He shot the man in the throat from fifteen feet. But the other man had raised his rifle too and got off a blast. How could he miss? Nix hurled himself toward Smoot. The right side of his face was bleeding. But he was laughing. Resumed roaring. He was beyond rifle lead, reckoned Smoot.

— Give me that, darlin', shouted Nix.

He ran a brief way and snatched the rifle from the man's hands. The man stumbled and ran back into the tarpaulin shanty. You could see where he bumped the sides of the canvas as he crawled inside it to another hovel connected behind.

— Yellow Fernando and your yellow men! Give me some more, I tell you! Hiding there behind them! Shame! Yellow, yellow!

Nix reached down and seemed to pick up the whole cooking fire at the mouth of the tent. He hurled it onto the roof and the tarpaulin went up instantly.

This time the plane came right over the hotel and the shanties themselves. Nix never looked up.

— Say now? screamed McCorkindale forward to Python Weems.

A sort of pipe tumbled out of the air right over the head of Smoot, fluttered into the church door and broke on the first pew beside Smut and Griffer, who had never uttered one word. The whole church went up, forward, backward, left and right, and straight up. Some of the splinters nicked the bottom of the Sopwith Camel. McCorkindale turned and saw the rest of the building collapse in upon itself.

— What? McCorkindale screamed forward, mean-eyed in his goggles.

Python Weems had called something back.

— Said you got a show all right, but it was really designed for your high troop concentration!

— All right!

Weems said something else. McCorkindale lifted his ear flap.

— Did you see that man in that steeple? shouted Weems.

Gabby was blown out into the street and woke riddled with splinters. The blast had flattened Smoot, too, and he was deaf, so that he heard no more of Nix's shouts and could only watch the quick and vast progress of the fire over the roofs of the shanties. He saw Nix go into the fire and become a part of it as it tired in the first hovels. The rose dress might be on fire, too. He was knocking greatly back and forth, clearing the way of flaming tarp and householdery. Then he went in deeper where the fire burned hottest. Even out here it was withering.

Fernando was on his knees behind a Chinese boy wrapped in a blanket. He himself was now on fire. The roof had flapped down on him and his black wedding suit began burning. His hat took up like a torch, and he cast it away, pounding his smoking head. Then the sawdust was on fire under him, agonizing his knees. A strut fell down and sat evilly right on his cheek.

Luther Nix came in the area thrashing and hollering. The head of Stella smoldered on the rifle, but he dropped it when he saw the wrapped child before his knees. Smoke and tatters had fouled his eyes and he looked again.

— Eh? said Nix.

Fernando shoved the child to the side and shot Nix four times in the stomach.

When Smoot saw Nix walk out of the smoke, the dress was burned off him and he was in only the pieces of a blackened undershirt. He did not look too interested in anything anymore. Then Smoot noticed he was punctured, not walking well, and bloody at the mouth.

Fernando came out some yards behind him. He was a burned wreck too, with an urchin in a blanket stepping behind him where it wasn't hot.

— Is it over then? I'm burnt up bad, said Fernando.

Nix sat down in the splinters and lumber around Gabby. Smoot had regained some hearing. Nix and Gabby seemed to be having some sorrowful conversation.

The dwarf stood beside Nix and knew he was going to die.

— Wasn't equal. There was a child. My angels, this should have been a neat little thing.

Nix glanced up dully at Fernando.

— Don't shoot me again. Give me a little more history here. Me and Gabby, bound for hell. His lips bubbled and Smoot finally surrendered, himself.

— Here's some history, Mister Nix, said Gabby.

Gabby had pulled out the great knife from Nix's sheath and fell on him, ramming long lengths of the blade repeatedly into Nix's liver. The old scout knew what he was doing. Nix screeched with each thrust. Smoot never thought he would hear this. But the man was still alive. He lay there, torn up and burned, but his eyes watched the sky and the dark sun, smoke flowing across it.

— Here's some more history, partner, said Gabby.

He began cutting Luther Nix's head off.

Fernando hobbled over and snatched the knife from him.

— Don't do that, old man.

Fernando was at the last of his strength. He almost toppled over. Then he raised up and stum-

142

bled toward the hotel and Fingo's office. His face, especially the right side of it, was pink-flaked and gruesome. He got a ways off before Edwin Smoot called to him.

— What about me? I'm a man!

Fernando returned, with pain and great loathing in his eyes, though there was now a change beyond despair. He sorted out the low Smoot from the lumber and blood and a kind of pity nestled on his features.

— That's always been a hard one for me, Smoot.

— Ain't I a killer? Ain't I shot down your . . . cunt? Ain't I blowed off your uncle's arm?

— Well. Fernando raised the gun without much determination.

— Not the gun. I want it like Mister Nix.

He was looking at the long knife in Fernando's hand.

— I ain't never been a knife man, Smoot. And I ain't got the strength.

— I'll shoot you where you stand, nigger! cried Smoot.

Fernando looked around again.

— Smoot, I'm not a nigger.

— In my world you are! You ain't never known my world! This ain't over! I'll shoot you where you stand!

Fernando turned again and came back, a last time.

— You probably would.

The pistol was out in his burned claw, but the

hammer fell on a spent round and clicked. The next one, live, splattered Smoot's heart. He was at peace before he hit the dirt.

★

L. P. Sheheen, often mistaken for a drunk, was the town fool who abhorred drink and kept a clean shirt on. He would enumerate with a curious zeal lacking in passion altogether a host of facts, a sort of history with the heart torn out of it. Neither by seeming will nor concern, he seemed to accumulate facts in a glut of the esophagus poured forth in an even vomitus knocked from him at a quarter to three every afternoon.

So he was yesterday's diary, like it or not, flat and unleavened for the most part, though the man tended toward Presbyterianism. Hardly a fact escaped him, this was the wonder, for he never seemed to be anywhere. Then he would float from some corner and his jaw would be going up and down: power, greed, lust, money, God, infamy, dust, ambition, death, the issues nicked off dead accurate and almost uninflected. He stood in the bullet-golden street the afternoon of the next day, babbling eastwardly, grim-jawed twenty-four-hour monitor, hogs circling him:

> — The sun was dark and hot. But their guns were long. There was no playing of billiards and no shouting, two days after our Lord's Birthday. The whores were in their whore rooms, quiet. Doctor Fingo was away, his hand on his smoke. You could

smell China over there. The piano was not playing. The church was not singing. The hogs, you hogs, did not know. The guns clicked and had eyes. The preacher was in the airplane with another man, who was a stranger. The yellow car of the sheep rancher sat tired at the horse trough, without smoke. The airplane was using the smoke now.

— The low man Smoot was there with those stranger-relatives. The courthouse was gone, flat black, with the airplane angry over it, cutting up the black wind. But you hogs walked back and forth and did not know. The bank said Bank and hid its money and the judge's morphine bottles over that great hole where folks threw their money down to, looking unhappy. Where they paid for dirt and rooves and their women would get bigger making more of them but not smiling about it, wishing the cactuses would do it for them. A woman will cry both ways, having it and having them. I know, though it is not for hogs' knowing, a woman's nook is so dreaded it makes a man holler and she's got to hang pretty cloth of all kind over her like a man don't need flowers nor lace over him. You see a woman she wears even a bonnet over her shameful face, bent over more for each child and looking at the ground talking to the Snake itself. The hole in the bottom of the bank, the hole in a woman, the hole right under us which is Hell of boiling reptile venoms and hairy fire, that is what is and that's always it no difference since God wrote out the world.

— Fernando fired the courthouse then went away and then the rough stranger-people, boughten thwartness of aiming men come on the rail or coach or tuckered horse, not looking at the Bank with its great hole, but that was funny because the

Bank was the whole thing, my hog and sow children, suffer thy farrow too, the Bank, they walked
just past it not even glancing at it like not glancing
at your mother sitting in the middle of the room.

— But nobody hired the Indian. He came in
seemed just for mean fun except it wasn't no smile
on his face and he had the hair of something dry
out there which had been blown in. He did not
assort with no man. That colored quartet commenced singing and come out of the barbershop to
trail him around like tall birds watching his fate but
not quite knowing the words to it yet. He did not
want them and he went away into fire and left
them. The Indian had doeskin waders on and
parched loins. He was the color of a dried-up hole
of water in the desert. One of the colored quartet
come up ask him what was the words to his fate
and the old Indian look a hole through him come
out the back of Amos's head and burnt up a child's
pet lizard on the hitching rail.

— How it begun was not wrote out well for
Fernando. We have callous disregard sometimes
here in the West. Some say there was no glory in
him or none of it at all, it was all ignominy and
things simply gone that used to be there. They say
was he hiding behind the Chinese child or was he
saving the Chinese child. They say murder just a
form of laziness extremed out. They say firing the
courthouse was just rapid laziness. Say the airplane
flying angry and concerned and the nitroglycerine
had no glory in it either, just a unwelcome gnat
over a frozen headache of a town where nobody
couldn't get no grip on heroism nor even a cause. I
was right near the old sheepherder without one
arm when he yelled out I can't swim, I can't swim,

you heard him too, oh my swine. There you heard, that was all it, a old man without one arm on the dry earth yelling I can't swim is what it all means, but you know and will never say, my hog listeners.

— The last to fall was the low man Smoot. He said to me once what he said to no other man. The salvation of a dwarf ain't available to regular earthlings, since he was low already and had a home in the roots where real things were. He could be near invisible where he stood, for most of the world chose not to look at him at all. So when he died he didn't go very far at all. And it would give his neck a wonderful rest from looking up. Some say there wasn't no glory in shooting a dwarf, neither. When the sun was not black no more and they could see, nobody minded much the others, but they hated to look at the body of the dwarf. Them as did look say he was pretty and pitiful and it made them cry.

— We will be here at the same time tomorrow, my children.

★

Agnes Dunning Nitburg sat beside her giant son Robert in his open buckboard with spring seats. The day was fresh and blue. Nandina's dogs ran a long way with them, then turned back, all the glorious eight of them, for water back at the manse. The automobile behind the buckboard had alarmed and interested them for a while, but they could not smell their mistress. Two Texas Rangers rode in the auto. One remarked again on the sad

147

death of Nandina. The dogs seemed lost and pathetic.

— And by the way, said the driver, —that old woman doesn't even believe we're here. I mean, she's got no credence in motored cars.

— A certain blindness ain't that bad out here. What I say. *Keff. Hack.* The man speaking was a crack shot, but a morbid whiner and hypochondriac allergic to Texas dust. He was red-nosed and teary-eyed under the Stetson hat as the stuff came in the windows. He claimed grandnephewship to Kaiser Bill and deplored this barren plat in favor of the Prussian woods and greens.

— Would you marry it? Wealthy blindness.

— Maybe if she'd cut her hair.

— She wants to worship.

— If she can find something left of the divine.

— Well it's all curious. We've got twelve bodies and nobody's signed one paper yet.

— Maybe it's the last of something, said the German. Your damned woolly West.

— Two things I think I'm really tired of. It hadn't even barely started the century and every other goddamned fool is going around saying *last*. The last of this the last of that. And the other thing is smart fucking krauts. Promise me you're the last one. And give me the last of that whiskey. We're looking at Volstead and the woman vote, Kaiser.

They watched the woman get out at the flattened church. The steps were left but there was a great hole in the floor and pews were blown away ten rows up. The giant son helped her up the steps. She went as far as he would let her with the cane, sunglasses gleaming in the morning sun, cracking the splinters with her high lace-up granny shoes. The church, blown at the mouth, retained its rear belly and main ribs. The steeple was still in the street, though some of its boards had been used for coffins. This did not involve the Chinese. Agnes Dunning Nitburg was on the gangway of a torn ark, is how it looked. Shredded hymnals and stacked pews were within her main grasp. Mc-Corkindale had been smoking cigarettes and tamping them out on the front pew, one of the few whole ones. She heard him move.

— Where is he?

— Me? asked the minister.

— I mean God. He still owes me and I want him.

— Mother Agnes, you're spared the sight.

— You seem to be in the air, young man.

— A murderer . . . standing in the filth of his own bomb.

— What's left, pastor?

— Maybe just that idiot in the street talking to pigs.

— Get God back in here immediately! I'm paying.

— Maybe folks aren't talking to God just yet.

— Then you . . . pretend, until he comes. I want music, I want the forms, I want the sad widows, I want the lustful minister, I want the hypocrites and the unpleasant children. All of it.

— You knew?

— Get blind long enough and you can smell it all, what you don't hear.

★

As for the judge, he never came back to town. But he didn't do much else either, except stare at the place on the picket fence where the head had been for a few months. He was not insane, Fingo figured. He could feed and clothe himself and make normal conversation. His wife said he was too mean to go insane, but the big son came and took her to live in the hotel. She delighted in dominoes with the "girls," pretending she did not know what the women were. They played badminton with her, too. She was a merry proprietor. Several of the sluts would attend church with her, and this was written up by a winking "local-color man" in the Austin newspaper.

Judge Nitburg still had a great deal of money.

But he told Fingo once that he could not think of one thing to buy.

Fernando Muré was a burned-scarred half-crippled recluse for two years at Navy Remington's ranch. He and the old man took care of each other, with the help of several Chinese.

The Chinese had not gotten the hotel and they followed him out to the ranch, haranguing him from outdoors day and night. Remington was

150

forced to put them to work as shepherds and kitchen workers. He gave them the barn. Things were fairly pleasant.

Philip Hine, the photographer, had lived through the fall of the steeple. He was explaining his point to Nermer and McCorkindale and Woods in the hotel dining room. Whispering, really, because Agnes Nitburg was sitting and reading braille barely twenty feet away.

— I'm a voyeur, you see, he said.

— You are? asked McCorkindale.

— Freely admitted. A peeping Tom. I'm speaking time and distance. Now really, what if a woman, say just an average sidewalk-walking woman, came in here right in your face, took off her clothes, I mean jaybird naked and just stood there with her things hanging out.

— Well. Not really so good, said McCorkindale.

— Offensive. Insane. Inappropriate.

— But, see, a woman at night across the way through gauze curtains, lighted from behind, doing the same thing with, say, just a little grace, just a little — here we are — slowness. See?

— Yeah. Must be one of dose meself. Voyoor, said Woods.

— Time and distance. Distance *from* the woman. The *time* it would take to *get* her. The whole thing becomes something else entirely. And who is to say not more real?

— So? asked Nermer.

— Fernando and all of you. It's been two years. Every day, more light from behind, more softness, more gauze. It's time we held the dance of history. You're all heroes, and folks will miss your kind. History won't let you hate yourselves anymore.

It was an agreeable theory and Philip Hine took it over to Fernando, fifty miles away. He was at the river fishing with Hsu, the Chinaman. His hair was full of silver now and his face was slack and grotesque on the right. He had a paunch. He walked painfully. His hands were black with worm dirt. He sat and listened to Hine courteously while the river lapped green and merry in the cove under the willows.

— None of that is right, Mister Hine, though thanks. You don't even seem to be wanting no money for it, either. Others has. *Have,* he corrected himself. — Thing is, it was all wrong and I am a villain. *Except.* I'm here studying up how I can make the next years fine ones, by my little Stella. I mean to be something extraordinary and make a high mark for good.

— But what will you do? Honestly your face . . . your looks, your whole legendary physical attributes. Well, forgive me, sir, but they're all *gone.*

— Yeah. Muré smiled, still with good teeth. — Maybe this time I'll have a whole lot better chance.